T0129953

Going Round Again

Going Round Again

John Biddle Backtracks

Keith Mapp

authorHOUSE®

AuthorHouse™
1663 Liberty Drive
Bloomington, IN 47403
www.authorhouse.com
Phone: 1-800-839-8640

First published by AuthorHouse   06/09/2011

ISBN: 978-1-4567-7873-6 (sc)
ISBN: 978-1-4567-8059-3 (ebk)

Printed in the United States of America

Albert Einstein once said that one definition of insanity is to keep on doing the same thing, in the same way, over and over again, whilst hoping that the outcome will be different.

That must also be one of the definitions of commuting by train.

CHAPTER ONE

John Biddle and Angela Wicks celebrated and consummated their marriage in the Venezuelan capital city of Caracas which, as it turned out, was the worst thing they could possibly have done.

To say that what happened to them there was Angela's fault would have been unfair to her, would have been an overstatement of the facts, because to say so would imply that she knew what the consequences of her actions were likely to be, whereas in reality that was not the case at all. But it was true to say that without her insistence that some aspects of their adventure should be conducted entirely on her terms it could, and probably would, have all turned out differently.

John's part in the adventure had begun some time before hers did. Hers started with the delivery of a parcel that came from him, containing three things—a letter, a plane ticket to Caracas and a mobile phone. The receipt of those three things had turned her world upside down and plunged her into a fit of confusion and indecision that had only ended when she had come to her senses and started to wonder why she had gone to the airport and found herself sitting on a plane waiting for a man—one that she had not even had the nerve to ring and talk to on the phone he had sent her—to arrive there and settle down into the seat alongside her. And as the time when that plane was due to leave approached, and he had still not shown up, her anxiety levels reached breaking point and she almost lost her nerve altogether and nearly got up to get off.

Then, at the last possible moment, everything changed, and John arrived there to be with her. At first she did not recognise him as he had grown a beard since she had last seen him—a completely unexpected act and totally out of character—but it was, as he told her later, a necessary part of what he had been doing since he had last seen her, several weeks before, in The Oxford Arms in Asham.

John barely had time to push his small suitcase into the overhead locker and shut it before the aircraft doors were closed and the crew began their final preparations for departure. She let relief flood over her and threw her arms around him as he settled into the seat next to her.

'You came,' she said. 'You really came.'

'And so did you,' he replied with a broad grin spreading across his face.

Fifteen minutes later they were in the air and heading westwards into the clear blue sky, towards the Atlantic Ocean, towards Venezuela, Caracas, and their new life together—a life they had toasted before take-off in the airline's complimentary champagne. Then they sat together, hand in hand, in companiable silence, until the seat belt signs were turned off, the cabin crew came round for the first time, and John asked if it would be possible for him to make a phone call.

'Yes sir; of course. I'll just get you a phone.'

When she came back, John took the phone the stewardess handed him, plugged it into a socket in the arm of his seat and dialled a number, then sat and waited as it connected. While he did, an amusing thought struck him and he laughed out loud.

'What were you laughing at just then?' Angela asked him when he had finished the call and rung off.

'Well,' he said, 'if you're not doing anything for a while I'll tell you, and I'm willing to bet you'll laugh too.'

During the course of the next few hours he told her everything there was to tell about what he had been doing since he had last seen her; about Perma-way, The Book of Excuses, being followed, train delays and Roamer-Phone; about Wright Arse, finding websites, passwords and spreadsheets; about the money the Perma-way directors had been making from the deal with the phone company and the money he had taken from them with his so-successful blackmail plot; and about why he was now sporting a new beard that made him look, in her opinion, like a fugitive master-criminal running from justice because, in reality, he was exactly that, as the million pounds in used notes locked away in the suitcase in the locker above their heads would prove to her if she cared to take a look at it.

With the little breath she had left, most of it having been taken away by the story he told her, in the hushed tones of co-conspirators—essential, as none of what he told her was anything that either of them could afford for anyone else to overhear—she told him that it would not be necessary and that she would take his word for it. And even after he had told her how he had done it all, using the trains, the smoke bomb, the mobile phone and GPS signal jammers, the handcuffs and the skimpy pink leather outfit he had bought in the sex shop, she still found it all unreal, and hard to believe that the two of them were millionaires and that, if they were careful with the money, they were quite literally made for life.

After the excitement of the early part of the flight, the rest of it passed uneventfully, as a not unwelcome anti-climax, and it was in the gathering dusk of a tropical sunset that they made their final approach to and landing at the Aeropuerto Internacional de Maiquetia Simon Bolivar, to give the airport serving Caracas its full and proper name. On one side of the runway they could see the flat land of the narrow coastal plain running away down to the deep, deep blue of the Caribbean Sea. On the other side the land rose sharply upwards to the impressive bulk of the coastal mountain range, the northward extension of the South American Andes, behind which the city of Caracas had been built, in a long, high valley that lay between those peaks and the next range of mountains to the south. Angela experienced a growing sense of unreality as the plane made its descent towards the unknown city ahead of them on an unfamiliar continent. John, who had been living in a world of unreality for quite some time by then, merely added the experience to his expanding collection and began to prepare himself for the next one.

Their arrival at the airport was routine and uneventful, and full darkness had fallen by the time they had made their way from the plane through the terminal to the taxi rank outside. On the way, they had stopped at passport control, at the baggage carousel to collect Angela's suitcase, passed through the customs hall, where they drew nothing more than the usual disinterested glances and perfunctory attention of the officials, and paused briefly at the Bureau de Change to convert some of John's ill-gotten gains into the notes of the local currency.

As they left the air-conditioned comfort of the terminal building, and its glass doors slid shut behind them, the heat and humidity of the tropics wrapped itself around them for the first time and held them in its warm and sticky embrace, an experience they were going to have to get used to as a regular part of their new way of life. Already perspiring gently, even after only a few seconds of exposure to the heat, they turned and walked along the front of the building towards the distant taxi rank. Ordinarily, John would have regarded the hiring of a taxi for a journey that could equally well have been completed by public transport as an extravagance, but on this occasion he was quite willing to agree with Angela that the additional expense was justified, as they had no real idea where they were going once they reached the city, and finding a hotel to stay in would be so much easier with the help of a friendly cabbie—if they could find one who spoke some English, that is.

The taxi driver they picked out did speak a little English, and Angela spoke a little holiday Spanish. Between the two of them they managed to overcome their linguistic differences well enough to agree a price for him to take the new arrivals to one of the international hotels in the city centre where the desk staff would speak English, or to be strictly accurate, American English.

Driving up through the mountains to Caracas was not the edge-of-the-seat stuff John had feared it might be when he first caught sight of their height and bulk through the window of the plane. Instead of the narrow, winding, cart track of his imagination, the road was a modern, well-engineered four-lane highway with, at that time of the day, only light traffic using it. As a spectacle, the journey was disappointing—diminished severely by the darkness, which stole away numerous views that would have been spectacular if only they had been visible. Also missing was the creeping sense claustrophobia that could be felt when it was light, as the mountains closed in on the road from both sides to surround, dominate and then swallow it up on its approach to the two tunnels it passed through on its climb upwards to its summit and its subsequent descent downwards into the city.

At the far end of the second tunnel the land flanking the road on either side began to open out, and they realised they could see the lights of the city spread out ahead of them. As they drove further on, the road dropped down onto the valley floor and they saw lights on either side of them; the lights of the small, flat-roofed, single-storey houses that the poor and working-classes lived in, packed tightly together on disorganised terraces cut into the still steeply-sloping valley sides. Still further on, the highway ran past and then into more affluent urban areas where the lights were brighter and more frequent, the houses were bigger and less tightly packed, and mixed in with an assortment of apartment blocks, industrial and commercial units, shops, schools, churches—the full range of buildings that formed the glue that cemented the fabric of a society together and made it all work. And all the while the volume of traffic increased and their speed began to fall. Finally, the houses petered out altogether, the buildings grew progressively taller, and they arrived in the brightly-lit commercial district in the city centre, where the sort of hotels they were looking for were to be found. They left the long, straight city street the highway had evolved into, made several turns to right and to left, then pulled off into a parking bay in front of the main entrance to the glamorous-looking PanContinent Hotel.

The taxi driver helped Angela unload her suitcase and accepted his payment from John with a slight bow, then got back into his car and drove off into the traffic. The two of them made their way in through the glass revolving door, across the air-conditioned lobby to the reception desk. Seeing them approach, the girl behind the desk smiled and said

'Buenas noches, senor; senora. Como puedo ayudarle?'

'Buenas noches; dice usted el ingles por favor?' Angela replied ('Good evening; do you speak English please?' in Spanish.)

'Yes ma'am,' the receptionist drawled. 'How may I help you?'

'We'd like a room please,' John told her.

'Two rooms please,' Angela corrected him. 'Single rooms.' John gave her a sidelong glance, but said nothing.

'Do you have a reservation?'

'No, I'm afraid not,' John answered.

'And how long will you be staying with us?'

Angela and John looked at each other enquiringly. It was something they had not discussed; just as they had not discussed the details of their sleeping arrangements.

'A week,' they both said at the same time.

The receptionist tapped numerous keys on her computer keyboard. 'I'm sorry,' she said. 'We have no single rooms available at all for that time; there's a medical convention coming to town and the delegates have everything booked up. We do have several double rooms, or . . . ' She tapped on more of her keys, then watched as the computer did its stuff. 'We have a small suite, with two bedrooms, a sitting room and a shared bathroom. I can give you a special rate so it's slightly cheaper than having two double rooms would have been.'

John looked at Angela again and she nodded to indicate her approval. She was calling the shots here. He would happily have settled for just one of the doubles, and had not thought for a moment that she would want to do anything different. They went through all the formalities of checking in. Passports and tourist entry cards were collected, to be returned later; registration forms were filled in and signed; keys were handed over; then they went to the lift, up to their floor, along the corridor and into their rooms; tired, hungry and ready to rest after what had been a long and eventful day for both of them.

As they were both so tired, neither of them felt inclined to go down or out to find something to eat so they ordered a meal from room service and settled down in the shared sitting room to eat it together.

'This is very nice,' Angela said, looking round the opulently decorated and furnished room.

'True,' John said. 'But why all this?'

'Why all what?' she asked innocently.

'All this; the suite; separate bedrooms: why not just a double?'

'That wouldn't be right—not before we're married.'

'Who said anything about getting married?' he asked her.

'I just did: and we are: so you'd better get used to the idea.' She said it lightly, playfully, but fully meaning every word of it. She had waited a long time for this; for him to get down off the fence he had spent so long sitting on and demonstrate some firm interest in her and commitment to her. Now it had happened she was not going to let him change his mind and get away, and that meant marriage, and soon.

The determination in Angela's voice took John aback, as it was something he had not given any thought to. In fact, he had not given very much thought at all to how the start of their adventure would affect Angela or how she might react to it. He had just assumed that her presence on the plane, waiting for his arrival, was a sign of her agreement to do everything just the way he had planned it. But he was wrong, as he was finding out, in no uncertain terms. And not wanting the day to end with cross words and disagreement, he decided to say nothing just then, but rather leave things as they stood, thinking that there was plenty of time for him to change her mind later, leaving the two of them free to start a life of glorious unmarried bliss. So after the meal they went their separate ways to their separate rooms and settled down for their first night of their new life together—apart.

John took some time to fall asleep, re-running the events of a momentous day in his mind, hardly daring to believe that it was him who had been involved in them all:—blackmail, armed robbery, assault, smuggling, elopement; all words and subjects that in his life had only ever appeared in the books he had loved to read on the trains, and in the TV detective stories he liked to watch in the evenings; not something he had ever imagined he would be a part of. And yet he was, and the case full of money standing alongside the bed was testimony enough to the fact that he was; John Biddle, master criminal, blackmailer, armed robber, man of violence, smuggler. As for the elopement—only time would tell about that.

Angela also lay awake for some time, finding her new surroundings strange and unsettling. This start to her new life with John was not what she had been imagining for so many years, as she had pictured it all happening in Asham, amongst their friends and the familiar surroundings of their old lives. This new life was something she was going to take some time to get used to, she thought, but she was determined to try, for both their sakes; and having a million pounds to try it with was going to make it all somewhat easier, she decided.

In the morning they got up, got dressed, and went downstairs to the hotel dining room to have breakfast together and try to decide what they were going to do that day, and the next, and the next . . . There were some obvious things to talk about. John's main concern was where they were going to live. As he pointed out, they could not stay in the hotel indefinitely. Angela agreed, but added that they could not move in together until after they were married. John decided to make his objection at that point, before things got too far out of hand, and tried to persuade Angela that it would be safer for them not to marry.

'Safer?' she said incredulously. 'What on earth could be dangerous about us getting married?'

'There'll be all sorts of forms and paperwork for us to fill in, and that's how the Arses could find us. Don't forget that I've just blackmailed their client out of a million pounds. They're bound to be upset about that, and I wouldn't mind betting they'll be looking out for any sign of us so they can come and try to get it back.'

'All the way out here?'

'Yes, all the way out here. They've got links with the CIA, you know. They could be very dangerous. They've already threatened to kill me once.'

'Now you're just being melodramatic and paranoid,' Angela told him. 'Do you really think the CIA would be bothered with two small-fry like us when they've got so many other things to worry about?'

'Just because I'm paranoid doesn't mean they're not out to get me,' John muttered gloomily. Then he went back to chewing his toast.

'Look,' he said, after a few minutes during which neither one of them spoke. 'I'll make you a deal: if we can find a place to get married where there won't be any paperwork, and I'm satisfied that we won't be discovered that way, then we'll get married; then we can rent a house somewhere and start living our new lives. How does that sound?'

'That sounds wonderful,' she said brightly, and leaned across the table to kiss him lightly. 'It'll all work out: you see if it doesn't. Now, how do we go about finding out where we should go to get married, where we should look for a house, and where we can go shopping? You need to get some new clothes to wear. Oh, and when we get back upstairs, please get rid of that beard, before I have to do it for you.'

Reluctantly, rather than have to carry the case full of money round with him wherever they went, John also let Angela persuade him to leave it in the safe keeping of the hotel, in its safe, that was actually a small strong-room in its basement. Then they were free to enjoy themselves and the city without the constant need to worry about where the case was and who might or might not be taking an interest in it and wondering what might be inside it. He had also collected their passports from the reception desk and given in to the urge to phone Mr Everest, his solicitor back in the UK, to ask for arrangements to be made to repair the front windows of his house, where Adrian Wright and his Arse men had broken them with their fake petrol bomb. Everest was delighted to hear from him and to have the opportunity of pretending to play spies with the exchange of the passwords they had agreed on. He promised that the work would be done at the first possible opportunity, and that the cost would be added to John's account, to be settled later.

The question of how they should set about achieving everything they wanted to do that day was decided for them as they left the dining room and Angela spotted a poster in the lobby advertising guided tours of the city, conducted in a multitude of different languages to cater for every conceivable type of visitor there could be to the place.

An hour and a half later, with tickets in hands, Angela and a clean-shaven John joined the back of a queue of English-speaking tourists in a square near the hotel to wait for the bus that would carry them round and introduce them to the sights and delights of Caracas over the course of most of the rest of the day. Immediately in front of them in the queue for the bus was a family that was obviously from England; John knew that because the father was a shaven-headed, beer-bellied thirty-something dressed in the replica football shirt of Richdale Rovers, the current English Premier League Champions. On the front of the shirt was a statement to that effect, that they were the champions, which was, in John's opinion, just another way of saying "Our foreigner players are better than your foreign players" or "Our Russian billionaire chairman gave us more money than your American, or Arab, or Thai, or whatever, multi-squillionaire owner gave you".

All in all, John thought, it would be more appropriate to call it The Biggest Bank Balance Premiership and leave it at that. At least it would be an honest statement of fact. And in the meantime all the English managers and players are left floundering down in the lower leagues, where they squabble amongst themselves every season and nothing important ever happens.

On the back of the shirt in question was the name of the club's latest expensive Eastern European import, star striker Sticcit Indanett. Isn't that the ultimate admission of personal failure? John thought. To be spending your life walking around in a shirt with someone else's name on the back?

Further down the queue, in amongst a collection of Americans, Australians and assorted English-speaking others, was another family that was obviously English: there could no doubt about that because the father/husband was making it obvious by conducting a loud conversation on his mobile phone with, it appeared, one of his work colleagues back in the UK. To say that what was being discussed was mundane, inane and pointless would have been to make an understatement, and nothing that was said appeared to be anything that could not have been left until the man got back to his office, or could not have been dealt with by one of the others who were still there.

From his past experience, John knew that this activity would be described by those who took part in it as "keeping in touch" or "keeping in the loop" (management-speak version). Those who did it would claim that they did it because they were worried that their colleagues/department/company would not be able to cope while they were not there. John and the rest of the rational and sane knew that they did it because they were petrified that their colleagues/department/company *would* be able to cope while they were not there. And looking down the queue at the man as he stomped backwards and forwards with his phone clamped to the side of his head with one hand while testiculating wildly with the other (testiculate; to testiculate; verb;

definition—to wave one's hands and arms wildly in the air whilst talking bollocks) John could see that the machine he was using was the inevitable one, the stereotypical device so much loved by middle-management and the (in their opinion) indispensable one; a device, the letters of whose name, when rearranged, almost spelt out what John thought they really were—the Brainless Wankberry—or was that just the people who chose to use them in this way?

While they all stood in line waiting for their tour bus to arrive, everyone, including his fraught wife, left to cope on her own with their two boisterous little boys, was hoping that the Wankberry's call would soon come to an end and they would be left in the peace and quiet they had hoped for when they had visualised this trip; but they were disappointed, because when the bus did come and they all got on it, the pointless and inane conversation droned on, threatening to drown out the tour guide's commentary on the city they were about to be introduced to. Angry glances and requests that the man should be quiet were met with agitated gestures from him pointing out that he was on the phone—as if anyone there needed to be told that!—but did have the effect of producing a reduction in volume to a level where it was just tedious rather than bloody annoying. And it continued that way through the first part of the tour and through the first stop for a quick look at a notable church somewhere in the centre of the city: but it ended as they got back on the bus again.

The instrument of their delivery from suffering was, surprisingly, the football fan who, as a result of his action, rose many levels in John's esteem and earned the gratitude of everyone present. As they all got back on the bus the football fan, seeing the Wankberry lagging behind, paying more attention to what he was saying than where he was going or what he was supposed to be doing, partially blocked off his re-entry so that when the doors of the bus closed, the annoying pillock himself was inside it, but the instrument of everyone's torture was still outside. As the doors snapped shut on his wrist, his fingers jerked open and the phone dropped down the outside of the bus. The pillock, suddenly deprived of his reason for being, panicked, and forced his way off the bus through the still partially-open doors. He was last seen, as the bus pulled away, kneeling down and shouting loudly between the metal bars of a drainage grating set into the tarmac, that his phone had fallen through, trying to carry on the important conversation he had been sharing with everyone else in the bus in the lead-up to this happy event. The wife watched her husband while all this was happening with a resigned expression on her face and did nothing to stop either him or the bus. With the loss of their oppressor, the mood of the passengers on the bus lightened, and the rest of the day passed happily for all of them, even the estranged wife and her boys.

At the end of that day Angela and John knew the basics of the city's history and, more important to them, how its modern manifestation was laid out and worked. They knew where they should go to look for a house to rent—at the eastern end of the valley, where the middle, upper and professional classes tended to congregate and the houses were finer, bigger and better-built. They knew where the shopping districts were and how to go about getting the best bargains in new clothes for John and, eventually, Angela. They also knew that there was a small Anglican community in the city, with a church and a charming and easy-going vicar, which is where Angela had decided they should go to look for the 'no-strings' wedding that John had agreed to.

At the end of a long, hot day they both wanted to get back to the hotel for showers, food and rest—in that order—but they had to wait just a little longer as the new clothes for John took priority because he had none to change into after his shower. So they went wearily to the nearest of the big department stores and failed miserably to haggle a good price for a set of decent but basic clothes that John could spend the next few days wearing, until they could afford more time to go shopping properly for a more extensive new wardrobe. That evening they ate in the hotel's restaurant, had some drinks at the bar and then went upstairs to go their separate ways, tired but happy, and looking forward to the next day, church- and house-hunting.

The following morning, after breakfast, they hailed a taxi outside the hotel and managed to make the driver understand that they wanted to be taken to the Anglican church. The car crawled along slowly through the tail end of the rush hour traffic, as they looked out and up at the offices and banks of the commercial centre, with the odd hotel dropped in here and there to break up the monotony, then at the shopping districts with their eclectic mixture of the familiar multi-national brands and unfamiliar local names. Then they were out into the edge of the eastern suburbs, where the traffic was thinner and moved more freely, pulling up outside what looked like a traditional English parish church, uprooted from its home in the old country and dropped complete here into this unfamiliar tropical setting. Inside, they found the vicar at his desk in the back of the vestry, with time to see them and listen to what they wanted. He was a charming, easy-going, West Indian man who insisted they call him Luther, and who told them it would be no trouble at all to marry them on the coming Saturday afternoon.

'We have two weddings here already on that day, my friends,' he said. 'The second is between two of my church-going parishioners, and we can easily fit you in after them, and the congregation will stay to join and celebrate with you, bless you both and act as your witnesses. The church will be beautiful. The people will be happy. It will be a lovely occasion for you both.'

At that point John deliberately asked about the paperwork, on the pretext of making sure that it was not too late to complete it all, as that day was Thursday, and the wedding was to be on the Saturday, in only two days' time.

'Oh, you don't need to worry yourselves about that, my lambs,' Luther told them. 'Everything is very easy here and it's not needed. All I need to do is to see that you are who you say you are; then everything will be set.'

John and Angela slid their passports across the desk. Luther looked at each one in turn, reading carefully through all the details and staring hard at the photographs, before comparing them with the real person sitting opposite him. Then he closed them, smiled and returned them to the lambs they belonged to.

'Thank you my friends,' he said. 'That's perfect.'

After that they discussed the fees for the wedding, which turned out to be very modest. John paid in cash and made a reasonably large donation towards the upkeep of the building, then they stood up, shook Luther's hand, and left. Angela clung to John's arm, hardly able to contain her excitement. John wore a rueful grin.

'There,' Angela said, 'I told you it would be alright and there was nothing to worry about. Just think; next time we leave here it will be as Mr and Mrs Biddle!'

Inside the church, unseen by the happy couple, Luther slid open his desk drawer, pulled out some of the irksome forms that Angela and John had no need to bother themselves with, and began to fill them in on their behalf, drawing all the information he needed from his prodigious memory, having read it from the important pages of their passports. As he did it, he sang quietly and occasionally giggled to himself. He loved to use his one great trick, his memory trick, to release his lambs from this burden, leaving them free to concentrate on what was really important about getting married; the love of God, their love for one another and the procreation of another generation of God's little lambs. This was a man who truly loved his job, and bucking the systems of mammon by pre-dating paperwork and forging a few lamb's signatures here and there, also from memory, was a bit of a chuckle too.

For Angela and John, the journey back into the city was not as swift and efficient as the journey out had been, even allowing for the traffic. The area the church was located in was a little off the beaten track for the city taxis, so they had to walk quite a way before they located a taxi rank. When they found one, it was in a small, local commercial centre, where a group of shops and offices stood around three sides of a square, which had a railway station on its fourth side and a small bus station in its centre. One of the shops, John noticed, was occupied by a firm of estate agents. Pointing this out to Angela, along with the fact that this was one of the eastern suburbs they had heard about the day before, and suggesting it was worth a try, he said he thought they should look in the window at least, to see what the local market could offer in the way of houses to rent.

They walked over to the glass and were looking in at the pictures and adverts there, all written in Spanish, when the door opened and a young man emerged, wearing a sharp business suit, a neatly-laundered shirt and an expensive-looking tie.

'Good afternoon sir, madam,' he said in only slightly-accented English. 'I am Rodrigo, the under-manager here. Can I be of any assistance?'

How do they do that? John asked himself. We've not yet spoken a word, but already they know we're English. Do we carry signs around, invisible to us, announcing that we're English, that only non-English people can see? Or are we, as a nation, so badly dressed that we stick out like the proverbial sore thumbs? I could understand it if I was wandering around wearing a football shirt with someone else's name on the back, but I'm not; so how do they do it?

In truth, John was mistaken in thinking that Rodrigo had identified them as English. He had not; he had just identified them as being foreign and, whether the French might like it or not, as English is the world's universal second language, the first attempt at addressing any foreigner is nearly always made in English.

'Yes. Thank you,' John answered. 'We're looking for a furnished house to rent. Do you do that sort of thing here?'

'Oh, yes Sir. Would you and your lovely wife like to come inside and we can discuss your requirements, please?'

'Angela?' John asked.

'Yes; thank you,' she said.

Rodrigo ushered them inside and sat them down in his office, then proceeded to ask them what, exactly, they were looking for. As they had not even discussed this between themselves, but had come in at Rodrigo's invitation, on the spur of the moment as it were, they did not have a ready answer for this, but rather made it up as they went along, assisted by prompts from their host, intended to help them decide on something he might be able to provide them with. And as they talked, cups of coffee for them to drink and property particulars for them to browse through were brought in at intervals by various smiling assistants. Eventually they had a small pile of particulars of properties that were the right size, looked nice, were said to be in good neighbourhoods and were within the budget John had set—somewhere within the extra five thousand pounds a month he had told Adrian Wright Arse he wanted in addition to the million pounds in cash he already had. Rodrigo suggested that after lunch, provided at his expense of course, they should go out to look at some of them. Perhaps, while they ate, they could decide on their favourite three or four, and go to look at those.

After an excellent meal, Rodrigo handed one of his assistants the keys of his large, air-conditioned Mercedes and Angela and John spent most of the afternoon visiting the houses they had chosen to look at. One amongst them stood out as their favourite—a single-storey villa with a deep veranda running full width across its front, standing in its own gardens on a hillside not far to the east of the estate agent's office, in what appeared to be a very nice area, judging from the green and leafy, neat and tidy gardens around all the houses there, and the quality of the cars parked in their driveways and car-ports. Inside, it was bigger than they really needed, but it felt cool and calm, and they both liked the extensive use of highly polished dark wood—for the floors, doors, door frames and wall panelling.

Satisfied with what they had seen, they settled back into the Mercedes and were driven back to Rodrigo's office, hoping to seal the deal and find out when they could move in. After a little mild haggling, which is always expected apparently, they had agreed the price—well within John's budget—and were told they could move in whenever they wished as the place was currently empty, provided they paid a small deposit there and then, and promised to pay the balance of the first six months' rent within fifteen days. They agreed, but John had a question.

'Would it be possible for us to pay this in cash?' he asked.

'Ah yes,' Rodrigo laughed. 'You are the great train robbers, no? Senor, your cash will be most welcome here, thank you.'

So it was agreed that they would return the following morning with the full payment for the six months' rent, receive the keys immediately and make preparations for moving in straight after the wedding on the Saturday. When they told Rodrigo the reason for their hurry he said it was absolutely charming and promised to have a bottle of champagne on ice waiting for them when they came back the next day.

Back at the hotel, with almost all of their objectives achieved, they asked at the front desk about the practicalities of changing the amount of money they needed from Sterling into Bolivars. That would not be a problem, the desk clerk told them; the best place would probably be the National Bank, three blocks along the street, where all currencies could be exchanged, for payment of a modest percentage in commission.

That night they went out to eat, and returned to the hotel again flushed with wine and their success, and both slept a long and contented sleep.

The next day was Friday, the day before the wedding, and there was a lot to do to get everything ready. They went to the bank to change the money they needed, having been to the hotel safe first to take it out of the suitcase. Then they went to the estate agents' office to pay their rent and collect their keys. Rodrigo himself drove the Mercedes to the villa and produced the champagne he had promised. He toasted their happiness, gave them his card, promised unprecedented levels of service and attention should they ever need anything more of him, and left them to enjoy their new home.

One important feature of the villa, that John had noticed as soon as he walked into the study, was the heavy, robust-looking safe that stood in the far corner from the door, under one of the windows. Such things were not normally a feature of British homes but, when this part of the city had been less law-abiding than it was then, they had become a standard feature of the homes of most of the better-off families who lived there. No longer as necessary as they once were, most remained in place in case of a return of more turbulent times. This was to be the new home of John and Angela's small fortune—unless or until one of them could think of something more productive they could do with it. The move was to be made on the Monday following the wedding, when they finally checked out of the hotel.

Several hours after Rodrigo had left, after they had spent some time in each of their new rooms, Angela had a shopping list of essential items they would need to add to what was already there to make their new house their home, and they were off into the city to buy them. Rodrigo had left a card with them for a local taxi firm with an office staff who spoke reasonable English, so they used the phone in the house to summon one of the firm's cars to collect them for the trip into town.

One shopping trip and one trip back out to the villa later, the day was almost over. They had everything they thought they needed to begin their married life together in their new home, plus new clothes to wear for the wedding itself. In the evening they forwent the traditional ritual of stag and hen parties, opting instead for a quiet dinner in the hotel, then went their separate ways, to their separate rooms, for the last time.

In the morning the sun was shining down on a sparkling city and it was promising to be hot once again. Angela and John's domestic arrangements made it all but impossible for the groom to avoid seeing the bride on her wedding morning, so neither of them tried too hard to avoid the other. John spent the morning reading. Angela spent it getting ready, and was still almost late. At two o'clock in the afternoon the taxi they had hired for the rest of the day arrived and collected them from the hotel. John held the door open for his bride-to-be as she got in, while the driver loaded her suitcase and his carrier bags of clothes into the boot, then they drove up to the church, and to Luther.

Everything at the church was as the vicar had promised it would be. Angela and John were made to feel like old friends of the congregation there. They sat through the first wedding, in a pew at the back; then stepped forward when it was their turn to make their vows and be married. Members of the congregation stood in as witnesses, the father of the bride and the best man, just as Luther had promised they would. Vows were made, rings were exchanged, registers were signed and the new Mr and Mrs Biddle took their leave of the church through its main front door.

At the invitation of the bride and groom of the previous wedding, they went into the adjacent church hall to join in with their reception, as honoured guests. Luther retreated into his office to make and sign certified copies of the new entries in the register before dropping them into an envelope, addressed to the British Embassy in Caracas, already containing his forged forms relating to Angela and John's marriage.

In the early evening, Angela and John took their leave of the wedding party and drove off in the taxi to their new home. John left their bags just inside the hallway, where the taxi driver had put them, but reached out and picked up the new Mrs Biddle, then carried her over the threshold in the time-honoured manner, kicking the heavy front door closed with his heel behind them. Neither one of them, in their happy state, gave a single thought to anything that might have been going on back in the UK just then, and least of all what might be happening to a certain Mr Adrian Wright.

CHAPTER TWO

Adrian Wright hated John Biddle with an intensity he could taste; could almost bite off and chew on; almost take between his teeth to grind and crush to nothing: which is roughly what he now had planned for John if, when, he could ever catch up with him.

Until Wright had met John Biddle he had had a career; had had a life. Now, after their last encounter, in the toilet compartment on the train, an encounter which had seen Wright so conclusively defeated, on every conceivable level, both his career and his life lay in ruins around him. It was not just the fact that he had failed to live up to the trust his employer and their client had placed in him, or the fact that he had lost that client a million pounds in untraceable bank notes, it was also the way he had been humiliated by that bastard bean-counter Biddle, being left in the toilet compartment to be arrested, dressed in . . . well, dressed in something he could not even face describing to himself, let alone to anyone else who might demand to be told what had happened to him.

On that fateful day he had had everything under control, right up to the time when Biddle managed to creep up on him unseen and push the muzzle of the gun into the small of his back. That had been a big surprise, and from that point onwards, everything had been out of his control. Wright knew now that he had been complacent, had totally underestimated his quarry, and had been forced to play the rest of the game to Biddle's rules and not his own. But who, honestly, would have thought, based on the evidence of Biddle's character and achievements up to that point, that he would have had the gumption or guts to arm himself, then plan and carry out the theft—because that was the way Wright still thought of the loss of the money, as a theft.

Taking the cash with him on the train was, Wright could see now, a reckless thing to have done, and he only did it because he had blind faith in his own planning and in the abilities of his back-up team—the team that Biddle had left trapped, first on the southbound train heading for the airport, and then on a northbound one on its way back again. That had been the point at which the doubt had begun to nibble away at Wright's confidence; a confidence then completely destroyed during the scene that unfolded in the toilet compartment on the second northbound train, that had seen him left handcuffed to the rail on the wall wearing just a skimpy pink leather thong and bodice that Biddle must have picked up in a fit of depravity in some seedy back-street porn-monger's in the preceding few days. And when Biddle backed out through the closing door, leaving the compartment filling with smoke, taking the money with him, Wright knew that the game was hopelessly, irrevocably lost, and that he was well and truly in the proverbial shit.

For several long minutes after Biddle had left, nothing happened, except that Wright had had to bend further and further over, trying to stay below the level of the cloying, choking smoke that was rapidly filling the compartment, blocking out the light from the fluorescent tube in the ceiling and making it difficult to breathe. Then he heard someone banging on the door, and a raised voice asking if there was anyone inside and if they were OK if there was. Wright tried to answer but could not, because he had a leather gag fixed around his head, filling his mouth and stopping him from making anything more than a pathetic whimpering noise.

The banging continued for a short while then stopped, and the door slid open. Daylight streamed in through the opening and smoke poured out into the carriage outside. Framed in the doorway, Wright could see the figure of the train guard, his mouth agape in disbelief at what he was seeing huddled against the back wall of the compartment, beside the toilet pan, as the smoke cleared. Then the guard disappeared and the waiting began again. Wright's senses, sharpened by the adrenaline coursing through his body as a result of the stress, bordering on panic, he was experiencing while trying desperately to work out how he was going to extricate himself from the mess he then found himself in, heard a door slam and a train move away on the opposite track, the down the line, heading south towards the airport. Then footsteps approached and the guard reappeared, this time accompanied by another railway worker who Wright assumed must be the train's driver.

'Well bugger me,' the driver said, turning to look at the guard. It was obvious that neither one of them knew what they should do, this not being the sort of situation that was covered in any of the training manuals they had ever read. Then the driver looked down and spotted the gun on the floor.

'You'd better call the police,' he said, pointing down at it.

The police arrived in force and at full speed some ten or fifteen minutes later, after the guard had activated the emergency release on the doors and left the train to ring for them on the station's land line, as neither his mobile phone nor the driver's were willing to work for some reason. With rising dread of what he was now going to suffer, Wright listened to the wail of the approaching sirens, the screech of tyres on the tarmac of the road and forecourt outside the station, the thunder of heavy boots on the platform and the train floor then, worst of all, the clicking-off of safety catches as they primed their weapons and the tiny space he was trapped in was invaded by the full might of the North Weald Constabulary's Armed Response Unit.

As they rushed in, the remains of the smoke canister were crushed underfoot, the pistol was sent slithering across the floor to disappear from sight where the grating was missing from the drain and The Book of Excuses fell off the edge of the basin onto the floor: so much for the possibility of the painstaking collection of evidence from a carefully-preserved crime scene. (The pistol was not found by the police that day and was not seen again for several weeks, when it was picked up by a young urchin from the trackside, having fallen there from the drain-pipe in the floor of the carriage when the police finally allowed the train to be moved up the line into the depot north of South Suburbia to be thoroughly searched. It was then used in a series of successful raids on sub post offices and small bank branches in South London and the southern Home Counties. The urchin used the proceeds of the raids to fund his university education, and some years later became the most successful criminal defence lawyer seen in Britain for many a long year, mainly defending the (alleged) perpetrators of armed hold-ups and thefts of small amounts of cash from sub post offices and small bank branches. The gun was never seen again.)

Having stopped shouting and thumping around, and having made a rapid assessment of the level of threat they faced from the perpetrator, the members of the North Weald Armed Response Unit (all two of them) carried out a staged, controlled retreat, backing up to position themselves on either side of the doorway to allow their senior officer to enter.

'All clear Guv',' one of them bellowed out through the door opening, straight into the ear of his Inspector, who had just then chosen to poke his head round the doorpost to find out what was going on.

'Fuck me, what the Mother of God is that?' he exclaimed, stepping into the compartment, poking at his half-deafened ear with a finger as he did.

'One perp., disabled and unarmed,' reported the other policeman, adding rather unnecessarily that the scene of crime was now safe and secured.

At the order of the senior man, the two armed policemen withdrew, to be replaced by two others, these both dressed in plain clothes, whose names, it appeared, were Detective Chief Inspector Flagg and Detective Sergeant Brennan.

After that, for a while, Wright was reduced to little more than an exhibit; a central part of the crime scene, but not required to play an active part in it, as photographers came and went, people in white suits came in and out, picking up tiny pieces of this and that with tweezers and putting them into evidence bags, then leaving again. The Book of Excuses was lifted carefully off the floor by white-gloved hands, dropped into a bag and taken away. The driver and guard came in, were spoken to by Flagg and Brennan, did some pointing and left.

Eventually it was Wright's turn. The gag was removed and taken away for forensic examination and DCI Flagg stood in front of him.

'Now sir,' he said. 'Perhaps you'd be good enough to give us your name.' Wright told him and Brennan wrote it down. 'Well Mister Wright,' Flagg said. 'We'd like you to accompany us to the police station in North Downham to help us with our enquiries: or we could arrest you and take you there anyway. Which would you prefer?'

'I'll come,' Wright said.

'That's good,' Flagg told him. 'Brennan: get him free.'

Brennan got him free, but not by unlocking the handcuffs. Instead, he got out a long and heavy-looking screwdriver and took the rail off the wall. Wright was then led unceremoniously out of the toilet compartment and off the train, across the platform and out into the station forecourt to a waiting police car in full view of a crowd of gawping onlookers and baying pressmen who had collected there in the hour or so since the police had arrived. Wright tried to shield himself from the flashbulbs and telephoto lenses being thrust in his direction and the frenzied shouts of the photographers and journalists, but Brennan held firmly onto the chain of the handcuffs and all he was able to do was turn his head away from one into the full gaze of another. Then he was in the back of the car, sandwiched between two stern and silent uniformed officers, speeding up the slope, away from the station towards North Downham. Two more cars fell in line, one ahead and one behind, with lights flashing and sirens screaming as they cut through the traffic on their journey northwards.

On arrival at the police station the convoy of cars pulled up inside the walled rear courtyard and its massive gates were pulled shut behind them. Wright got out and was told to follow one of his escorts through a door at the back of the building, past two lines of gaping, sniggering policemen and women who had obviously heard what was coming and the sight they were about to be treated to. Once inside, he was taken along a corridor to the front desk to be booked into the daily log.

'Name,' said the desk sergeant, looking him up and down with a barely suppressed smirk.

'Adrian Wright,' Wright told him.

'Any pockets to empty or offensive weapons about your person?' the sergeant asked, and laughed. Wright just glared at him.

'Take him down to cell three,' the sergeant told his escort.

'Just hang on a minute,' Wright protested. 'Why are you sending me to a cell? I'm the victim here. I've been robbed at gun-point, assaulted, made to dress in this absurd and disgusting costume, then paraded publicly in front of God knows who, to be photographed for the perverse enjoyment of God knows who else, and now you want to lock me up as though it was me who'd committed a crime. Well I protest!'

'I'd save your breath if I were you, sir,' the sergeant told him, placing unnecessarily heavy emphasis on the word 'sir' to make it crystal clear that, in his opinion, the title barely applied to the bizarre apparition that was standing in front of him. 'DCI Flagg says you're to be detained until he orders otherwise, so that's exactly what's going to happen. If you don't like it you can take it up with him the next time you see him.'

'And when's that likely to be?' Wright asked.

'That's something he hasn't seen fit to share with me, but I dare say it'll be when he's good and ready to find out just what exactly it is you may or may not have done or been up to. Until then you'll just have to wait . . . in cell three.'

The sergeant nodded to the escort to take Wright away. Wright tore his arm away from the man's guiding hand and thumped both of his, still 'cuffed together, down onto the top of the desk.

'Then the least you can do is take these off, and give me some decent clothes to put on.'

'Of course Sir,' the sergeant said, with the same emphasis on the word "Sir". 'Do you have the key?'

'No,' Wright told him sulkily.

'And neither do we; so until one of us finds it, or a locksmith or blacksmith appears, you're stuck with them. And as far as your clothes are concerned, we're not running a charity shop or some kind of shelter here and we don't carry a stock of alternative clothing for people who suddenly find their leisure-wear unsuitable for being arrested in, so you're stuck there as well. Now please go down to your cell before I have to have you carried there.' Wright acquiesced.

Cell three was not the most luxurious place he had ever been in; but it did at least have the merit of being warm, providing him with a place to sit down, as he was now beginning to feel very weary, and it was private, if you discounted the spy-hole built into the heavy metal door that was in regular use by someone or, more likely, any number of different someones, come to take a look at the latest "exhibit" to be detained at the pleasure of the North Weald Constabulary.

Time passed by slowly, very slowly, with no prospect of imminent relief from the abject misery Wright was feeling about the position he found himself in, and his growing hatred of John Biddle, the cause and architect of it all.

Eventually, after what felt like an eternity passing, he heard footsteps in the corridor outside, the scrape of a key in the lock and the sharp "click" as the bolt slid back when the key was turned. The door swung open and a uniformed officer entered the cell.

'Come with me please sir,' he said, and led the way outside. Another officer, who had been waiting outside the door, fell in behind and the three of them set out along the corridor. At its end he was shown into an empty interview room, told to sit down and wait; so he did. When Flagg and Brennan came into the room a little while later they first walked in opposite directions round the table that occupied the centre of the room, like a pair of what used to be called Red Indians circling a doomed wagon train, then sat down opposite Wright, facing him. Brennan reached out and turned on the tape recorder.

'First interview with Mister Adrian Wright: DCI Flagg and DS Brennan present,' he announced, then gave the time and date. Flagg and Brennan sat and looked at Wright expectantly. Wright just stared back at them silently.

'Well?' Flagg said eventually, breaking the lengthening and increasingly tense silence. 'Is there anything you'd like to tell us?'

'I was robbed,' Wright said, setting the scene for the version of the story he had decided to tell.

'You were robbed,' Flagg echoed. 'Of what, exactly, were you robbed?'

'Of a substantial amount of money; in used bank notes; in a canvas holdall.'

'Would you like to be a little more exact?' Flagg asked him. 'How much money, and what was it for?'

'It was . . . it was a million pounds. It was a payroll, for a group of railway workers who prefer to be paid their wages

33

in cash.' It sounded lame and limp to Wright, so God only knew what it sounded like to the other two.

'A million pounds in used notes,' Flagg repeated slowly, as though savouring the sound and feel of the words as they rolled off his tongue and across his lips. 'And who did this money belong to; not you presumably?'

'No,' Wright said. 'It belongs to my employer.'

'Who is? . . . ' Flagg asked after an expectant silence.

'Perma-way,' Wright told him quietly.

'And how do you come to be dressed like that?' Brennan chipped in, speaking for the first time. 'Assuming that's not your normal attire for transporting large amounts of cash, of course.'

'The robber made me put it on,' Wright told him.

'Any idea why?'

'No, not really; unless it was . . . ' he nearly said vindictive, but that would have opened up a whole new line of questioning because it would imply that Wright and the robber knew one another, and he did not want to either name Biddle or admit that he knew him. Biddle would be his, and so would the glory of reclaiming the money; as soon as he could get himself out of this place and this mess. Instead he said 'to help him to escape.'

'Would you like to explain that?' Flagg asked him.

Thinking on his feet, making it up as he went along, and finding that it fitted, Wright told him, 'The longer you spend interrogating me, the more time he has to make his escape, before you start to search for him. This . . . outfit,' he spat the word out 'is an attempt to make that process take longer than it otherwise would.'

'So it was a 'he',' Brennan said. 'Do you know who 'he' is?'

'No,' Wright said, prepared for the question; one that might have tripped him up a few minutes earlier.

'Any idea where he went?' Flagg asked.

'No, but the airport's not far away.'

'Description,' Flagg said, nodding to Brennan, who reached into the inside pocket of his jacket and pulled out his notebook so he could write it down. Had he been in a better mood, Wright might have been tempted to say 'A large, flat area with buildings, and strips of concrete where aeroplanes land,' but he was not in a good mood.

'Medium height and weight,' Wright said. 'With shortish mid-brown hair.'

'Clothes?'

'Dark trousers, probably jeans. Black shoes; leather; lace-ups. Red zip-front jacket—looking new or newish; not faded the way red does as it gets older.'

'Age?'

'Mid-forties, I'd say.'

'Anything else? Any distinguishing features or marks?'

'Nothing that I can recall.'

'What was the money in?'

'A dark green canvas holdall with brown leather handles. A typical old-fashioned type of bag.'

'Size?'

'Medium; fifteen inches by ten by six, perhaps.'

'OK Brennan,' Flagg said. 'Airports, London terminal stations, ports; all the usual.'

Brennan got up and left the room. Flagg told the tape recorder he had gone and what the time was, then leaned back in his chair, straightening his legs and folding his arms across his chest, as though he was relaxing; which he was not.

'Is this a regular thing for you?' he asked in a chatty tone of voice. 'This carrying around large sums of money in cash in such an unsafe manner?'

'No, not regular,' Wright said. 'I do it occasionally, but I wouldn't say it's unsafe. Drawing attention to yourself usually turns out to be less safe.'

'Ever been robbed before?'

'No; this is the first time; and the last, hopefully.'

'Did he find it easy? I don't see any marks or injuries.'

'He had a gun.'

'Did he now? That's interesting. The guard claims he saw a gun, but we haven't found one. How do you explain that?'

'Well I don't know where it is now, but there was one—I can assure you of that.'

'Is the guard a friend of yours; you know, a mate?' Flagg asked, suddenly leaning forward across the table and fixing his gimlet-like eyes on Wright's.

'No, of course not,' Wright said. 'I'd never seen him before he opened the toilet door after the robbery.'

'Never? Not even when you got on the train in the first place?'

'No. Well I suppose he was there, but I don't remember seeing him.'

'He remembers seeing you; and your 'mate': very chummy he says you looked.'

'I don't know what you're trying to imply Inspector, but I had a gun in my back at the time.'

'Alas,' Flagg said with regret, his palms open wide in a gesture that indicated emptiness. 'No gun.'

'But there was one, even if you and your plods can't find it now,' Wright snapped. 'So perhaps you'd better look again!'

'What's this?' Flagg asked him suddenly, lifting The Book of Excuses up off a shelf hidden under his side of the table and banging it down loudly on the top.

For a second Wright was unable to speak, as he scrabbled around mentally for the right answer. 'It's mine,' Wright said. 'It's a project I'm working on.'

Flagg opened the cover and began flicking through the pages. 'What's it all about?' he asked.

'It's a record of reasons why trains get delayed,' Wright told him. 'Starting in the early days of the railway and continuing up to the modern day.'

Flagg carried on turning the pages, looking at each one briefly. 'Why did you have it with you?' he asked.

'I was taking it to my office: to work on when I'd delivered the money. I collected it at the same time.'

'Why aren't these entries in chronological order?' Flagg asked, running his finger over the writing on the two open pages in front of him.

'I don't know. That's one of the things I've been asked to look into.' Wright looked up as the door swung open and Brennan came back into the room. He was glad of the interruption as he was beginning to find Flagg's line of questioning uncomfortable. Flagg told the tape machine that Brennan was back.

'Where's your office?' Flagg asked next, his interest in The Book apparently forgotten.

'In Overway House; above the station in South Suburbia.'

'And where did the money come from?'

'Bridges Junction. I was taking it from the depot there to Overway House.'

'Isn't that the wrong way round?' Flagg mused. 'Wouldn't it make more sense if it went from the head office, this Overway House, to the depot, where the hourly-paid workers who would want cash are more likely to be based?'

Wright paused, having to think on his feet to find answers that sounded plausible to questions that were beginning to stretch the web of lies he was spinning towards its breaking point. 'That's not my field of expertise,' he said, hoping to sidestep the issue, 'I'm really only a contractor, employed short-term to carry out specific tasks.'

'Specific,' said Flagg slowly then, after a pause, 'I'd have said that looking at a book listing reasons for train delays and carrying bags of used banknotes around the countryside were tasks that were far enough apart in nature to suggest that your duties were far from specific; wouldn't you?'

Wright shifted uncomfortably on his chair and coughed into his hand to cover the pause while he struggled to think of the right reply. 'The book is what I was hired for: the money was incidental. I went down to Bridges Junction to get the book and was asked to pick up the money while I was there.' He relaxed.

'But you implied earlier that you've done this kind of thing before,' Flagg interposed.

'No; I said it was done; but this is the first time I've been asked to do it.' Brennan opened his mouth as if to say something, but Flagg cut him off. 'We need to speak to your superiors, to let them know what's happened. Who should we speak to and how do we get hold of them?' he asked.

'You'll need to speak to Stephen Dent, Financial Director for the Region. He's based at Overway House. I don't have his number on me now I've lost my clothes and mobile phone, but you'll find the Perma-way number in the phone book. Ring that and ask for him and the switchboard will put you through. He'll probably be waiting for some news from you.'

'Thank you; I'll do that,' Flagg said, with just a faint edge of sarcasm in his voice. He was a senior-ranking detective after all, and finding people was a major part of his job. 'Now if you'd like to go with Brennan here, he'll take you back to your 'room'. It's probably best for your dignity and our peace of mind if you stay there until Mr Dent or one of his associates turns up with something more suitable for you to wear.'

They all stood up. Brennan and Wright walked to the door, with Brennan leading. Just as Wright was about to go through into the corridor, Flagg said 'Just one more thing Mr Wright; what were you going to do with the book and all those reasons for delays?'

Wright just stood in the doorway, open-mouthed, while he tried to think of an answer. 'Analysis,' he said eventually. 'Analysis of trends: cause and effect; to find out where we're going wrong and what we need to do to put it right.'

'Thank you,' Flagg said. 'You can go with Brennan now.' Flagg also left the interview room, turning and walking away in the opposite direction from that his DC and their 'guest' had taken, and as he did he could hear raised voices coming from the direction of the front desk, at the end of the corridor. Heading towards it to find out what was going on, he met the desk sergeant coming the other way, looking red in the face and flustered.

'Is there a problem Sergeant?' Flagg asked him.

'Yes, Sir,' the Sergeant replied. 'There's a gentleman out front demanding to see you immediately: says his name's Dent; Stephen Dent; and he doesn't want to take 'no' for an answer: and he's got two hulking great PCs from the Transport Police with him.'

'Is that so?' Flagg asked. 'And what does Mister Dent want to see me about?'

'Won't say, Sir; but he says as soon as you know he's here you'll want to see him too.'

'We'd better not disappoint him then,' Flagg said. 'Show him into one of the interview rooms and tell him I'll be there shortly.'

'And the two PCs?'

'Send them down to the canteen; and make sure they pay for their own coffee.'

Fifteen minutes later; minutes during which Flagg did nothing at all but wait for fifteen minutes to pass, he pushed open the interview room door to reveal a pacing, angry and impatient man he assumed was Stephen Dent. 'Mister Dent?' he asked, holding his hand out to the other man. 'I'm DCI Flagg. I believe you wanted to see me.'

'Yes, and about time!' Dent snapped at him, ignoring the hand. 'Your Sergeant told me you'd see me straight away.'

'Yes, well I'm sorry about that Sir,' Flagg said, not expanding on whether he was sorry he had not been there straight away or sorry that Dent had been told that he would. 'But I'm here now, so what can I do for you?'

'I understand you have one of my employees here.'

'Yes, a gentleman by the name of Adrian Wright. He's . . . '

'Well I'm here to insist that you release him from your custody and turn him over to the officers of the Transport Police who've come here with me, as the matter falls within their jurisdiction and not yours,' Dent demanded loudly, cutting Flagg off in mid-sentence.

'He isn't in custody Mr Dent. As I was going to say, if you'll allow me to, he's here voluntarily, helping us with our enquiries. Do you think he should be in custody? And if you do, may I ask why?'

'No, no,' Dent blustered. 'Not at all. I thought . . . I thought . . . Well anyway; this is a railway matter and so should be dealt with by the Transport Police. And as a matter of interest, what's Wright said to you?'

'He says he was robbed, sir. What do you think happened?'

'Robbed; yes, of course. Now, Inspector, can we have our man back please?'

'I don't see why not,' Flagg said after pausing for a moment's thought. 'The incident in question took place on railway property, so the Transport Police has jurisdiction as you say, so I wouldn't be able to resist a formal application from them, even if I wanted to, even if he had been arrested.' And so saying he got up, walked to the door, opened it and called out for the custody officer.

When he arrived, Flagg told him to go and get Mr Wright from cell three, find a white paper evidence suit for him to wear for his journey home, and get the 'cuffs taken off him with the bolt cutters.

Wright was produced shortly afterwards; the Transport Police officers were called up from the canteen and Flagg left them with the custody officer, going through the paperwork needed to secure Mr Wright from the time he had spent as their 'guest' and making sure that he was reunited with all of his possessions before he left; especially The Book.

Flagg and Brennan watched from the window of Flagg's second floor office as Wright and Dent, accompanied by their escorts, left the building, walked across the car park in front of it and got into the back of the large, black car that Dent had arrived in. The escorts got into the front and the doors all closed. The detectives could not hear what was being said, due to the distance, the height and the double glazing, but it was clear that heated words were being exchanged between Wright and his boss, and it was Flagg's guess that the argument between them would go on for some time after the car had swept through the open gates, turned onto the road, and been swallowed up by the early evening rush-hour traffic.

'My copper's nose tells me that all is not as it seems here Brennan,' Flagg told his DS. 'Get the transcript of that interview typed up as soon as possible; then go through it with a fine toothcomb looking for contradictions and discrepancies. And get the plods in the office to go through the records to find out anything and everything they can about our Mr Wright and his friend Mr Dent.'

In the back of the car, Wright's name appeared to have been changed to Fuckwit. Stephen Dent was livid: incandescent with rage; with an anger that could not be sated by anything that Wright might have to say for himself. Wright sat and listened as the storm blustered and blew and, finally, diminished from tornado to mere gale. Then, after making sure that the glass screen between the front seats and the back of the car was in its raised position, he turned to face Dent.

'Let's just calm down and take stock of where we are Stephen,' he said. 'You've got The Book back. Yes, we've temporarily lost the money, but the project is still intact.'

'And you know that for certain, because . . . ?'

'Because Biddle told me so: he knows exactly what we're up to—the delays, the phone calls, and the money they generate—but instead of blowing the whistle on us he's decided to blackmail us; one million in Sterling, which he's now got, and five thousand a month, to be paid into a numbered Swiss bank account. For that he keeps what he knows to himself and lets you carry on—unhindered.'

'While he lives the life of Riley off the fat of the land at our expense!'

'But only for as long as it takes us to find out where he is and get back what belongs to us, to put and end to this game of his.'

'Takes us! Takes us!' Dent screamed. 'There is no 'us'! You're out of the game, Wright: you had your chance and you blew it. Now sod off out of my sight and stay there. I don't want you anywhere near me or the project or the railway; unless it's to bring me our money back and that bastard Biddle's head on a pole! I may continue to employ the rest of the Arses or I may not; I haven't decided yet. But if I do give them a chance to redeem themselves their numbers won't include you! Now get out and go away.' Dent leant forward and stabbed at the button to lower the glass screen.

'Stop here,' he snapped. 'Mr Wright is getting out.'

'But you can't,' Wright pleaded. 'You can't just leave me here, in the middle of nowhere; it's miles from where I live; I've got no money or anything; we've got to plan to find Biddle and get the money back; we've . . . '

'I've told you,' Dent said in a menacingly controlled voice. 'There's no 'us'; there's no 'we'; now fuck off before I have to make you.' He leant across Wright and pushed the door open as the car came to a halt against the kerb. The two PCs in the front seats turned round to stare expectantly at Wright who, admitting defeat in the face of superior numbers, did as he was told. Dent slammed the door shut and the car pulled back out into the flow of traffic, straight into the path of an oncoming bus, whose hooting driver was treated to raised fingers on arms extended through both front windows of the offending vehicle. A short way back up the road a small, dark-coloured saloon pulled into the kerb and paused as its driver watched and waited to see what Wright would do next.

Wright started walking. The second car stayed where it was for a few minutes then started moving slowly forward again.

Wright, shoeless, angry, tired, dejected, plodded along the road feeling highly conspicuous in bare feet and the white paper suit the police had given him to wear. It would have been fine for a journey home in Dent's car; but this? Ahead of him a small, dark-coloured saloon dropped out of the stream of traffic and stopped against the kerb. As he approached it, the driver leant over and wound the passenger-side window down.

'Excuse me,' she called out as he passed. 'Am I heading the right way for Bigton please?'

Wright turned and looked down to his right, at the pretty, blonde, twenty-something who had called out to him. As he did not reply straight away she repeated her question. 'Is this the right way for Bigton?'

'S-sorry,' he stammered. 'I was miles away for a minute there; it's been a bit of a day one way and another. Bigton; no, not really; your best bet is to head east, towards South Suburbia, and look out for signs for the motorway. That'll take you straight there then. I can't do much better than that; this isn't really my area; sorry.'

She looked up at Wright for a moment or two, as if trying to make her mind up about something. 'Could you use a lift somewhere?' she asked. 'You don't look as though you're dressed for a long walk, and something tells me you've got a long way to go.'

Now it was Wright's turn to pause: then he decided it was too good an offer to turn down.

'That would be great,' he said. 'Thanks. I actually live in Pooley, not far away from the end of the motorway, so if you drop me off near home I can give you directions from there.'

'OK,' she said, smiling up at him as she pulled on the inside handle to open the car's nearside door.

Wright couldn't believe his luck as he settled into the passenger seat and she pulled back into the traffic. He longed to be back at home, safely locked up in his flat, after the pig of a day he had had. Tomorrow, after a long sleep, if that was possible, he was sure everything would look different; better; but right now? All he wanted was to get home.

'Bad day?' she asked. 'You look . . . what can I say? a bit rough around the edges.'

'I'd rather not talk about it,' he told her. 'I'd rather not even think about it.'

'Nice outfit,' she persisted. 'Present from the police?'

'Yes,' he said, 'I was robbed, and they needed my clothes as evidence.'

'Poor you; were you hurt?'

'No, not really, just roughed up a bit,' and as he said it he lifted his hand up to the bump and bruise on his head where Biddle had hit him with the gun. She glanced his way as he did.

'Ooh, that looks sore,' she said. 'There are some right nasty people around nowadays. Did they take much?'

'No, not really: wallet, keys, that sort of thing; nothing that can't be replaced.'

They chatted on amiably as she drove, following his directions; turning east and following roads that led, eventually, into Pooley. By the time they got there he was feeling a lot better; flattered by her attention and beginning to feel a bit better about the situation he was in. He tried to get her to drop him off in the High Street, but she was insistent that she should take him all the way to his door; particularly after the day he had had. Once they had stopped, he told her how to find the end of the motorway that would then take her on to Bigton.

'Thanks for bringing me all the way home,' he said as they turned into the road he lived in. 'I'm just up here on the right; number thirty-three.' Pause. 'I don't suppose you've got time for a coffee or something?'

'That's very sweet of you,' she said. 'But I think I'd better press on. I've got a dinner-date in Bigton tonight and I've got to get ready when I get there; you know, put on the glad-rags and war-paint.'

'He's a lucky man, and I hope he's grateful.'

If only you knew, she thought. Last thing now—'You are lovely . . . and by the way, I'm Sasha,' and held out her hand. He took it and shook it awkwardly.

'I'm Adrian: Adrian Wright.'

'Well, Mr Wright; it's been nice meeting you. Perhaps we'll meet again sometime. I've been looking for a Mr Right for some time now,' and she laughed. 'Now I must get going.'

Wright opened the door and got out, pushing it shut behind him. As Sasha drove off he crossed the road and walked up the steps of the tall Victorian terraced house his converted flat formed a part of. Inside the front hall he made his way to the door of his neighbour, Mrs Johnson's, flat, hoping that she would be in and that she would not have forgotten where she had put the spare key to his front door, which he had given her for safe-keeping not long after he had moved in.

Sasha drove to the end of the road, turned left and slotted into a parking space on her left a short distance from the junction, alongside the railings of the park that stood opposite the terrace that housed Wright's flat and that flanked the road she had just turned into. The park would make it easy for her to take the photographs she needed without being too readily seen, but that could wait; first she had to get her copy filed. Pulling a small dictating machine from her handbag on the back seat and thinking back over the events of the day—the mad dash from the newsroom to Lord's Copse in the wake of the Armed Response Unit; seeing Wright emerge from the station entrance in the pink leather outfit; following him back to North Downham police station; then tailing the black car; and the absurdly-lucky pick-up after whoever it was in that car had dumped him so unceremoniously—she turned the machine on and started to speak. 'Police and railway officials remained tight-lipped tonight about the details of an unsavoury incident on a train at Lord's Copse Station earlier today that appeared to have involved a local man in some kind of bizarre assault. Giving his name only as Adrian . . . '

The following morning Wright set out on what he was thinking of as his comeback. The way he looked at it there were two ways he could deal with the situation he found himself in; he could give in and go under; or fight, and fight to win. He chose the latter. The first thing he did was to ring his mobile phone from the land-line in the flat. He sat and listened to it click, then connect, then ring, and ring and ring. Having nothing better to do, he just left it ringing. It took about five minutes, but eventually it was answered.

'Hello,' said a voice Wright did not recognise.

'Hello,' Wright said. 'Who am I speaking to please?'

'It's George,' said the voice.

'George; my name's Adrian. That's my mobile phone you've got there George. I lost it yesterday and I'd like to have it back please. It's an old model and not worth much, but I'm willing to pay you something for your trouble if you can look after it for me until I can come and collect it.'

'You say you'll pay me,' said George warily. 'How much?'

'Well; that's a difficult question to answer,' Wright told him. 'How much do you think it might be worth?'

'How about a hundred quid?' Wright breathed in sharply. A hundred was a bit steep, but he needed the phone for its SIM card with his contact names and numbers on it. Damn! Why had he never thought to buy himself one of those devices you can get to back-up your phone memory and SIM card? 'Fifty,' he said.

'Not enough,' George told him. 'You want it more than that, or we wouldn't be talking.' They argued back and forth for a few minutes more; then settled on seventy-five in cash, no more questions asked. They arranged to meet in Bigton, where George said he worked, on the promenade, at lunch time, twelve-thirty, at the end of the pier.

Wright listened to George end the call; then put his phone down. Picking up a train timetable from the coffee table, he leant back in his chair and started looking up train times between South Suburbia and Bigton. Choosing the train before the one he really needed to catch, just in case they were running late (not that that would ever happen, would it?) he worked out what time he would have to leave the flat, with a stop at the bank on the way to draw out the cash he was going to need. Luckily he had always split his money between two bank accounts, and only ever carried one set of their cash-cards around with him when he went out, so the other was still in his possession. Eventually, he knew, money would be a problem if he did not get himself another job, assuming that yesterday's fiasco would lead to him being fired from his employment at Arse, but for the time being he could live off the contents of his bank accounts and his savings.

The taxi he rang for took him into South Suburbia in the middle of the morning, depositing him in the High Street outside his bank, where he used the cash-point before walking on the last few hundred yards to the station. Sasha followed the taxi in her car, making sure she thought she knew where it was heading before phoning her office to ask Jim, one of her colleagues, to get himself down to the station to take over tailing Wright for as long as it took to find out where he was going. Jim would recognise Wright from the photographs Sasha had taken the day before, although he was wearing clothes that day, rather than the skimpy leather outfit, and Sasha had given her co-worker the registration number of the taxi. Their office was also in the High Street in South Suburbia, and that proved to be lucky for Jim, as he saw Wright getting out of the taxi outside the bank when he shot out through the front entrance of the Suburban Advertiser's building, just four or five doors away. Jim sauntered along slowly as Wright got his cash out; then sped up to walk at the same pace as his quarry as he made his way down to the station. When they got there, Wright walked up to one of the vending machines and set about buying his ticket. Jim, tall, slim, ginger-haired and bearded, formed a queue of one behind Wright and looked over his shoulder as he did, then pretended to buy his own ticket as Wright walked away, went through the automatic ticket barrier and started to walk down the ramp towards the platform where the fast trains to Bigton came in. Jim opened the barrier with his regular season ticket and followed, reporting Wright's destination to Sasha on his mobile as he did.

'He's gone down onto the platform Sash, so it's odds-on it's Bigton he's going to. There's a non-stop fast due in in just under fifteen minutes, so I'll stay with him until it arrives and he gets on it. Do you want me to go with him?'

'No thanks,' Sasha told him. 'I'm just heading down to the top end of the motorway now, so if I put my foot down I should get there at just about the same time that he does.'

On another day that would have been over-optimistic wishful thinking on her part, but on that day Sasha was lucky, as a combination of good weather, light traffic, summer holidays for many of the members of South Weald's Traffic Police Division and a set of broken points just outside Bigton station meant that she was parked-up in a waiting-only area not far from and with a good, clear view of the station entrance when Wright walked out through it.

Wright was glad that he had chosen to catch the earlier train, otherwise he would have been late for the meeting with George and might have missed the opportunity to reclaim his phone. As it was, even after the delay on the way down, he was ahead of time, and was able to take a leisurely stroll down the hill towards the seafront.

Sahsa sat in her car and watched him start off down the long, straight slope towards the sea. She gave him several minutes' head start, then pulled out and followed. Just before she caught up with him she found a parking space on a meter on the opposite side of the street and pulled into it. She got out, locked the car, fed some coins into the meter, then set out to follow Wright on foot.

When he arrived at the end of the pier, at twelve twenty-five, Wright simultaneously realised two things: that he had no idea what George looked like, and that George had never seen him either. The only thing he could do was take up a position from where he had a good view of the area, then look around for someone else who looked similarly lost, hoping that that person would turn out to be the man he was waiting for.

Sasha tried to stay out of Wright's line of sight by standing more or less directly behind him and some distance away as she watched him. And as she watched she saw two men, who obviously did not know one another, eventually meet up to make some kind of exchange. As they did, she took a series of photographs to add to the collection she already had.

'George?' Wright had asked, approaching the man he had singled out as the one most likely to be the one he wanted.

'You must be Adrian.'

'Yes; have you got it?'

'Yep. Here it is,' holding out the phone. 'Have you got the money?'

Wright took it out of his jacket pocket and held it out. George took the money and Wright took the phone.

'I suppose you'll want these too,' George said. 'The phone was in the jacket pocket.' He held out the bag he was carrying, which Wright now recognised as Biddle's; that had contained The Book of Excuses the day before, and was now filled with Wright's lost clothes.

'Thank you,' Wright said. 'That's good of you.'

'No trouble,' said George. 'They're not worth anything, and they're no use to me.' Then after an awkward silence he concluded 'I'd better get back to work then.' He turned and walked away. After checking that his wallet and cards were still in the jacket pocket, Wright walked slowly back in the same direction, towards the station, apparently following George, who seemed to be one of that increasingly rare breed, an honest crook. Sasha followed Wright following George. In line astern they turned away from the sea, walked back up the slope, across the station forecourt and, one by one, in through the main entrance. Inside, Wright stopped and stared, open-mouthed, as George first stopped to buy himself a sandwich, then returned to his post on the customer service desk of the station's lost property office.

'Bugger it!' Wright exclaimed under his breath; then turned away towards the destination board to look for a train to take him home, and bumped straight into Sasha who was coming the other way with a coffee in her hand. 'Sasha,' he said. 'What a lovely surprise. Are you following me, or am I following you?'

'Adrian,' she said, feigning surprise. 'Fancy seeing you here! I almost didn't recognise you with your clothes on,' drawing strongly disapproving sidelong glances from the nearby queue of grey panthers on a day's outing to the seaside, who saw just a middle-aged man and a girl looking young enough to be his daughter apparently discussing their recent sexual exploits out in public where just about anybody could hear them. Disgusting! Wright blushed, but Sasha was implacable.

'What are you doing here?' she asked him, taking his arm and steering him towards the coffee stand. 'Come and have that coffee you offered me yesterday.'

'They found my phone,' he said. 'On a train, when they cleaned it.'

'That's great. What's that; been shopping?' she asked, pulling at the top of the bag he was holding.

'Nothing,' he said quickly, snatching it away from her, but not before she had managed to glimpse what was inside. She dropped the subject and asked him what he wanted to drink, to divert his attention, as they reached the head of the queue.

From the counter they moved over to stand at a high table with no chairs, from which Wright could see the destination board showing the expected arrivals and departures at the station.

'How was your dinner-date?' he asked her.

'It was fine,' she said.

'And the company?'

'A lovely man; but not the one, I think; not my Mister Right.'

'Well better luck next time.' He drank his coffee and made ready to leave. 'My train goes in a couple of minutes,' he told her.

She reached down, pulled a pen and a piece of paper out of her handbag and scribbled quickly. 'My number,' she said. 'Call me sometime; for a drink or dinner or something. What's yours?' He told her and she wrote it down in the front of a small diary, also pulled from her bag.

The train Wright caught in Bigton sped northward towards South Suburbia, stopping at Howards Heath, Bridges Junction and High Weald International Airport on the way. As it left the outskirts of the seaside town behind it, Wright pulled out his recently-reclaimed mobile phone and looked to see if he had missed any calls or messages. Its liquid crystal screen told him he had missed one call, and had a text message telling him so. He dialled in to his voicemail box, pressed the button to listen to the waiting message, then swore loudly as the voice he heard turned out to be John Biddle's.

'This is John Biddle, calling for Adrian Wright. Adrian, I just wanted to call to leave you a message. I just wanted to say hello; to let you know that I'm fine; and to tell you that, well . . . I'm on a plane.'

You bastard, you bastard, YOU BASTARD! he thought, listening to the sound of the disembodied voice and the sharp click of disconnection at the end of it. I'll get you; one way or another; you see if I don't!

CHAPTER THREE

Wright's train arrived back in South Suburbia without further incident. He got off and walked up the ramp into the main passenger concourse on the bridge above the tracks. On the far side of the ticket barriers the newspaper vendors had arrived and set up their kiosks and billboards. The front page headline of the early edition of the local rag caught his eye and sent him into another fit of rage and confusion. He quickly bought a copy and retired into a quiet corner to read it and despair.

The headline

"ARMED POLICE LEAD RAID ON LOCAL TRAIN"

sat squarely above a picture of him being led out of the entrance to Lord's Copse station in handcuffs and the pink leather outfit, his face clearly visible to the camera. Underneath, the story read

"Police and railway officials remained tight-lipped last night about the details of an unsavoury incident on a train at Lord's Copse station earlier in the day that appears to have involved a local man in some kind of bizarre assault.

The man, identified only as Adrian, was taken from the train handcuffed and wearing just a pink leather thong and bodice after it was raided by members of the North Weald Police Armed Response Unit.

The incident, which is reported to have begun when an armed man brought the train to a halt, triggered a widespread security alert that disrupted services on the London to Bigton line for the rest of the day and also involved officials at the Airport."

Wright skimmed through the rest of the article on the front page, which appeared to say nothing more that was not mere speculation or a repeat, in different words, of what had already been said; then turned to the inside page where the story was flagged as continuing. As he opened the paper he almost dropped it in surprise, because the text was illustrated with a photograph taken looking along the road where he lived, from the park fence side, with the building his flat was in almost in the centre of it, and with a caption underneath that read "The man arrested at the scene, and later released from police custody, is believed to live alone somewhere in this quiet suburban street in the West Park area of Pooley."

Oh my God, he thought. Where did they get all this from? It must have been the police; nobody else knew; unless it was Dent, of course, and I wouldn't put that past the man.

Hurrying out of the station entrance, Wright turned left, away from the High Street, and entered the older part of town, where the smaller, independent shops and businesses are located. The old-fashioned barber's shop he went into was not his regular place, so he was not known there and had little chance of being recognised, but that did not stop him from burying his face in a two year-old motoring magazine while he waited, in case someone came in who had seen it on the front of the local paper. When his turn came in the chair, he had to be brave.

'Yes sir, and a-what can I a-do for you?' the Italian barber asked him.

'A complete change,' Wright told him. 'Shave off the moustache; give me a number two cut all over; and lose the grey, I want it darker again.'

'Yes, Sir,' the barber replied enthusiastically. 'I make you look a-ten a-years a-younger when I finish.'

'I hope so,' Wright answered, 'that's what my new girl wants.' The barber's reflection winked an eye at him conspiratorially in the big mirror on the wall.

Wright sat and watched as the moustache, an old friend, disappeared; the not-quite-so-short-back-and-sides hairstyle he had sported since he left the Army in the late 1980s changed into something very different which, he had to admit, he did not dislike; and the colour changed back to something close to what it had been in the eighties as well.

Leaving the shop feeling as different as he looked, he went further into the old shopping area to search for his next port of call. It took a little while, but eventually he settled on a small gentleman's outfitter selling things that were different from his normal, rather formal, attire of blazer, collar and tie and grey flannels, but which would not take him as low as dropped-crutch jeans, huge upholstered trainers the size of small sofas and T-shirts with obscene slogans plastered all over them. What he chose were dark blue chinos, classic white polo shirts, a black zip-fronted leather jacket and a pair of dark grey, casual-looking shoes that were rugged and built for easy walking. The overall effect comfortable and cool; rather than the in-your-face 'young' look some men of his age (foolishly) choose to go for.

Better, he thought, looking at his new self in the long mirror in the fitting room. Almost unrecognisable: just what I was hoping for. Now to get on. Keeping his new clothes on, he packed all the old ones away in the carrier bag the shop assistant gave him when he paid; then took his new identity home in a taxi.

Back in his flat once again, having gone in through the alleyway at the back of the house rather than using the front entrance, where he might be seen by the press if they were still lurking around there, he settled down in his chair with his train timetable. Scribbling notes on a piece of scrap paper perched on the chair-arm alongside him, he started to put together an itinerary for the ill-fated journey he had made the morning before. Was it only then that it had all happened? he asked himself. It seems like so much longer ago than that; a measure of how much has happened in that time, I suppose.

He began with his departure from Bridges Junction at just after nine o'clock, tracking the train he took up the line to North Downham where he left it and, after a short wait, got onto the southbound train which Biddle (bastard!) had then forced him to get out of at The Boltons. There they crossed the bridge to the up platform and got on the next northbound train, staying on it until Lord's Copse. Biddle then left the train, and Wright was left to the tender mercies of the train crew and the police. At this point Wright had to force himself not to dwell on the cringe-making embarrassment of what he had gone through after Biddle had left him, but concentrate on where the bastard himself might have gone.

Thinking through what little he knew, he reasoned that Biddle must have gone straight from Lord's Copse station to the airport, and he must have done it by swapping to the train that came through on the southbound line while the fiasco with the toilet and the smoke bomb was being played out; that was the only way the times worked out. Referring to the timetable again, he reasoned that the most likely time for Biddle to have got to the airport was 11.15am, the arrival time there of the train he must have swapped onto.

From there, assuming that he was being honest when he had made his phone call, and that he already had his plane ticket with him when he arrived at the airport, Biddle would only have needed to check in, go through passport control and security, then walk down to the gate and board. So the phone call, received on Wright's mobile at 12.45, number withheld, could have been made either from Biddle's mobile phone immediately after boarding, before the plane's engines were started, or after take-off, when the seatbelt signs went out and the crew went through the cabin for the first time asking if there was anything anyone wanted or needed. So if he really was on a plane, and giving him a minimum of fifteen minutes to get from station platform to gate, and giving the plane a reasonable length of time to push-back, taxi, join the runway and take off, that plane must have been scheduled to leave sometime between 11.30 at the earliest and, say, 1.15 in the afternoon at the latest.

At that point Wright got up and moved across to the desk where his computer stood. He sat down, turned the machine on and logged on over the internet to the website of High Weald international Airport. Following links through several of its pages, he eventually arrived at a table that listed the flights scheduled to leave that day. His shoulders sagged in disappointment, as he had hoped to find a full list of departing flights shown there, but he could only see part of the story—the list of flights scheduled to leave between then and the rest of the day. The part he was really interested in had been deleted progressively earlier in the day, as and when those flights left. The next morning, he reasoned, a full list would be shown again, but that was almost twelve hours away. There was nothing he could do about it but wait.

That time of waiting was spent cooking and eating, then showering, reading and sleeping. Surprisingly, he managed each one of them comfortably, having expected to be far too agitated to have much of an appetite for food or books, and fully prepared for a restless, sleepless night for the same reason.

In the morning he took his breakfast to the computer and re-trod his steps from the night before, finding that, as he had hoped, the full day's complement of flights was listed there for him to look at. Taking a pen and paper from the desk drawer under the computer, he wrote down the names of the countries and cities the flights he was interested in were going to that day. He knew that flight schedules changed from day to day, so any list he wrote that day, being a Thursday, would not match exactly the schedule for the Tuesday of that week, but some of it would, and he was really only looking at that point for an indication of the size of the task he was facing in trying to work out where Biddle might have disappeared to.

He looked, he wrote, then he added up, and he found that between 11.30am and 1.15pm on that day, 46 flights were scheduled to leave, heading for 41 separate destinations in 17 different countries across the world. Clearly he was not going to be able to find the bastard Biddle by just choosing the flight he had taken, then hopping on it to follow him. So with that thought in mind, he got himself ready to go out, and was just about to leave when the phone rang.

He picked up the receiver and snapped 'Wright,' into it.

'Am I speaking to Mister Adrian Wright?' a businesslike female voice asked him.

'Yes, you are,' he replied.

'Employee of Amalgamated Risk Services (Europe)?'

'Yes. Can I help you?'

'You can indeed. My name is Sharon Froode. I am the Human Resources Director at Amalgamated Risk Services (Europe). I have been asked to read this statement, addressed to you, from the Director General of the company. Its content will be confirmed in a letter to be delivered to your home address shortly. The statement reads as follows:-

(1) Following recent events involving the loss of one million pounds belonging to our client, Perma-way, you have been suspended pending further investigation.

(2) Following adverse publicity surrounding those recent events and the loss of your anonymity you have been found guilty in your absence of gross misconduct and your contract of employment with Amalgamated Risk Services (Europe) has been terminated with immediate effect.

(3) All monies owed to you up to and including the date of your termination will be paid in the normal way, on the normal payroll date at the end of the month.

(4) You are reminded that certain terms of your contract, specifically those relating to client and company confidentiality agreements and any national laws regarding secrecy, including, but not

limited to, the United Kingdom Official Secrets Act, outlive your contract termination and continue to apply to you. Any breach of these requirements will be pursued vigorously at law and may result in prosecution, financial penalties being imposed, or imprisonment.

Have you understood what I've just told you Mister Wright?'

'Yes,' Wright said dejectedly, seeing no point in arguing: the events she referred to had happened, and Arse had decided they were all his fault and were not about to change their minds just because he disagreed, so what was the point?

'Good,' said Ms Froode. 'Written confirmation will be delivered to you shortly. Goodbye.' And that was it; the end. It was over; his career was over, with little he could see in the way of future prospects.

As he put the phone down the doorbell rang. He went to the front door, opened it a crack and looked out. It was a motorcycle courier, holding out a slim envelope, that was addressed to Wright, in one hand and a clipboard holding a form he was required to sign to acknowledge its receipt in the other. The envelope was from Arse; he knew that without needing to look. It was the letter he had just been promised in the phone call.

'That was bloody quick,' he told the courier as he scribbled his name on the receipt with the pen tied to the clipboard on the end of a length of tatty old string.

'My pleasure,' said the courier into the heavily padded inside of his helmet, leaving Wright hearing nothing more than an incomprehensible mutter.

Wright dropped the letter onto his hall table without opening it—there was no need, he had already been told what it said—as the courier descended the front steps, mounted up and tore off up the road with a deafening roar and a cloud of exhaust fumes. Wright pulled his front door closed and went out the back way to walk to the station.

Surprisingly, to him at least, on the way to the airport his mood lightened and he began to enjoy a perverse sense of freedom; a feeling that he was no longer beholden to the whims and vagaries of others, that the choice of where he went and what he did was entirely his to make, without reference or responsibility to anyone but himself. He knew, of course, that it was all an illusion and could only last until his money ran out, but until then he decided that he would make the most of it and enjoy it as much as he could.

His arrival at the airport also felt different. He had been there a number of times in the past, usually as a passenger, coming or going on trips in and out of the country; but he had never seen it before as a venue for a massive re-creation of a game, remembered from his childhood, of hunt the thimble. Getting off the train, he tried to see the place through bastard Biddle's eyes; somewhere to be got through as quickly as possible, but also somewhere he might have had to hide a bag full of money that he was not taking with him but would be coming back for later. Wright had decided to leave the rushing part until 11.15, when the train that Biddle must have got there on would arrive at the station. In the meantime, the search for a possible hiding place would begin.

Taking the station itself as his starting point, Wright stalked up and down the length of each platform in turn, looking carefully for lockers or other places where the bag might have been left. There were no lockers, nor anywhere else that looked likely to offer a safe haven that Biddle could return to with any hope of finding that what he had left was still there and waiting for him. Wright left the platforms and moved on, up the escalator to the station concourse on the floor above. Standing under the destination boards he looked carefully around him, turning slowly as he did. He saw the plate glass windows facing northwards, up the railway lines beyond the end of the platforms; he saw the entrance to the footbridge with its stairs and escalators dropping down onto the platforms below; he saw the ticket office with its queues of tourists and their luggage waiting to be served; he saw shops, selling nothing particularly useful as far as he could see, but nevertheless very popular; he saw the entrance to the combined departures and arrivals area for the airport, with more shops beyond it; and finally a travel shop selling tickets and dreams. What he did not see was anywhere that bastard Biddle might have left the money.

Moving out of the station into the airport proper, he repeated the exercise in each area he came to; arrivals; the check-in areas for departing passengers; the bus station downstairs; the huge shopping mall that had been built upstairs. Then he took the shuttle the short distance to the second terminal and did the same thing there. The story was, he found, the same everywhere; the only safe haven he could find lay in the left luggage lockers, banks of which were located in both terminals. Now how could he get those open and search them?

By then it was approaching 11.15 am and it was time to go back to the station to wait for the arrival of the train Biddle had been on when he got there. The destination board told him it would be coming in on Platform 3, so that was where he went. It arrived on time, and as it slowed to a stop alongside the platform edge, Wright looked down at his watch. Then he moved off, walking quickly, as he did not think that Biddle would have been running for fear of attracting attention to himself. He went up the stairs onto the bridge, across the station concourse and through the opening into the departures area. Once there he went straight to one of the check-in desks and took note of the identity of the person at the back of the longest queue, then stood to one side and watched them make their way slowly to the front, check-in, make their way through passport control and into the security hall where the hand-luggage scanners were located. Changing his position so that he could see the person whose progress he had decided to monitor, he waited until their hand-baggage had been swallowed by the scanner, and they had walked through the gateway formed by the structure of the metal detector, then looked at his watch again. This, combined with the walking times to the various departure gates inside the terminal, obtained from signs placed just inside the passport control area, confirmed what he had already estimated, and told him that the times and flights he had picked out earlier were just about right.

In a mixed mood, he turned away and headed back to the station to begin again. On the one hand it was nice to have your theories proved right in practice, but on the other hand that still left Biddle with a huge number of flights and destinations he could have chosen from, which did nothing to help Wright's hunt for him and the money.

Back on the station platform, Wright repeated the exercise he had just carried out, this time turning right as he left the station and taking the shuttle service to the second terminal. On arrival there he went straight to departures, picked out his passenger, then watched and timed them as they passed through the check-in and security procedures. When they had gone he pulled a small notebook and pen from his jacket pocket and carefully wrote down the findings of his investigations up to that point. He really had no need to as he rarely forgot anything important; but he also subscribed to a belief in Sod's Law, knowing that if he wrote everything down he was sure not to forget it, but if he did not make notes he most definitely would.

What next? he thought to himself. A little lateral thinking, perhaps? What else can be done with money here? And looking around he saw the Bureau de Change; a place where money could be converted into other currencies. What would be the benefit? He had no idea, but it would not hurt, while he was there, to find out how much could be exchanged in one transaction. So that was what he did, going to all of the different outlets in each of the terminals in turn, finishing up back in the first terminal, not far from the station entrance. He was just writing down the findings of this latest piece of research in his notebook when he sensed the presence of a person hovering at his elbow. Looking up from his book, he found he was flanked by not one, but two tall, wide, athletic-looking men dressed in dark jackets and grey trousers, carrying radios and looking vaguely threatening.

'Good afternoon, sir,' one of them said. 'We're from airport security, and we'd like a word with you please. If you'd like to follow my colleague here, we can go somewhere private for a chat.'

The physique and demeanour of these two men suggested that it would be unwise to refuse their request, and the presence of armed policemen not far away, who would without doubt side with the representatives of airport security in any dispute or disagreement that might blow up, helped him to decide. 'Take me to your leader,' he said: so they did.

His two escorts took him through a door at the end of the passenger concourse that was marked "Private—No Unauthorised Access" and was secured by a lock operated by a swipe-card reader. The man in front slid his card through the slot in the front of the machine mounted on the wall, waited for a buzzer to sound, pushed the door open and stepped through into the brightly-lit corridor beyond it. Wright went next, followed by the second escort. At the far end of the corridor they turned sharp left into a room that was not unlike the interview room at the police station where Wright had spent so much time earlier in the week. Without being invited, he sat himself down on one of the four chairs gathered around the table that stood in the centre of the room.

'OK,' he said. 'Who's going to tell me why I'm here? What is it that I'm supposed to have done?' He was not feeling intimidated by any of this because he knew he had not done anything wrong.

'If you'd just like to wait a few minutes, sir, someone will be here to talk to you; then you'll have the opportunity to say your piece.'

Those few minutes passed by and, at the end of them, another man arrived, bringing with him a slim, buff folder containing, Wright assumed, the inevitable forms to be filled out to record the proceedings that were about to take place. The man sat down and, without looking up, opened the file and took a pen out of his jacket pocket. 'Your name please, Sir,' he said to Wright, clicking the top of his ballpoint with his thumb as he did.

'Could you tell me why I'm here please?' Wright asked in a measured tone of voice.

'We'll get to that in a moment: if you'd just like to tell me your name please.' The man with the pen began to fill in his forms, with date, place, time and other basic information preliminary to the insertion of his "suspect's" name.

'And if I don't?' Wright asked.

'We have the right to hold you here on suspicion while we summon the police. They have the right to search and detain you further pending enquiries. It's much easier if you'll just co-operate.'

'Suspicion of what, exactly?'

'You've been observed, for quite some time, acting in a suspicious manner, on the CCTV system, sir. You don't appear to be here with the intention of catching a flight, and you don't appear to be here to meet anyone. You've been asking some rather odd questions about the left luggage lockers and about the amounts of money that can be exchanged in the various bureaux in the various terminals. Taken together that adds up to a pattern of behaviour that's not normal, and so is treated as being suspicious. That leads us to want to ask you some questions about what you're doing here, and why; beginning with your name and going on from there.'

Wright still made no reply. The man looked up for the first time, raising his eyebrows as he did, having been concentrating on the file and papers in front of him until then. A flicker of recognition sparked in his eyes, followed by a slow smile spreading across his face. 'Wright,' he said, 'Your name is Adrian Wright. You don't recognise me do you?'

Wright stared long and hard at the man sitting opposite him, but still said nothing.

'Ex-Sergeant Phil Patterson,' the man said. 'If I remember rightly, the last time we met was in that bar in

Aldershot; the night the whole platoon got banged up in the slammer after you started that fight.'

'Phil Patterson,' Wright repeated slowly, remembering for the first time in a long time the bar, the night, the fight. 'The fight I had to start to stop you from being massacred by that Marine whose girlfriend you groped. That night cost us all a small fortune in bribes, you sex maniac.'

'Yes, but wasn't she worth it? She was a dream,' Patterson said, smiling and mimicking the contours of the girl's ample curves with his hands.

'That's not the way members of the Military Police are supposed to behave,' Wright said, grinning and holding his hand out across the table. 'How the devil are you; and what are you doing here?'

Patterson shook his hand; then turned his attention back to the paper on the desk. 'I'm Head of Security for this part of the airport,' he said, 'and Deputy Head for the whole shooting match. Now it's your turn: what the hell are you doing here?'

'Can we do this in private?' Wright asked.

Patterson looked up at one of his two colleagues; then inclined his head towards the door. The two men left, closing the door behind them as they went, leaving Wright and Patterson alone in the room. Wright relaxed. 'I work for a firm of security consultants,' he said, getting out one of his Arse business cards and sliding it across the table. Technically, to his way of thinking, he was not lying, as his dismissal would not be real until he saw it written down in black and white, and so far he had not, because he had left the letter in his flat, unopened. 'I'm following the trail of a man I think came through here on Tuesday, between 11.15 and midday. What I was doing was working on a couple of theories, to see if they could be anything more than just theories.'

'And hence the coming-and-going, the clock-watching and note-taking,' Patterson said. 'What about the questions at the currency counters?'

'More theories,' Wright said, and said no more.

'So you think your man was carrying money with him?'

'I do, but I don't know how he would have got it through the security checks, so I was looking to see if there was some way he could have taken it legitimately, or left it behind so he could come back later to collect it.'

Patterson paused and took a deep breath, as though thinking about something unpalatable, which he was. 'I think I can help you there; and if we're both right it'll help set my mind at rest over a couple of things too.' He paused again before going on. 'At about the time you're interested in, something strange happened on one of the security scanners. The woman working on it got the shock of her life when she saw the skeletons of two rats running around inside the machine. The way she reacted was understandable, I suppose, but disappointing from our point of view given the training she's had. She screamed and jumped away from the machine. Everyone in the hall turned to stare at her, and . . . ' he held his hands out sideways, palms upturned, to indicate that he did not know what else might have happened.

'How did the rats get there?' Wright asked.

'In the pockets of a jacket that someone had put on the belt. It was . . . '

'Red,' Wright finished for him.

'On the inside,' Patterson corrected him. 'It was red on the inside; light blue on the outside, and reversible. It was inside the scanner when the rats were first spotted, and when it was examined later, traces of rat's urine were found inside the pockets, as well as on the outside of it. Rats are all incontinent, you know, so they pee all the time. These two were carried to the scanner in the pockets of that jacket and let out inside it, as a distraction from what was following it on the belt.'

'Which was a bag full of used fivers,' Wright told him.

'Are you sure?' Patterson asked.

'About as sure as I can be.'

'That puts my mind at rest: I had visions of something far worse. How much do you think there was?'

'About a million,' Wright said, 'Give or take some small change. Where did he go?'

'We don't know, and I wish we did. The cameras in the security hall sweep that room in a random pattern, but have a manual over-ride in case someone wants to look at something specific. When the woman screamed, the operators all took over and looked at her to see what was going on. None of them saw what else happened, so we've got nothing on tape: believe me, I've looked.'

'Anything else?' Wright asked.

'I've got a canvas holdall with a small animal cage and a pair of gloves inside, recovered from a bin in one of the male toilets here. The gloves are thin but tough; something like Kevlar I'd say; possibly military.'

'Can I see them?'

'You can; they're in my office,' Patterson said, picking up the folder of papers and Wright's card from the table, getting up and leading the way to the door. Once in his office, back down the corridor, Patterson shut the door and turned the key; then opened a locked cupboard. 'No-one but me and those two out there know about all of this; and that's the way I'd like to keep it.' He got the holdall out of the cupboard and placed it on the desk.

'That's what he had the money in when he arrived at the airport,' Wright said. 'I think we can assume that he had all this very carefully planned: the rats were already here, in a left-luggage locker probably: our man arrived, swapped the money over to another bag, more secure than this one, put the rats in his pockets, dumped this lot and went to security to spring his surprise. He put the jacket on the belt ahead of the bag with the money; the rats got out; then scream, panic, everyone stares, our man steps up, grabs the bag and disappears into the glorified shopping centre that masquerades as a main departure lounge. No-one notices because they're all too busy gawping at the screaming female and wondering what the hell's got up her skirt.'

'Are you sure you're sure about this?' Patterson asked.

'One hundred percent, now I've seen that,' pointing at the holdall. 'I'd stake my career on it,' which, of course, he already had, and lost, but Patterson did not need to know that.

'Good: I was shit-scared it was a bomb.'

'But you'd know if it was by now: it would have gone off.'

'Not necessarily. It could have been hidden somewhere, on a long time-delay trigger. Some of these aircraft don't get looked at that closely that often.'

'Well you can stop worrying on that score: it wasn't a bomb, it was cash; believe me, I know.'

'Thanks; it's a relief to know that. Is there anything else you need?'

'If I told you his name, could you find out where he went?'

'Not without a court order I couldn't. The Freedom of Information Act turns out to be just the opposite, but the Data Protection Act works very well when it comes to stopping us from finding out anything that might actually prove to be useful, and the airlines use it to protect the so-called privacy of the celebrities and crooks they ferry around the world; unless the celebs want to be photographed and gossiped about, that is, in which case everyone knows who's going where or been where.'

With that the business between them appeared to have been concluded. Each one thanked the other for the help they had been; then Wright made ready to leave. As he did, he reached out and took his business card off the desk. Holding it up for Patterson to see, he said 'This meeting never happened, and we haven't seen each other since that night in the bar. I don't know anything about rats, and Amalgamated Risk Services doesn't exist.'

'Absolutely,' Patterson told him. 'And I won't say goodbye because you were never here in the first place.'

On the train on the way back home. Wright took stock of where he was, and what he knew about Biddle and the money. What he did now know for certain was that the bastard had flown, and taken the money with him. What he still did not know was where he had flown to, and he seemed to have no way of finding that out. There were still 41 destinations in 17 different countries to choose from, in all parts of the world, and there were umpteen different airlines that had gone to those places on the day in question: and if someone in Patterson's position on the inside was not able to get information from the airlines, what chance did he have from the far side of the outside?

At the end of all this, he reached the conclusion that some lateral thinking was needed. If he assumed that Biddle had left the country, which was the obvious thing for him to have done, other possibilities opened up, involving contacts Wright had made over the years, and which he could still use, provided he did it quickly and got to them before word got round that he had been fired. So when he got back to the flat he phoned the particular man he was thinking of—his private contact at the Foreign Office.

'Hello Norman; this is Adrian Wright. Can you talk?'

'Not right now. Can you phone back in half an hour?'

'I can. Same number; your mobile?'

'That's it. Speak to you later.'

Half an hour later he tried again. This time Norman was in a position where he was able to speak.

'I need a favour,' Wright told him.

'Go ahead: no promises, but I'll see what I can do.'

'A man named John Biddle flew out of High Weald International on Tuesday, around midday. I want to know where he went.'

'Do you have any other details: travelling companions, airline details?'

'No, nothing I'm afraid.'

'It's difficult. I can't make any promises; contrary to what some parts of the sensationalist press would have us believe, this isn't a police state; we don't log everyone in and out, you know.'

'I know, and it's a long-shot, but if you do hear anything, could you let me know?'

'Will do: same number?'

'Yes: same number; and thanks.'

Wright needed something to do to occupy his mind and use up his energy while he waited for a call back from Norman; a call that might or might not come; so he decided to go to Asham to break into Biddle's house, to see if there were any clues to be found there. So, the following morning, he went back to the station and caught a train on the branch line that ran there out of Bridges Junction, heading towards the coast at Smalltown-on-Sea.

Wright got off the train and stepped down onto the platform at Asham station, fully aware of the fact that, once again, he was following in John Biddle's footsteps, but was a long, long way behind him. He did not know much at all about Biddle, but what little he did know included the fact that he had commuted from Asham to South Suburbia for the best part of twenty years (or was it the worst part?); taking the same trains at the same times, morning and evening, day in and day out, week in and week out, year in and year out; an unimaginable feat of endurance for someone like Wright, who thrived on variation and change.

He walked up the concrete steps onto the footbridge above the platforms, turned right, crossed over the tracks and then took the second staircase down to ground level on the other side. The streets behind the station were quiet; almost empty. The residents were mainly at work; most of their cars had gone with them, and commuters were no longer allowed to park in the spaces they left behind them since the introduction of the council's parking permit scheme several years earlier.

Wright crossed over in front of the pub on the corner and walked towards Biddle's house on the opposite side of the road, wanting to be able to see it clearly from the outside without being seen to be taking too much of an interest in it. As he approached it he could see there was a white van parked outside, and two men at work in the front garden. Drawing closer, he could see that the van had writing on its side:—"SunnyGlaze—Window Repairs, Renovations and

Replacement—Established 1974" and giving an address and phone number in North Downham.

Now that's interesting, Wright thought to himself as he walked past, and changed his plan of action to suit the change in circumstances that followed on directly from the van's presence there.

Being summer, daylight lasted well into the evening that day, and Wright could not help thinking that the kind of task he was about to embark upon would have been better suited to the bleak days of the winter months, when it got darker more quickly and everyone seemed to go home earlier. As it was, he had to wait until almost midnight to break into the premises of SunnyGlaze, using a poorly-secured door at the back of the workshop; then making his way forward to the office that faced out onto the street at the front. He picked his way between piles of stored timber, racks of sheets of glass and neatly-kept workbenches, holding his pocket torch out in front of him in one of his gloved hands to guide him into the office. Snapping the torch off, he stepped over to the front window and closed the Venetian blind to block off the glow of the streetlights outside; but also, more crucially, to stop anyone outside from seeing in.

Turning his torch back on again, Wright swept its beam around the inside of the room, stopping when it reached a pair of old, four-drawer filing cabinets standing against the back wall. They were both locked, but in only a matter of seconds he had snapped the locks out of both of them, using the screwdriver he had brought with him as a lever, and in just a few minutes more he had found what he was looking for. Thanking his lucky stars that this had turned out to be a very traditional small business, with nothing more than rudimentary security precautions in place on its premises—locks on its doors rather than intruder alarms, dogs and security guards, and neatly-filed papers in folders rather than computer-based order- and invoicing-systems—he slid open the drawers of the cabinets one by one, beginning the search for what he was hoping he was going to find there.

Their filing was, he found, impeccable, which made his job very easy and he gave a mental vote of thanks to the person or people who had set it up and looked after it all. The orders and invoices were filed by client name, in alphabetical order, which did not help him to begin with, as there was no paperwork for anyone called Biddle; but then he found another section that recorded the client names cross-referenced with the addresses where the work was to be carried out, so that the paperwork could be found either way, from the address or from the client name. From there it was simple: he looked up Biddle's address, 27 Ashvale Road, Asham, and pulled out a card telling him that the client was a Mr Everest of the firm Everest and Goodbody, Solicitors. Turning then to the file of client names, he found them and their address; 26 Chambers Street, North Downham.

Straight away Wright knew he had found not only someone who was likely to know where Biddle had gone, but who was almost certain to be the holder of the second of his computer discs, containing details of Perma-way's mobile phone scam; and as he realised this an alternative, a much more lucrative alternative, to simply recovering the money and returning it to Perma-way made its way steadily into his mind. If, he decided, he was to find Biddle and the money, and reclaim both copies of the disc at the same time, what was there to stop him from taking Biddle's place as the blackmailer of Perma-way and doing what Biddle had so cleverly planned, instead of him? A happy thought indeed!

With his task there finished, he put the papers back into the folders in the drawers and shut them, then walked back through the workshop to the door at the rear. He clicked the torch off and waited while his eyes adjusted to the darkness, looking and listening all the while to make as sure as he could that it would be safe to leave when he chose to go. He need not have worried himself, it was deserted outside and as quiet as the grave, and he made his way back easily to where he had left his car, a few streets away. The car in question was one that he had bought for himself that afternoon, as soon as it became clear that he would need to be in North Downham in the middle of the night, after the trains and buses had stopped running. What he bought was a small family saloon; stable, agile, economic to run and surprisingly quick, but also dark-coloured and nondescript; just the sort of thing his training at Arse had told him was good for this type of operation, just in case a speedy exit was needed. No such thing was necessary that night though, as the roads were clear and there was no pursuit to bother him. Wright drove home in a good mood, feeling that he was beginning at last to make some progress in his search of the haystack that was the world for the needle that was the bastard Biddle.

In the middle of the following morning, after a good night's sleep, Wright was woken by the sound of his mobile phone ringing on his bedside table. He fumbled around, trying to find it in the half-light of his bedroom, behind the still-closed curtains. He grabbed it, hit the button to answer it, and the ringing stopped. 'Hello,' he growled into it, still only halfway back to life from sleep. It was Sasha.

'Hello Mr Wright,' she said breezily. 'I haven't seen you for a while.' She meant it, she and Jim had not yet discovered the back way in and out of his flat, and had not knowingly seen his new persona either. Wright was confused: what could a young and attractive girl like this see in a middle-aged man like him, and yet . . . why should he question her motives? He had not had much in the way of female company and attention of late, so why not just make the most of it and enjoy it while it lasted, whatever those motives might be, and worry about the future when the future arrived.

'Are you OK?' she asked him. 'You sound as though you're still half asleep.'

'I am,' he said. 'I've only just woken up.'

'I hope it was a good night,' she said, assuming that he meant he had been out on the town. He grunted.

'Are you doing anything today?' she asked him. 'How about meeting up for lunch? If you're not busy, that is.' Now he was awake.

'That would be good,' he told her. 'If you're sure.'

'Of course I'm sure; I wouldn't ask if I wasn't. Where are you?'

'At home of course; I've only just woken up.'

'Those two things don't necessarily go together,' she said, and giggled. 'I thought it best to check. Shall I come over and pick you up?'

He thought for a moment, then said 'Yes; if you don't mind, but not at the flat. I've got to go to the . . . post office; there's one on the far side of the park outside my place. Would over there be alright?'

She agreed it would, and said she would see him there in an hour, long enough for him to get up, shower, shave and grab a coffee before leaving.

When he came out of the post office, having got there early and waited inside until he saw her arrive, she did not recognise him at first, and she had a moment's fleeting panic when he walked across to her car and opened the door. When she realised it was him she gasped in genuine surprise, taking in the smart new clothes and the short, dark hairstyle.

'Wow!' she said. You've had a makeover. It looks good. What brought that on?'

'I fancied a change; and it was long overdue.'

She lifted up her mobile phone and took a photograph of him as he settled himself into the passenger seat.

'What was that for?' he asked.

'So I'll recognise you next time I see you,' she said. So Jim will recognise you next time he sees you, she meant. 'Where shall we go then?' she asked him. 'Do you have to be back at any particular time?'

'Not really,' he said. 'What about you?'

'No; I don't work at weekends. Let's go down to Bigton; there are lots of good places there for lunch.'

'What do you do when you're not on a weekend off?' he asked her as she pulled away from the kerb and set out towards the motorway.

'I temp.' she said. 'Mainly admin and office work, but I'm up for anything really, as long as it sounds like fun. I like the variation; you know, different places, different people; it makes life interesting. What about you?'

'I'm in security. I work for a firm of security consultants.'

'That sounds interesting. Who do you work for? Would I have heard of them?'

'I don't suppose so. It's a secret anyway: if I told you I'd have to kill you; and I wouldn't want to do that,' and he laughed.

She stayed quiet, seemingly satisfied by the answer, while deciding that to push it further right then would be counter-productive and that she would have to wait and find out another way.

They drove down to Bigton for lunch, as she had suggested. The restaurant they chose was good, as was the food. He enjoyed her company and was flattered by the attention; at her interest in him. She seemed to be enjoying herself too. After lunch they strolled along the front chatting; with her subtly trying to find out more; with him being unintentionally evasive. Later, after coffee, they drove back to Pooley and she dropped him off at his flat. She thanked him for an enjoyable afternoon, leaned over and placed a light kiss on his cheek. He turned towards her and tried for more, but it was her turn to be evasive.

'I can see I'll have to keep my eye on you,' she said, laughing; and she meant it.

CHAPTER FOUR

Martin Everest had no family to speak of, at least none that could be described as close, his wife having left him many, many years before when he proved himself to be barren, so she could start to look for a man she could have children with. As a result, Everest never left his office early to rush home, there being no loving arms for him to rush home to, and he dedicated himself to his work. So it was getting quite late that Monday evening when he began to think about packing up and leaving his office.

Margaret, his ancient secretary, had long since left to feed her beloved cats and settle down in front of the television to watch the early-evening soap operas she enjoyed so much; so it was a surprise to Everest when he heard the outer door of the office open and close, then the sound of the bolts on the inside being slid home to secure it. He got up, walked over to the door of his own office and swung it open to reveal a stranger, a man, coming across the outer office towards him.

'Are you Everest?' the man demanded.

Everest looked him up and down, taking note of what he saw, and not liking it very much—the close-cropped brown hair, the nondescript, expressionless face, the black leather jacket with its zip undone revealing a white polo shirt underneath and, most concerning, the gloved hands in the middle of summer.

'Are you Everest?' the man demanded again.

'I am,' he replied. 'And to whom do I have the pleasure of speaking?'

'That's not important,' the man told him, pushing himself forward into Everest's office, forcing the solicitor to retreat. 'I've got some questions to ask you.'

'I'm sorry,' Everest said, rallying, and attempting to hold his ground. 'I'm about to close up and go home. Can you come back tomorrow?'

'No I can't. I've got questions to ask and I want answers now. Do you understand me?' As he said it he stepped forward and pushed Everest back again. The solicitor stumbled; then sat down heavily in one of the chairs that stood in front of his desk for visitors to sit in. It creaked loudly as his weight dropped into it. The stranger leant over him, looming threateningly.

'Where's John Biddle?' he demanded.

'Who?'

'John Biddle.'

'I don't know anyone of that name,' Everest said, his heart rate beginning to rise and his body beginning to sweat.

'Yes you bloody well do,' the man told him. 'He's one of your clients, and you've just paid to have the windows of his house repaired; in Asham.'

Wheels turned slowly in Everest's mind, the edge of his wits being dulled by his rising stress level, a racing heartbeat and an intense feeling of sickness that had started to spread upwards from his stomach. Eventually he made the connection between the repair of broken windows and the man he knew of only as Asham-Smythe, whose whereabouts he did not know.

'How do you know about the broken windows?' he blurted out.

'Because it was me that broke them,' the man said, leaning forward aggressively, thrusting his face forward and down, coming to a stop only inches from Everest's. 'Where's that bastard Biddle?' the man shouted, 'Where's he gone?'

Everest squirmed and pushed back in the chair, trying to get away, then went rigid with fear as a devastating pain shot up his left arm, across his chest, up through his neck and tried to take off the top of his head. The chair creaked loudly again and then cracked and split as his now-rigid legs and feet pushed hard against the floor and started to topple him over backwards, as his whole body went into spasm. The chair legs folded underneath slowly as the wood they were made of tore itself apart, and the massive bulk of the late Mr Everest was deposited on the floor in the shadow of his desk.

Wright stared down at him in surprise, unable to move, or speak, or even think. He stayed like that for what could only have been a minute or so but felt more like an eternity, waiting for a sign that the solicitor was still alive; but no sign came; no groaning, no movement, no breathing. Wright bent down and picked up a pudgy wrist, feeling for a pulse. There was none: there was no hope for him; the man was dead.

Wright swore, then stood up and looked around him. The room was fitted-out in a traditional style, with wooden panels on the walls to picture-rail height, then white-painted plaster from there to the ceiling, which was also white. A row of filing cabinets, also in wood to match the walls, the desk and the chairs, stood in the back corner, furthest from the door. He walked over and slid open the top drawer in the first cabinet he reached. Working through the drawers one by one he quickly figured out Everest's filing system and almost as quickly worked out that there was no record of a client called Biddle. Trying again, he looked for Asham, and this time found one labelled 'Asham-Smythe'. Pulling out its slim cardboard folder he opened it and found nothing more than duplicates of the window repair paperwork he had seen several nights before in the office of SunnyGlaze. It was a dead end; literally.

More in hope than anything else, he went out into the outer office and searched quickly through the cabinets and cupboards out there; quickly because he did not want to be seen through the windows that looked out onto the street. He found nothing of any use; no Biddle, no Asham-Smythe, and no likely-looking computer discs. Then, feeling slightly guilty about what had happened, while telling himself that it was not really his fault, he went back into Everest's office, picked up the phone on his desk and dialled 999. When the operator answered he asked for an ambulance to be sent to the solicitor's office address, feigning a pained and frightened voice, saying he needed help immediately as he was having a heart attack and was about to die. He rang off and put the phone down. Finally, he bent down over Everest's body, took the wallet out of his pocket and slid it into his own. From there he walked to the front door, slid back the bolts, then opened it and walked away down the street when he was sure no-one was passing or looking.

Thinking that there was no time like the present, Wright drove towards the southern edge of North Downham, to where the address given on Everest's driving licence was located; according to the street map he had bought in the first petrol station he had come across after reaching his car. The centre of the town with its shops and restaurants gave way to an area occupied by car dealers, fuel stops, DIY stores and computer retailers, then estates of suburban semis built between the wars on the slopes of the gentle hills that surrounded the town, and eventually to leafy lanes flanked by bespoke detached houses occupied by the well-to-do. One of those belonged to Everest, and was just waiting for Wright to arrive there and search it. First though, knowing absolutely nothing about the man and who might or might not be waiting for him to arrive home, Wright had to find out whether or not the house was occupied.

Waiting for darkness to fall was, he reasoned, the best way to do that, so he could see if and where there were lights on in the place. The presence of lights after dark did not guarantee that anyone was there—modern electrical timers made sure of that—but a lack of light inside the house would be a sure sign that there was nobody in. But as it turned out, he did not have to wait that long, because while he was waiting the police turned up and rang the doorbell, presumably to break the sad news of Everest's demise to anyone who was there to receive it. They drove up in their car, turned into the drive, stopped, and two uniformed officers, one man, one woman, got out. They walked up to the front door and rang on the doorbell but got no reply. They then rang on the doorbell and rapped on the knocker, with the same result. Finally they circled the outside of the house, knocking on side and back doors and rattling their handles, but it was all locked up and there was no answer. The female officer reported in on her radio, they got back in the car and left.

Wright waited for several minutes after the sound of their engine had died away to nothing, then slipped out from behind the bushes alongside the head of the drive and set off round to the back of the house. Using the end of a garden hoe that Everest had carelessly left leaning up against the side of the potting shed, wrapped in an old compost bag to deaden the noise, he smashed the glass in the back door then reached inside to unlock and open it.

His first pass through the house was, in accordance with his training, by way of a reconnaissance mission; to establish its layout, discover escape routes, should he need them, and confirm that the place was deserted. It was, so his search proper could be conducted thoroughly and at a leisurely pace. He began in a room that was clearly a study, quickly breaking open and searching a filing cabinet then a simple safe that offered nothing much in the way of a challenge. Neither produced the result he was hoping for. The master bedroom was the next place he went, finding nothing more than a collection of rather tasteless pornographic magazines featuring muscular young men with glistening, oiled bodes. The lack of a woman in Everest's life had obviously not served him well, or had, perhaps, been the result of this secret interest of his. This same pattern, but without the presence of any more of the magazines, was repeated in the other rooms in the house: Wright found nothing of any possible use: the evening had been wasted and left him no further forward.

For Flagg and Brennan it had been a quiet week after the bizarre events of the previous Tuesday, with the armed raid on the pervert on the train at Lord's Copse. There had been the usual brawls in pubs, a couple of assaults put down to road-rage and a number of burglaries reported—mostly domestic, plus one at a window replacement company on one of the trading estates on the edge of the town. Nothing unusual there, except in the last case, where a couple of filing cabinets had been vandalised but nothing seemed to have been taken. The monotony was broken on the Tuesday morning when one of the uniformed Sergeants rang Flagg to say he had a case he wanted to refer to the DCI, and could he come up to talk it through.

'Be my guest,' Flagg told him. A couple of minutes later the two of them were sitting facing one another across Flagg's desk, with cups of tea and the doughnuts Flagg had told the Sergeant to pick up from the canteen on his way up spread out between them.

'So, what have you got that you think we might be interested in then?' Flagg asked.

'On the face of it, it's just a death; a heart attack; one Mr Martin Everest, white male, solicitor, 63 years old, grossly overweight and unfit; in his office yesterday evening; ambulance called at just before seven; arrived at about ten past; dead when the paramedics arrived; called us out to attend; just routine—on the face of it.' He stopped.

'Only you think it isn't,' Flagg finished for him.

'Correct: and I'll tell you why. The heart attack victims I've seen before might have known it was coming and might have been scared of dying, but none of them looked like this one did; he was petrified of something: and then there's the phone call.'

'The phone call?' Flagg echoed.

'The call for the ambulance: I think someone else made it.'

'And what's so unusual about that? Lots of 999s are made by somebody else.'

'You're right, but not while pretending to be the victim.' Flagg must have looked confused, because the Sergeant carried on. 'Look; the quack says that this bloke would have died almost instantaneously, and the level of pain he would have been feeling would have made it virtually impossible for him to have done anything more than just grunt and fall over; but this one, if we can believe the evidence, managed to ring 999 and call his own ambulance.'

'How do we know it was him?'

'Because he said "*I'm* having a heart attack" and "*I'm* going to die", only he couldn't have done it—he wouldn't have been capable of making the call, or had the time to do it, or put the phone down neatly afterwards, which he also appears to have been able to do, if we're to take what we see at face value.'

'All of which, if you're right, makes it a suspicious death, and one we should be looking into.'

'Correct,' the Sergeant said. 'Do you want it?'

'OK,' Flagg said. 'What have you got?' The Sergeant slid a thin folder across the desk towards the DCI.

'Incident log, notes from the scene, photos, the preliminary medical report and transcript of the 999 call with time-stamp, operator's name etcetera. All the usual, really: and the audio record of the call itself is saved in the computer database; the reference for that's on the transcript too.'

'OK,' Flagg said. 'I'll take a look and let you know.'

Some time later, when Brennan came in, Flagg told him what the Sergeant had said, and asked him to whistle-up the 999 call. Flagg had to ask Brennan to do that because he could not; his limited computer skills did not allow him to. Brennan sat down in Flagg's place as the DCI got up to pace the room; which he liked to do when he was pontificating.

'So,' he said. 'The voluminous and heavy Mr Everest is all alone in his office, working late, when he suffers this huge heart attack and keels over almost instantaneously, taking a chair with him,' pointing to one of the photographs of the scene that had been in the file the Sergeant had brought up. 'But not before saying . . . ' He pointed at Brennan, who clicked on a button on the computer screen with the mouse and the cursor. The sound of the 999 call played through the speakers built into Flagg's computer: first the ringing tone, then the voice of the girl who answered the call, then the voice of the victim, announcing his heart attack and his imminent death; and Flagg knew at once it was a voice he should recognise because he had heard it before, but could not quite work out when or where or who it was.

'We know that voice, Brennan,' Flagg told his DS. 'Who was it?'

'I've no idea,' said Brennan, who knew his DCI had a better ear for these things than he did.

'Hmmm,' Flagg said, thinking hard. 'I know I should know who it is, even though he's tried to disguise his voice.' Then he paused. 'Right!' he said, 'Let's make sure we know who it isn't. Brennan, do you think you can copy that voice onto a tape recorder, or one of those MP5 things that everyone seems to have stuck in their ears these days? If you can, do it, then find out if Everest had a secretary and play it to her. Odds-on it won't be him. In the meantime I've got some thinking to do.'

Flagg did his thinking up at Everest's house, having gone there on a whim that his Copper's nose was telling him was the right thing to do.

Some time later, Brennan's mobile phone rang. When he answered it he found himself speaking to Flagg.

'Did you find a secretary?' Flagg asked him.

'I did, and it wasn't Everest's voice; just like you said.'

'Did she know whose it was?

'No,' said Brennan. She didn't think she'd heard it before.'

'No,' said Flagg. 'There are only two people alive who know who it is: it's owner's one of them, and I'm the other.'

'Are you going to explain that?' Brennan asked after a pregnant pause. 'Or do you want me to guess?'

'No, that's beyond your current powers of deduction, lad. Although you show definite signs of promise, you've got a long way to go yet. I'm up at Everest's house. It's been broken into, through the back door. It must have happened after the plods came up here yesterday looking for the next of kin. There was no-one in, but they tried all the doors and found it was secure. So our man came in after they'd left, and I think the place has been searched. He's looking for something: I wonder what?'

'You said you knew who the voice was,' Brennan prompted gently.

'Have patience, I'm getting there. After a quick look around the house, I wandered up and down the road a bit, and got myself accosted by an old dear who thought I was acting suspiciously. She's not happy: says I'm the second one in two days.'

'Second what?' Brennan asked him.

'Suspicious character, of course. Keep up!'

'And she saw this suspicious character and recognised him?'

'No such luck, but she did see his car, and remembered its registration number; or most of it at least. She says she's pretty sure about the letters, but she's getting a bit short sighted, and isn't so sure about the numbers. She says they were either 273, 275, 276, 278 or 279. So I got onto traffic and they ran a check for me, on that registration, with those five numbers as alternatives; and you'll never guess what they came back with.'

No, probably not, thought Brennan, but its odds-on you're going to tell me in the next few minutes; in your own round-about way. Brennan was right and wrong; Flagg did tell him, but not in a round about way.

'A car with one of those numbers was sold, yesterday, in Asham, to one Adrian Wright of our acquaintance—the pink leather pervert from the train last week. The dealer registered the sale and transfer of ownership first thing this morning, on the internet.'

Adrian Wright, Brennan thought. When you know it's him you can hear it through the attempt to disguise his voice and not be recognised. Well done DCI Flagg!

'Right,' Flagg said. 'Get the fingerprint boys up here; and to Everest's office as well. If there are any prints to find I want them found. And get a picture of Wright to take round to the shops and offices down there to find out if anyone saw him. I'll do the same up here. There were plenty of photos taken outside the station on Tuesday, so one of the rags is bound to have a reasonable one of his face.'

'Are we going to bring him in?'

'No, not yet; it's not a murder yet; just a suspicious death. Wright was looking for something and he thought Everest had it, or at least knew where it was. He went to the office to put the frighteners on—too well as it turned out. He didn't find what he wanted, so he came up here to the house; but not until after he'd made the call for the ambulance, so he might just have a shred of human decency left in him. I want to know what he's up to before we do anything else, so let's take the time to do the leg-work first. I'll see you back at the nick later and we'll have a proper chat, OK?'

'OK,' Brennan confirmed; then started making calls to get forensics organised.

Flagg and Brennan met up again in the DCI's office late in the afternoon, to discuss what they had found out and decide where their investigation was going to go next.

'Did you manage to get any prints?' Flagg asked his DS as he took the mug of tea Brennan was pushing across the desk towards him.

'We did, but none of them matched the ones we took off the cup that Wright used while we had him here. We found Everest's, his secretary's, lots of unidentified and lots of smudges. The smudges appeared to be the most recent as they were laid on over the others, and that was the same at both the house and the office, so if Wright was there it seems he was wearing gloves.'

'Of course he was there,' Flagg said. 'I know he was there. I know he killed Everest; or at least what he did killed Everest; I just can't prove it yet.'

'So what do we do now?' Brennan asked. 'Did you find anything useful while you were up at the house?'

'Possibly,' Flagg said. 'What I found was that our Mr Everest had an interest in young, fit male bodies, so I think there might be a link between him and Wright that involves what happened on the train last week.'

'How do you work that out?' Brennan asked him. 'Wright seems to have been the victim of that little whatever-it-was, and he can hardly be described as young or fit, in any sense of either of those words.'

Flagg thought for a moment or two; then said 'Think back over some of the cases we've dealt with over the years and ponder human nature for a minute. How many times have we come across restless, unsettled middle-aged men looking to spice their lives up a little bit and deciding to have an affair to do it. They may well have spent hours drooling over the centre-folds in Playboy while they made up their minds, but how many of them ended up with a supermodel or actress rather than just another version of the dowdy middle-aged wives they were trying so hard to get away from? Not many, I can assure you. The same applies here. What you might want and what you can get aren't always the same thing; not by a long way.' Flagg may have thought he was thinking on his feet. Brennan thought he was making it up as he went along, ignoring the obvious gaps between his theory and the evidence.

'Anyway,' Brennan said. 'The descriptions Wright and the guard gave us of the "other man" tallied quite closely, and neither one of them described anyone sounding remotely like Everest.'

'Details, Brennan: mere details.'

'I wouldn't class anything of Everest's size as a mere detail,' Brennan muttered.

Flagg heard him but decided to let it go. 'So what do we do now?' Flagg asked, echoing Brennan's earlier question; then going on without pause to answer it himself. 'We put Mr Wright under observation; that's what we do.'

Brennan's heart sank. This was clutching at straws, and he knew that when Flagg said "we" he actually meant "you": the leg-man in these cases was always the DS, never the DCI, and if by chance they did get a result, the plaudits all went the other way round, to the DCI and never to the DS. 'OK,' he sighed. 'When do I start?'

'As soon as possible,' Flagg told him. 'I'll get you some help as soon as I can: one of the spare plods will do—out of uniform of course. I'll want to know . . . '

'Where he goes and when he goes there; who he sees when he gets there and for how long; what he went there for and, if possible, what was said while he was there. I know; I've done it all before.'

'Then what are you waiting for? Off you go; get to it.'

Brennan got up and went, taking his unfinished tea with him, to drink in the canteen before he left the building. While he was there he picked up several packs of sandwiches, knowing that he was in line to miss yet another meal. At this time of year it got dark late and Flagg would want him on station outside Wright's flat for as long as the daylight lasted; wanting his money's-worth from his DS; his full pound of flesh as it were.

Brennan ate his sandwiches sitting in his car, in the road where Wright lived, watching the front entrance of the building his flat stood in, in case he should enter or leave it; waiting for it to get dark so he could go home.

Inside the flat, Wright was at home doing what he had been doing for the previous few days; nothing in particular, other than wonder what to do next in the hunt for the bastard Biddle. Just then he had no leads; nothing to go on at all. Everest had proved to be a dead end, quite literally, and he had found nothing at the fat solicitor's house that was of any use to him. If he had felt any remorse over the man's death it had passed quickly, leaving him unmoved, blaming the solicitor himself for what had happened, because it could all have been avoided if only he had told Wright where Biddle had gone. He had chosen not to do that, so he had died, and it was all his fault and no-one else's. In the still quiet of the sitting room the phone rang. Wright reached out and picked it up. 'Hello; Wright,' he said.

'Adrian; it's Norman,'—his contact at the Foreign Office. 'Your man appears to have taken himself off to

Caracas. On Saturday last he was married to one Angela Wicks, in the Church of St Mary the Virgin, in one of the eastern suburbs of the city, by the reverend Luther Smith.'

'How good is this? Is your source reliable?' Wright asked, excited by what he had heard, but not wanting to rush off on a wild goose chase if the information was dubious in any way.

'First class,' Norman told him. 'It came in from the Embassy there this afternoon, in a routine update of known movements of British Citizens abroad. That's where your man was on Saturday afternoon; although by now he could be almost anywhere.'

'Thanks Norman; that's great,' Wright told him, experiencing an enormous sense of relief now that something positive was happening. 'I owe you one.'

'You owe me more than one, old man,' Norman told him. 'By the way, what's this rumour I've been hearing on the grapevine that you're becoming persona non grata around the place?'

'Vindictive rumour, that's all. I must have upset someone I shouldn't have. 'Bye.' And he hung up before anything more could be said.

Caracas, Venezuela. Now does that fit, and how do I get there? he asked himself as he turned to his computer and made a connection to the internet. Once again Wright found himself following in John Biddle's footsteps as he found and logged onto web pages for High Weald International Airport, following links for Destinations; Caracas; Airlines; Novice Airlines, the only airline that flew there direct; and finally Novice's flight schedule to Caracas, where he found their 12.05 Tuesday and Thursday flights listed. The Tuesday flight fitted perfectly with the time schedule Wright had worked out for Biddle, and so must have been the one that he had flown on to leave the country. Wright booked himself a seat on the coming Thursday's flight, a day and a half from then.

For the rest of the evening Wright planned his trip to Caracas in as much detail as he was able to from the confines of his flat, treating it as some kind of military expedition. From the internet he printed out copies of maps of the country, the region, the city and the suburb where the church the bastard and his bride had got married in was located. He booked himself into a modestly-priced hotel nearby. He wrote himself a list of the minimum in terms of clothes and effects he thought he would need for the short time he expected to be there. Then he went to bed rejoicing, because things were moving forward once again.

In the street outside, Brennan watched the flat as the front room light went out. He waited ten minutes or so until he was satisfied his man had turned in for the night; then started up his car, switched on the lights, pulled out and headed for home. Further along the street, Jim, Sasha's colleague, whose turn it was to stake out Wright for the paper, did the same thing going in the opposite direction. As the two cars passed, Brennan did not recognise Jim—he would not, as they had never met. Jim, who knew Brennan by sight and probably would have recognised him in daylight, missed seeing the DS as it was already too dark by then.

Wednesday dawned bright and cheerful, and Wright woke and got up, feeling very much the same way. What was on his agenda for the day? A good breakfast, sorting out the things he needed to take to Caracas, and hunting out a suitable bag to take them in; then a trip to the local supermarket, as he had almost run out of food and there was still a day to go before he left for South America.

Brennan was also off to an early start, having arrived "on station" shortly after dawn, prepared for a long day of tedium watching out for Wright. To his pleasant surprise, however, his day brightened considerably just after breakfast time, when the passenger door of his car was opened and the delectable body and person of WPC Withers slid itself gracefully into the passenger seat alongside him.

'Morning Sarge,' she said. 'Care for a nibble?'

Now of all the officers in the North Downham station—indeed, of all the officers in the whole division—this was probably the one that Brennan would most have liked to see "out of uniform", but not in the way Flagg had meant when he had used the term. Now here she was, sitting in his car next to him, wearing a pair of tight denim jeans and a plain white V-necked T-shirt that hugged her figure in all the right places and showed off her ample cleavage to full advantage, filling his senses with her perfume and her presence, and carelessly using dubious phrases like "care for a nibble?" It was as much as he could do to keep his mind on the job in hand, and it took him several moments to realise that she was holding out an open box of doughnuts she had just picked up from the bakery next to the post office on the far side of the park for him to choose his nibble from.

'Ah, oh, yes please,' he spluttered, picking one out just before he made a complete fool of himself. After that he had no idea what to say, other than asking how she managed to keep her fantastic figure the shape it was in if she included such rubbish in her diet. As it was, they just sat side by side in silence while he pulled himself together and decided he should give her a briefing. (Perhaps there would be an opportunity for a debriefing later—in his dreams!)

'Did DCI Flagg tell you why we're here?' he asked her.

'Yep; we're watching one Adrian Wright; picture here,' holding one up. 'To see where he goes, what he does, who he sees and, if possible, find out what they talk about.'

'Correct. Spot on,' he told her.

'Why?' she asked. 'What's he supposed to have done?'

'I'm afraid I can't say at the moment,' Brennan said. 'DCI Flagg's orders; but you can take it from me that if he did it, it's serious: oh yes, it's serious all right.'

'OK,' she said. 'Flagg's a good DCI and I respect his judgement.'

'Oh, bollocks!' Brennan exclaimed.

'Well that's not really fair,' she said. 'I know he's not everyone's cup of tea, but you have to admit, he does get results.'

'No, no; it's not that: our man's on the way down the street in his car and he knows me. I can't afford to be spotted. Brace yourself.' And so saying he swung round to face her, leant over, gathered her in his arms and kissed her, long and hard, in the way he had seen TV cops do it in the same situation. When Wright had safely gone by and they surfaced for air, WPC Withers was quite out of breath.

'Wow,' she said. 'Where did you learn to kiss like that?'

'I didn't. I . . . I . . . I mean I can't,' he stammered.

'You bloody well can, you know,' she told him. 'Look, I'll prove it,' and she reached out to pull him back over towards her.

'Not now; not now,' he exclaimed, flustered. 'We've got to follow Wright; not practise snogging,' realising as he said it that he might be throwing away one of life's little golden opportunities. 'Later?' he added meekly.

'You're on,' she said, smiling across the seats at him. 'If we're going to be doing this regularly I think it's only

right that we should practice to hone our skills; don't you?'
Brennan started the car and set out after Wright, not sure
whether she meant surveillance or snogging.

Wright drove to his local supermarket. Brennan and
WPC Withers followed. Wright parked not far from the
entrance. They stopped further away, in a spot that gave
them a good view of both Wright's car and the doors of
the store. Wright's car door opened and the driver got
out: but it was not Wright, it was some trendy bloke with
close-cropped brown hair, wearing blue Chinos, a white
polo shirt and a black leather jacket. Brennan and Withers
both sat and stared.

'That's not him . . . is it?' she asked.

'It doesn't look like him,' he answered. 'Not the 'him' I
know anyway. We need pictures,' he said, leaning across her
to pull his camera out of the glove box. She leaned forward
and planted a kiss on his cheek.

'Exciting, isn't it?' she said excitedly.

'Yes,' he replied, and the surveillance isn't bad either, he
thought.

Brennan got out of his side of the car rather stiffly and
she joined him as they walked towards the store entrance,
bobbing along disconcertingly beside him. They stopped
off behind one of the trolley parks, from where Brennan
could get some good shots of Wright as he came out of the
store and walked towards them. Brennan used a full roll
of film on a series of pictures of the front, profile and rear
views of the man they thought might be Wright, but could
not be sure about. When they were done, the DS shot the
film out of the camera and handed it to WPC Withers.

'Get that developed—they do a one-hour service in
there,' pointing back into the supermarket. 'Then get a taxi
to take them back to the nick to show Flagg. I'll follow

him,' jerking his thumb at the receding figure of the man who could be Wright, or might not be. 'I'll see you later back at his place.'

'OK.'

'Good girl,' he said, pushing his luck (in for a penny . . . he thought) by giving her a light pat on the bottom to send her on her way. She showed no sign of objecting. He, the incurable romantic, began planning where they were going to live, when they would get married, how many children they were going to have . . .

Wright drove straight home and parked close to the end of the alley leading to the back entrance to his flat. Brennan followed him down there at a distance and realised that things had got complicated, now they knew there were two entrances to cover and would have to divide their resources to do it properly. He phoned Flagg to give him the good news.

'That's all right,' Flagg told him. 'There are two of you. Park the car halfway between the front door and the end of the alley and run to it when he goes out.'

Romance on hold, thought Brennan.

Wright flew out of High Weald International Airport en route for Caracas bang on schedule at 12:05 the following day. Brennan and WPC Withers followed him all the way to the airport, finding it more difficult than they had hoped, as he took a taxi and train, leaving his car at home behind him. Flagg would not be pleased to hear that he was expected to pay for a parking ticket for Brennan's car, but if he wanted Wright followed wherever he went, Brennan had no choice but to leave it on the yellow lines in the road outside South Suburbia Station and pursue his man on foot.

The two police officers followed Wright into the station, down onto the platform, onto the train, off the train, up the stairs, onto the bridge; then into the airport and all the way to the Novice Airlines check-in desks. When he left the desk and moved on through passport control they had no choice but to let him go, as they had no authority to go any further and, unless they were going to arrest him, which they were not, there was no point anyway. Returning to the check-in desk, Brennan was able to bully the girl there who had dealt with Wright into telling them where he had gone and what type of ticket he was holding. That would give them and indication of when he was expected to return to the country.

'He's got an economy class open return for Caracas,' he told Flagg when the three of them met up later in the DCI's office. 'We had to let him go; there was nothing else we could do.'

'But why's he gone out there, and what's he going to do while he's there?' Flagg wanted to know, pacing up and down his office impatiently, pounding the palm of one hand with the fist of the other. 'What's he going to do? And when's he coming back?'

'We've no way of knowing as far as I can see,' Brennan said. 'We'll just have to wait.'

'Hmmm,' murmured Flagg, thinking.

'Are we all agreed it's him?' Flagg asked.

'Why; do you think it isn't?' Brennan countered.

'No: I'm absolutely sure it's him. I can see it's him from the photos,' Flagg said. 'The same eyes; untrustworthy; up to something; some no good of some kind.'

'That's what the passport control people said too,' Brennan told him. 'I can't see it, but they pulled rank: "It's what we've been trained for",' they said. 'Snotty-nosed gits, I say.'

Flagg let him finish and then changed the subject. 'And how are you two getting along?' he asked.

'OK,' they both said. Like a bloody house on fire, Brennan thought.

'Good: good,' Flagg said. 'Withers; you can go back to normal duties until Wright gets back; then we'll have you back again. You can both clock off now: it's been a long couple of days. Back tomorrow, Brennan; early mind.'

He giveth with the one hand, while taking away with the other, Brennan thought, then went into the corridor with Withers to head off for the pizza they had promised themselves. When all this is over I might find I've got a lot to thank our Mr Wright for, he thought: he hoped. When they had gone, Flagg sat down at his computer and started trying to log onto the internet to look for particular types of websites emanating from Venezuela in general, and from Caracas in particular.

CHAPTER FIVE

The mechanics of Wright's arrival in Venezuela were the same as John and Angela's had been just over a week before, but without any of the sense of romance or adventure the two of them had been feeling then. Instead, his mood was one of grim determination; to get in, get done and get out as quickly and cleanly as was practically possible. Then he would have what he firmly believed was rightfully his; the disc, the money, the freedom, the future. He thrilled at the thought of what he could do with the cash—a cool million, less the odd thousand or two that the bastard Biddle would probably have spent by then—plus the extra income he could get for himself by using the contents of the disc to screw even more out of Dent and his crooked cronies at Perma-way in payment for his silence. He gripped the armrests of his seat tightly and tensed all of his muscles as a wave of excitement ran through him, as he enjoyed the sensation of being alive with so much to look forward to, savour and anticipate; including, he hoped, extending his relationship with Sasha when he got back home.

The old lady in the seat next to his, mistaking the outward signs of excitement for fear, tried to reassure him.

'It's alright, dear,' she told him, reaching over and patting his white-knuckled hand with hers. 'This aeroplane has a safety record that's second to none; and this airline has never had a major incident involving one of them.'

'Perhaps they're due one then,' he snapped back sarcastically, sending the poor woman back inside her shell with her bubble bursting, wondering if he might be right, and whether her chirpy confidence might not have been altogether misplaced. Touch-down was routine though, and the short taxi in from the end of the runway to the terminal building was uneventful. Wright collected his bag from the overhead locker and shuffled off the plane with everyone else, without so much as a backward look or a word of thanks to the cabin crew, despite their cheery goodbyes and thank-yous. He passed through the terminal, just as Angela and John had done, missing out only the baggage collection, area as he was travelling light and had only his overnight bag with him.

Once outside, he climbed into the back of a taxi driven by a man he immediately decided was an ignorant peasant for his lack of understanding of English. The driver, for his part, regarded Wright as an arrogant foreigner for his lack of even rudimentary Spanish. Eventually, Wright seemed to have been able to make the man understand where he wanted to go by pulling out the maps he had printed from the internet and stabbing repeatedly at the street his hotel was in with his forefinger and shouting 'Here! Here!' as loudly as he could. The driver had known from the start what he meant but pretended not to just to annoy him and distract his attention away from the exorbitant price he was about to be charged, from sheer relief at having succeeded in reaching his destination.

Once inside the hotel, Wright checked in, had a meal in the restaurant and a few drinks on his own at the bar, then went up to his room and turned in for the night.

In the morning he left early to walk the short distance to the church where Biddle and his new wife had got married the weekend before, following the route he had marked on his internet street map of the area. As he approached it he was pleased, and rather surprised, to see that it was just like any normal parish church back home, because that meant that, as the lapsed son of church-going parents, he would instinctively know the internal layout, and that removed some of the uncertainties associated with going into action on what he was thinking of as foreign territory.

When he got there, he walked straight up to the main front door, turned its large brass handle and pushed. It was locked, so he took the path along the side of the building, trying each of the doors he came to in turn, finding all of them locked too. Clearly he was too early and was going to have to wait for the vicar to arrive. He crossed the street and sat down on a low wall in the shadow of some trees, from where he had a clear view of the front of the church and along its side, where the door to the vestry appeared to be. Then he waited, with nothing else to do and nowhere else to go, as this church and its vicar were the only lead he had to the whereabouts of Biddle, his new wife, the money and the computer disc.

When the vicar did arrive, Wright almost missed him, as the day was already warm, he was sitting comfortably on the wall with his back leaning up against the trunk of a tree, tiredness from the previous day's travelling was catching up with him and was dragging him towards the edge of sleep. Gradually, without him realising it was happening, his head would drop, his breathing would slow and steady and his eyelids would begin to droop; then he would wake up with a start, knowing that he could not afford to be asleep when the vicar came or he might miss him altogether. And he almost did miss his arrival, but not quite, as he snapped himself awake just as the vicar was going into the vestry, pushing its door closed behind him. Wright stood up, stretched, and walked slowly across the road, along the side-path to the vestry door, and went in after the man he had gone there to see.

As he stepped into the church, with its familiar look, layout, and even smell, Wright was transported back to the days of his childhood; of sitting in the freezing cold of the English mid-winter, on the rock-hard wooden pews, listening to his parents' old vicar droning on endlessly about the wages of sin, about redemption and forgiveness, and he remembered why, as soon as he could, he defied his parents and stopped going to church and swearing an oath to himself that he would never set foot inside one again. Now here he was, breaking his promise; but all in a good cause, he told himself. For a moment he stood still and listened, waiting for a sign to tell him where the vicar had gone; then he turned to his right and walked through the doorway there, following the noise the man was making as he settled himself behind his desk and sorted through papers, pens and reference books in readiness to write the first draft of his sermon for the coming Sunday's services. He looked up as Wright knocked gently on the door to attract his attention.

'Good morning Vicar', Wright said, 'I hope I'm not disturbing you.' As he was the only lead to Biddle's whereabouts, this was a man Wright needed to treat with kid gloves. There must be no threats or intimidation, just polite enquiry, so the vicar would not be left with even an inkling of suspicion of Wright's true purpose.

'Not at all,' Luther replied. 'You are very welcome Mr . . . er . . . '

'Dent, Vicar', Wright lied. 'My name is Stephen Dent.'

'Come in Mr Dent. Sit down and tell me what I can do for you: and please; call me Luther.'

'I'm looking for someone Luther; a friend; someone I haven't seen for a long time. His name's John Biddle. I heard from an acquaintance that he was in Caracas, and that he'd recently been married, here, in this very church. I'm here on business for a few days and I thought it might be nice to drop in on them to offer my congratulations to him and his new bride.'

'Ah, yes,' Luther mused. 'Your acquaintance was right; I married them, John and Angela, just last Saturday. Such a lovely couple: a lovely wedding.'

'That's wonderful news,' Wright told him. 'Do you know how I can get in touch with them, to give them my congratulations?'

Luther leaned back in his chair, giving his prodigious memory the chance to work its magic. 'When they came to see me for the first time I remember them saying they were staying in the PanContinent Hotel in the city centre, but I think they've moved into a villa they've rented since then. You could try the hotel, in case they left a forwarding address: or, now let me think; they took a taxi from here after the wedding breakfast; now what was that cab company called? I know the car was green and yellow . . . what was its name? Yes; I have it—Taxis del este de la ciudad. That's East City Taxis in English. I think they shorten it to "Taxis del este" on their cars. They'll know where Mr Biddle and his new wife were taken to; but I don't know if they'll be willing to tell you.'

'That's a chance I'll have to take,' Wright said. 'If you don't know where the Biddles live, the taxi firm seems to be my only chance of finding them. Where can I find it?'

Luther picked up his pen and wrote out the address and phone number on a slip of paper, copied from a phone directory he pulled out of a drawer in his desk. He held it out for Wright to take. 'It's not far from here,' he said. 'But the best way to get there is to pick up one of their cars. There always seem to be a lot of them about.'

Wright took the paper, stood up, thanked Luther for his help and shook the hand that was offered to him. 'Could I ask just another small favour of you please vicar? If you see the Biddles in the near future, could you please not mention that you've seen me and that I'm looking for them? I'd like this to be a big surprise. If, of course, I can't find them, then I'll come back and let you know: then if you see them . . . '

Luther agreed readily, being a man who appreciated the pleasure of a nice surprise himself.

On the way back through the vestry, more from force of a habit inherited from his parents than anything more virtuous on his part, Wright dropped a few Bolivar notes onto the collecting plate on a side-table by the door; then stepped back out into the sunshine and heat. Now; how to find a cab? Turning back the way he had come from on the street outside the church, he started looking for the taxi-rank he thought he remembered seeing on the way there; convincing himself that there had been one, and that the cars there were all, or predominantly at least, painted in the yellow and green livery that Luther had described. There was a taxi-rank, and eventually he found it, down a side turning off the route he had taken from his hotel up to the church. But his pleasure at finding it was short-lived as he saw that none of the cars there were green and yellow; until, of course, he realised that he did not have to go to the cab company's office in one of their own cars; he could go there in one of anybody's. So he did; sliding onto the back seat of the first cab he came to and making the driver understand what he wanted by holding out the address Luther had given him and pointing at it while saying 'I want to go there,'—in English, of course.

'You don't need a taxi to get there, my friend; it's just at the other end of the next street; you can easily walk there in just a few minutes,' the driver told him in Spanish.

'I want to go there,' Wright insisted, with more pointing and a raised voice.

The driver tried again, but met with no success—just more of the same from the increasingly agitated Wright—so he gave up, shrugged his shoulders, turned and started the car's engine. To avoid embarrassing his passenger, the driver took a round-about route that delivered him to the door of the cab company fifteen minutes and two hundred metres from where they started. Wright paid the man his fare and tip without question, got out and walked into the office.

Inside, the atmosphere was hot and steamy as there was no air conditioning, and the single-storey building had a flat roof that heated the place up early in the course of the morning and kept it that way all day; but its front office was empty. Wright walked over to the wooden counter and rapped on it with his knuckles to attract the attention of anyone who might be in the back part of the building, on the far side of the wall behind the counter. He waited for a short while and was about to bang again, harder, when a dumpy, middle-aged woman shuffled out through the door opening in the centre of the wall and stood there staring at him.

'Si Senor,' she said.

'Do you speak any English?' Wright asked her.

'Si Senor; a leetle.'

'Good,' he said. 'I'm looking for someone; a friend; his name is John Biddle; he lives in Caracas, near here somewhere, but I don't know his address. He uses your taxis. Can you tell me where he lives?'

'What you say his name?'

'Biddle: John Biddle. He's English, like me. Do you know him?'

The woman pursed her lips and sucked in noisily while she was thinking; or pretending to think. Wright, knowing from experience how this all worked, took his wallet out of his pocket and slid a banknote onto the counter. He pulled out another and held it in the air between his thumb and forefinger.

'He's an Englishman, and there can't be too many of those living around here. He got married last Saturday and one of your cabs took him home with his wife; from the church; St Mary's.'

'Ah; the Eenglishman,' she said, reaching out for the note on the counter and putting it in a pocket on the front of her dress. 'I know heem now. I remember. He has new wife.'

'Where does he live?' Again the sucking noise. He held out the second note, above the counter, then pulled it back as she reached out for it. Slowly he got out a third and put it with the second.

'Write down his address,' he told the woman, making the action of writing with an imaginary pen on the notes in his other hand, then pretending to pass them to her, and snatching them away as she reached out for them. She gave in. She pulled a pen and a small pad from her pocket, rested it on the counter and scribbled down what Wright hoped was the address he wanted. Then she straightened up and backed away, tearing the paper off the pad as she did, making it clear there was no trust between them. The exchange was made at arm's length across the counter; his banknotes for her scribbled note. Wright turned away without uttering a word of thanks and stepped back out onto the street. She just stood and watched him walk away, then shuffled back into the back room to carry on with whatever it was she had been doing when he arrived.

For the office of a cab company, the area outside was somewhat devoid of cabs just then, and Wright had to wait quite a while for one to arrive. Even then it was not available to him immediately as the driver had come back to use the toilet, to have a drink and to get away from the cauldron that was the driving seat of his car for a short while; so it was approaching midday when Wright was finally dropped-off not far from the address he had been given; of the place where he would be able to find the bastard Biddle and his bastard wife.

The neighbourhood was a good one, with a cluster of single-storey villas set on the slope of a hill, each one standing in its own grounds, most of them with expensive-looking cars on the driveways outside them. The Biddles', pointed out to him by the cab driver who, luckily, also spoke a little English, followed the pattern, which was a good thing as far as Wright was concerned. As soon as he saw the house he started to plan his way in and out of it. The best approach was, he decided, from the road running down-slope across the front of it. Access could be gained to the garden either via the driveway that swept up the slope to the front of the place, dividing in front of it to serve both the front door and the empty car-port attached to its right-hand gable wall, or by hopping over the low, stone garden wall and using the cover offered by the trees and bushes on the other side of it. Access was unimpeded all around the outside of the villa, with no fences or walls dividing front from back gardens, and the single-storey layout meant there were lots of doors and windows to choose from for breaking-in. The walls at the back and sides, separating Biddle's villa from its neighbours, were also low and stone-built and the gardens beyond had yet more trees and bushes in them, so reasonable escape routes were available all round, with a fair degree of cover. Biddle had chosen his fortress poorly and had made Wright's next task much easier than he had any right to expect it to be.

Not wanting to get too close for fear of being seen, Wright found a place to sit and hide, just inside a clump of bushes and trees on the opposite side of the road from the Biddles' villa, and not too far along from it. He waited until he was sure no-one was looking, slid inside and made himself comfortable. From there he was able to watch the front of the house and the driveway for their comings and goings, and was sure to see them if they came out or went in because the driveway was the only proper access route to the place. His only problem was trying to stay awake in the heat and humidity of the day, just as it had been outside the church, earlier. Looking around, he found a stone with a sharp point on the top lying on the ground beside him. He moved it slightly to one side then rested his hand on it, pushing down until it hurt him, using the pain to stop him from drifting away into sleep.

The afternoon wore on and nothing happened; no-one came out of the villa and no-one went in; and nothing much else happened in the neighbourhood either. Wright's boredom was kept at bay only by his anticipation of the prize that awaited him when he was successful in reclaiming the money and the computer disc. Sleep was kept at bay by the stone and the pain in his hand.

Late on in the afternoon the area started to liven up, as children began to return from school with mothers and maids, then fathers and career women arrived back from their work in their cars and in taxis. Wright's concern that he might be discovered in his lair by roaming children proved ill-founded: this was an affluent area inhabited by middle-class people whose offspring came home to do homework, watch television or play computer games indoors—not play outside like street urchins. Along the road, a woman approached the entrance to the Biddles' driveway, turned in and walked up to the front door. She reached up, lifted the heavy brass knocker and rapped loudly with it. Wright leaned forward to make sure he could see as the door was opened, and he got his first sight of the bastard Biddle since he had backed out of the toilet compartment on the train at Lord's Copse station as it started to fill with smoke, and Wright's current troubles began. In his imagination, Wright lifted the high-velocity hunting rifle he had brought with him to his hide, looked through the powerful telescopic sight mounted above its long, slim and menacing barrel, took careful aim, squeezed gently on the trigger, pulling it tighter and tighter, then blew John Biddle's brains out with one perfectly-aimed and executed shot. On the doorstep of the villa, knowing nothing of the lurking threats against his person, either imaginary or real, John took delivery of an envelope that turned out to be a dinner invitation from the couple living in the house next door, handed to him on their behalf by their maid.

'Who was that?' Angela asked him, looking up from the magazine she was reading as he returned to his chair in the sitting room at the back of the house, overlooking the garden.

'The maid from next door,' he told her. 'We've been invited there for dinner tomorrow evening, to welcome us to the neighbourhood and to meet some of the people who live here.'

'Oh,' said Angela. 'Will that work? Will they speak English? Perhaps we'd better say no.'

'Too late; I've already said we'd go. The maid spoke English and the invitation was written in English so it seems a fair bet that they'll speak English for us. Now, what shall we do about food tonight? Would you like to go out, or shall we cook something here?'

'Let's push the boat out and go out,' she said. 'I fancy trying that little Italian restaurant we passed last night; and it's not as though we can't afford it.'

John agreed, so he went out into the hall to phone to book a taxi to take them there and bring them back afterwards. Then he returned to his chair to continue with his siesta while Angela read on, as there was still some time to go before they needed to dress and get themselves ready.

Outside, Wright continued to wait, sitting still and quiet inside his bush. He was hungry, thirsty and tired, but the longer he stayed there the less all that seemed to matter to him. The sun had long ago passed over the yard-arm and was about to sink down behind the hills to the west, signalling the onset of dusk and the approach of the darkness he needed to break into the bastard Biddle's villa and begin the search for his prize. He patted the pockets in his trousers and jacket, to make sure he had everything he needed with him. He did, and he knew he did, because he had been checking at regular intervals all through the afternoon and finding everything there, but at least it was a small something to do every now and then to keep the onset of boredom away.

At just before eight o'clock it was dark. Hearing the sound of an approaching car engine, Wright parted the bushes in front of him and looked out. A taxi, a green and yellow taxi, drove past the bush, continued along the road to the Biddles' driveway, braked sharply, turned and swung in. Biddle and his new wife came out and got in when it had stopped at the top, but not until Biddle had given the front door a good hard shake to make sure it was closed, and had a good look at the windows at the front of the house to make sure they were shut too. The taxi backed into the car port to turn round, then set off down the drive. Wright ducked down as it swung back onto the road and roared past him, flashing light through his hiding-place as it did. Then it was gone, leaving just a cloud of fine dust hanging in the air behind it.

Wright could not believe his luck; an empty house to search through at the first time of trying; although it was not, perhaps, such a coincidence after all because he knew that if it was he who was in possession of the million pounds-worth of used fivers, he would not be staying in to cook for himself either. He waited until he was quite sure the taxi had gone and was not coming back, and that there was no-one to be seen in the road or the nearby gardens. Then he crawled out of his bush into the road, stood up and made his way across to the corner of Biddle's front garden. After one more look around to make sure he was alone, he slipped over the low stone wall and disappeared from view among the shrubs and bushes there. Staying under cover, he worked his way round the side of the house to the back, where he had decided to make his first attempt at breaking-in.

Along the back there were two doors and a number of windows to try to get in through. The first door he came to was strong and robust and did not look likely to yield to anything less than a noisy attack with a sledgehammer. The second door was not as well made and was a poor fit in its frame. Wright pushed on it and found it moved back and forth, leaving a gap next to the lock that might allow him to open it using the burglar's regular tool, the credit card. He got out his wallet and pulled out his favourite card; the one he thought of as his mason's membership card. Why? because, as the old saying has it, masonry open doors for you. He slid the card into the gap between door and jamb, in line with the lock. He pushed on it firmly but carefully and felt it moving in, then bending, as its far end slid round the corner towards the lock. When it met firm resistance he pushed on it sharply. The lock clicked and the door swung open. He waited for a second or two to make sure it was safe, then stepped forward, pushing the door closed behind him.

Inside the house it was quiet and dark. There was no-one in and no lights on. Wright got out the tiny pocket torch he always carried with him and snapped it on, shielding the beam so it gave out only as much light as he needed to find his way through the house. Just as he had done in Everest's house when he had searched that, he went through the place twice; once to make sure he was alone and to plan the detailed search that would follow; the second time to carry out that search.

The room he had broken into was the kitchen; not a place of any great interest unless and until everywhere else had been searched first and revealed nothing. Beyond that was the hallway, with the other rooms leading off it; the sitting room, dining room, bathroom, bedrooms and a study, with a large leather-topped desk, rows of bookshelves on two of its walls and a large, old-fashioned-looking safe standing in the far corner, opposite the door. As soon as the pencil-thin beam of his torch came to rest on it, he knew that the money and the disc would be inside that safe, and that there was no real point in looking any further. He also knew that his quest could not be completed on that night as he needed either the key that fitted the large keyhole on the left-hand side of its door, or a safe-cracker, or some cutting gear to use on the lock or the hinges to get the door open or off. He had none of these with him, and no chance of getting any of them at short notice, so his triumph was delayed, by twenty-four hours at least.

Swallowing his disappointment, he decided that as he was there, and as he had the time to do it, he would be thorough and make sure his assumptions were correct. He walked over to the safe and tried the large handle on the front above the lock. He was right; it was locked. Then he systematically searched through the rest of the house, looking in every cupboard, drawer, nook and cranny; under beds; on top of wardrobes; in the pockets of clothes hanging in wardrobes. It did not take long because Biddle and his wife had little in the way of possessions, having arrived with almost nothing and not having bought very much in the time they had been there. All he found was their passports and the return section of their open return plane tickets in a sideboard drawer in the study, and although he was tempted to take them, just for the sheer hell of it, he resisted the urge, not wanting to alert them to the fact that he had been there.

Tomorrow, perhaps, he told himself, when I've opened the safe and got the money and the disc. And the more he thought about it the more appealing the idea became; bastard Biddle and his missus, marooned there, with no money, no passports and no tickets to get them back home. Tomorrow then; definitely tomorrow.

He left the villa the same way he had entered it, through the kitchen door into the garden, making sure it was closed behind him; leaving no sign that he had ever been there. He circled the house to the front, hopped over the garden wall into the road outside and walked away, keeping his eyes open for a taxi he could pick up to take him back to his hotel.

John and Angela enjoyed a nice evening out, eating in the Italian restaurant, then moving on for a few drinks and some light music in a nearby bar. They went home by taxi and got ready for bed without knowing that anyone had been in the house while they had been away from it. John went from room to room checking that the windows and doors were securely closed. In the study he checked that the safe was closed and locked, then he turned in, feeling happy and relaxed; content with his lot.

In the morning, while Angela and John first slept in, then laid in, then had a leisurely breakfast in bed, Wright was up and about, making plans and arrangements for his return visit to their villa; hopefully that night. Having found a member of the staff of his hotel that spoke a reasonable amount of English, he set about finding out where he could hire or buy an oxy-acetylene welding set. He was directed to one of the poorer quarters to the west of the city centre where there was industry and commerce rather than suburban housing. Here, when there was money to be made, his lack of Spanish was no obstacle at all and he soon had his welding gear—two large steel bottles, one containing oxygen and the other acetylene, both mounted on a two-wheeled steel sack-barrow and connected to the burning torch by the familiar rubber tubes. He also had a small car he had hired from a garage nearby. He wheeled his welding gear out of the building to the car and squeezed it in the boot, ready for the drive up to the Biddles' villa.

He was ready far too early, but rather that than start late and end up having to rush. Nothing could be done in daylight; there was no guarantee that the coming night would be the one when the chance to open the safe presented itself; and it was possible he might have to spend many long hours over the next few days watching the house for that chance to occur; so he decided to spend the day resting, or sleeping if he could. On the way across the city in the cab he had taken from his hotel, he had passed a large park, with tree-lined avenues running between big, open, areas of grass. That was where he decided to go, parking the car under the shade of one of the leafy green trees, rolling his jacket up to make himself a pillow and then leaning back against the trunk. And there he stayed for the next few hours, half-asleep, with half an eye on his hire-car, to make sure no-one felt tempted to interfere with it, and with half a mind dreaming about what his future life was going to be like, when he had the money, the disc, the girl, the lifestyle . . .

When Wright woke up he was hungry. It was well after lunchtime and he needed to eat because he had no idea when his next opportunity would be if he was watching the bastard's house waiting for the chance to break in. Leaving the car where it was, he walked back across the park to the road on its far edge, where he remembered seeing a line of restaurants. Not being particularly fussy about what he had to eat, he went into the first one he came to, sat down and began to read the menu.

On the far side of the city, the Biddles enjoyed a leisurely day of not doing very much at all, before beginning to get themselves ready for the dinner party in the house next door to theirs in the evening. Neither one of them had any idea that Adrian Wright was in the city; that he had already been inside their house and searched it; or that he was planning to return there with his welding torch and gas bottles at the first opportunity he could get. And neither one of them saw him arrive in the area in the late afternoon; park his car in a small side street a short distance away; then walk back and slip into his hide in the bush when he was sure no-one was looking, to begin his patient vigil.

Across the street, Angela and John got ready; showering; choosing clothes; dressing; changing minds; choosing more clothes; getting undressed; getting dressed again; going back to the original set of clothes and putting those on again; teasing hair; applying make-up; agonising over jewellery, handbags and shoes: and while all this was going on, John relaxed in the sitting room with a book and a long, cool drink. Eventually everything was ready and it was time to go. The Biddles stepped out of the house onto the drive. John locked the door and checked the windows, then turned and offered his wife his arm in a very formal and old-fashioned way, then together they walked away. Wright watched them go, knowing that all he had to do now was wait for the darkness that would cover his approach to the back of the house; and then . . .

Angela and John approached the front door of their neighbours' house and stopped. John reached out and pressed the bell-push. After just a short wait the door was opened by their host, and they were greeted warmly by him and his wife, who was standing just behind him.

'Senor Biddle; Senora Biddle; welcome to our home. It is very good to meet you. Please come in and make yourselves comfortable. Can we get you both a drink?'

They were led into the sitting room of the house, where other guests were already assembled; mainly other residents from the immediate area, plus some work colleagues of their hosts. The welcome could hardly have been warmer. The language was not a problem; everyone there was middle class, educated and in professions where English was spoken as the second, if not on occasions the first, language. Angela and John relaxed and began to enjoy themselves.

When darkness fell, the dinner was well underway, with large amounts of food to be eaten and a seemingly endless supply of wine to be drunk. Wright left the cover of his bush and walked back down the road to his car. Opening the boot lid, he reached in and pulled out the welding gear, dropping it down the back of the car onto the road on its trolley wheels. He closed the boot and locked it, then turned and began walking towards the Biddles' villa, pulling it all along behind him. At the corner of the garden he stopped and looked round, making sure there was no-one nearby. Satisfied that he was alone, he lifted the welding gear and its trolley up, slid it across the top of the low stone wall and dropped it into the garden on the far side. Then he, too, slid across the wall and was swallowed up by the vegetation.

He made his approach to the back of the house in the same way that he had the night before, sticking to the cover of the bushes and trees, pulling his welding gear behind him. The night was dark and still around him. Everything was quiet apart from the odd snatch of conversation or laughter and soft music drifting over from the house next door, where the dinner party was in full swing. He slid along the back wall of the house, wary in case anyone stepped out of the party into the garden, for a smoke or some air, and spotted him there. But no-one did, and he reached the door, snapped it open and disappeared into the kitchen. Once inside, he went into the dining room to collect one of the high-backed chairs from around the table, which he wedged under the door handle. Then he went back and did the same thing to the other two doors. That would make them difficult to open from the outside, and serve to give him advanced warning should Biddle or his wife come back while he was still inside the house, allowing him to make good his escape before they could get in, whichever door they decided to use.

With that done he went into the study and prepared to open the safe. He began by drawing the curtains over the window behind it. He was not going to turn on the light, knowing that the flame of the welding torch and the glow of the hot metal would give him more than enough to see by, but by the same token he did not want anyone looking in and wondering what was causing the flickering, ghostly glow they would otherwise have been able to see through the window from the outside. He pulled the welding gear towards him, positioning it comfortably close to the safe. He took out of his pocket the cigarette lighter he had bought for the purpose and stood it down on the floor in front of him. He reached out to the gas bottles and opened the valve on each one in turn. He picked up the torch in one hand and his lighter in the other. He turned the control knobs on the torch to start the flow of gas, then held the lighter up to the end of it and lit the flame. It danced and flickered yellow in front of him, casting eerie shadows that jigged around the walls and on the door behind him. A small shiver of excitement ran through him. He was ready to begin.

He put the lighter back in his pocket with one hand, holding the torch in the other. He slipped on the tinted safety glasses he had bought with the welding gear; there was no point running the risk of blinding himself when a little care could be taken to avoid it. He turned the control knob on the side of the torch and the flame changed from yellow, dancing and pretty to small, blue, focussed, roaring and hot. He leant forward and began cutting the safe door, in a wide arc from its edge, around the lock and back to the edge again. Sparks flew, smoke billowed and molten metal ran as he made the cut. The noise of the roaring flame filled his ears. The liquid steel running onto the floor set the boards smouldering then flaming in front of the safe as the cut grew longer and longer. He did not care about the floor; he was nearly there; nearly there; done! The lump of metal he had cut out fell to the floor, the lock still held inside it. Still holding the torch, he reached out with his foot and flicked the door open. The sudden in-rush of air turned the smouldering fire the heat from the door had started in the banknotes inside into an inferno that erupted out of the oven Wright had managed to turn the safe into. He dived to one side to avoid the searing, blinding heat as it shot out towards him. He only just made it, but scorched his face and hair, lost his eyebrows and dropped the torch in the process. His head hit the floor hard, leaving him dazed, groggy and disorientated.

When he came to his senses it seemed to Wright as though the whole room was on fire. The inside of the safe was an inferno, its contents beyond hope of rescue. The floor was ablaze in front of the safe. The books were burning on their shelves. The curtains were burning furiously and the windows had lost most of their glass. A dark pall of smoke was beginning to fill the room, quickly spreading from the ceiling downwards. All he wanted to do at first was lay on the floor, wrapped in self-pity, as he watched his hopes all burn away: the money was lost; the disc was lost; his future was lost; but then realised that his life would soon be lost as well if he did not get up and get out of there pretty quickly. He rolled over onto his hands and knees; then pulled himself up onto his feet, shielding his eyes and face from the heat of the ever-expanding fire as he staggered out into the sudden cool of the hallway, to the front door, out through the door and away down the drive.

At the dining table in the house next door the main course was finished, the cutlery and crockery had been cleared away and the diners were chatting and laughing as they waited for the sweet to be served. The maid hurried in from the kitchen, empty-handed but looking flustered and agitated. She broke into her master's conversation to tell him something that appeared to be urgent and important, gesturing towards John and Angela as she did.

'Senor Biddle,' the man said, standing up and placing his crumpled napkin on the table in front of him. 'My maid has just reported to me that your house is on fire.'

At first, John did not take in what his host was telling him and he just sat still as he began to realise what had been said.

'Please excuse me; it appears that I have to leave,' he announced to everyone present as he stood up; then he turned and began to run.

As John approached the bottom of the drive leading up to the villa, he met another man coming the other way. This other man was looking charred around the edges, was smoking gently all over, and looked vaguely familiar, although John was too distracted with concerns for the villa and his money just then to take any great note of it all. As they passed, John thought he heard the other man mutter something under his breath, that he only later realised was the single word "Bastard". Ignoring him, John ran up the drive and in through the open front door of the villa, heading directly for the study, where the safe stood, in the furthest corner from the door. The lobby and the study doorway were being kept free of smoke by the rush of hot air out through the shattered study windows, but John could see straight away from the glow in the doorway that the seat of the fire was inside the room he needed to go into, making his job all the more urgent; to get to the safe and rescue the money and, if possible, the computer disc. But as soon as he turned the corner into the room, crouching down to avoid the worst of the heat and the smoke, he could see that his task was hopeless; the floor was burning; the desk and its contents were burning; the curtains and walls were burning; the wide-open door of the safe showed that its contents, the bulk of John and Angela's fortune, was burning fiercely, and was clearly beyond rescue; and in the middle of it all were what he immediately recognised as two gas bottles, of the type used by welders, with the paint on their outsides blistering and peeling as it was cooked by the flames lapping along their sides, and by the growing heat of the fire.

Knowing that he was now at great risk of losing his life, as well as everything else, John turned to the sideboard standing beside him, just inside the door. Using his body to shield it from the heat being radiated by the fire, he slid open its top drawer and pulled out his and Angela's passports, with their return air tickets inside. Then he slipped out of the room and ran: down the hallway, through the open front door and out onto the veranda. At that point his world was turned upside down, as the gas bottles behind him exploded, with a blinding flash and a huge shock wave that blew the house to pieces and sent him flying through the air and into semi-consciousness.

When John had left the party, Angela followed him as quickly as she could totter on the heels she was wearing which, like her, had not exactly been made for running. She too passed the still-smouldering figure of Adrian Wright Arse in the road outside, not recognising him for who he was because she had never seen him before. Given the constraints of her shoes and her physique, she ran as though her life depended on it, which in a way it did, because if she had been more athletic and had arrived too soon and got too close to the gas bottles when they exploded, her life would have been at risk, just as John's was. As it turned out, she was slow enough to be safe, and the house erupted just as she turned the corner into the drive, and she was blown over backwards, deposited unceremoniously on her backside on the opposite side of the road under the canopy of a leafy tree, which then protected her from almost all of the pieces of the fabric of the house as they returned to earth with a noise reminiscent of large hailstones falling. John landed in an untidy heap not far in front of her, temporarily deafened and completely senseless to begin with, which was just as well, otherwise his impromptu flying lesson and, in particular, the prospect of the manner of its imminent end might well have frightened him to death.

While all this was happening, several blocks away, a terrified young girl was being held up at knife-point by a leather-clad, helmeted mugger who had stopped and climbed off his motor bike to confront her and snatch her handbag. Just as she was about to give in to him and let go of its strap, they both heard a resounding bang from not far away and he was hit on the side of the helmet by what turned out to be the ruptured shell of an acetylene bottle, sent flying into the air by the explosion that had caused the bang. Knocked sideways by the blow, he was pitched bodily over his bike and then head-first down the shaft of a dry well next to it, from where he was later retrieved and arrested by the police. John and Angela's bad luck was clearly that girl's good luck that night, thereby proving the old adage that every cloud has a silver lining.

While John lay barely half-conscious and Angela lay stunned, Wright made his way back to his car, defeated again; this time by his own lack of foresight; but still blaming the bastard Biddle for all his woes. His first thought was to get away from the place as quickly as possible—get in the car, drive to the airport, get on a plane going to virtually anywhere and leave—before Biddle realised who he was and the police started to look for him. When the two of them had passed at the bottom of the drive, Biddle had seen him clearly but failed to recognise him. The explosion he had heard as he headed back to the car, that could only have been the gas bottles erupting in the fire, may have killed Biddle, or may not. If not, it might not be too long before the bastard realised who it was he had passed on the villa's driveway, put two and two together and set the police on his trail. That might happen or it might not; but why take the chance when he did not need to; when the money and the computer disc, the only two things that could possibly have kept him there, were gone? He decided to get out while the going was good, so he drove straight to the airport, where he dumped the hire car in one of the short-term car parks, went into the terminal and booked himself onto a flight with Carib Airways to Jamaica, from where he could change for a flight to London. If all went to plan, he could be back home in just over half a day from then.

Back at the villa, things did not go quite so well for Angela and John. After the explosion, their neighbours summoned the fire department to deal with the fire, medics to tend to John's injuries, and the police to deal with anything else they could think of. By the time the local fire engine had coughed and spluttered its way up the hill, the villa had almost gone and the fire was beginning to subside. When the medics arrived, John was awake, wondering who he was, where he was, and why his head felt like it had been run through his mother's old mangle. When the police arrived they swarmed all over the garden chattering excitedly on their radios, and trampling evidence underfoot. They questioned the neighbours; then arrested Angela and John.

Wright boarded his flight at the airport an hour and a half after he arrived there; at just about the same time that Angela and John were being loaded into the back of the police car that would take them to the local jail. Wright sank down into his seat and buckled his seat belt; hugely relieved to be on his way home without being arrested and taken in for questioning, or worse; unspeakably frustrated to be doing it empty-handed.

Angela and John were taken from the back of the police car and put into a cell together for the night; and that was thanks only to the influence of their neighbour, a prominent lawyer in the city, who insisted they should be housed together, away from the rest of the prison population—the rapists, murderers, thieves, abusers, swindlers and perverts who are always to be found in every jail in every city in every country in the world.

As dawn broke, Wright was sitting in the main airport terminal in Jamaica, waiting for his flight to London to begin boarding. Angela was lying on her back, wide awake, on the rock-hard wooden boards that masqueraded as a bed, staring up at the ceiling of the cell. John was asleep, snoring loudly, on the bed on the opposite side from her; suffering from concussion, which Angela understood could be dangerous when combined with sleep, but the snoring proved beyond doubt that he was still alive, so she saw no sense in waking him up. Two of them worrying about what would happen next would, she reasoned, achieve nothing more than she could manage by worrying on her own, so she left him to sleep and did the worrying for both of them.

CHAPTER SIX

Stephen Dent was restless and uneasy. From his office window on the thirteenth floor of Overway House he stared out and down, onto the platforms of South Suburbia station and at the glint of sunlight on the railway tracks beyond as they snaked their way north, towards London. Normally this sight, and the trains shuttling back and forth along those tracks, in and out of the station far below, gave him a feeling of both power and contentment.

The sensation of power came from the knowledge that all of it was under his control, and he could make it do almost whatever he wanted it to, just by lifting a phone and telling someone he wished it to be so. The contentment came from the knowledge that it was already doing just what he wanted it to without his having to lift a finger; trains running to a timetable dictated by him personally; incurring delays, running late and making money from the deal he had set up with Roamer—Phone, his partners in crime in the scam he had orchestrated. And the other little bit extra helped quite a lot too: the bit only he, and not even his fellow Perma-way directors, knew about. But just then he was no longer feeling either powerful or content. The peace of mind he should have been enjoying had been taken from him by the actions of two people; John Biddle, the scheming, conniving little actuarial assistant—assistant, mind you, not even the real thing!—and the bungling incompetence of that arse Wright, or right arse as he was now, and forever would be, known.

It was Monday morning, almost two weeks after the incompetent arse Wright had let Biddle slip through his fingers, taking his, Dent's, million pounds with him to who-knows-where, as nothing had been heard of him since, in spite of Dent's instruction to the Chief Inspector of the Transport Police that he wanted Biddle found, alive if possible, but otherwise if necessary. Nothing had been heard of Wright either, but that was of no concern to Dent—if he never heard from Wright again it would be too soon—and anyway, Dent knew where he could be found if ever he was wanted for anything. And Dent was doing his level best to make sure that Wright would never work again—not even serving burgers in the local greasy spoon—so he was pretty sure to be at home if ever hell froze over and Dent found he needed the incompetent fool for anything. Dent turned away from the window, sat down at his desk and tried to push his discontentment down hard- and far-enough to be able concentrate on the day's work ahead of him.

At about the same time, Wright was sitting in his flat thinking about Dent. He had arrived home the day before; flying into London from Jamaica, then making his way home by train. His mission had been a failure. Everest was dead and his records had contained nothing that could be of any help to Wright. Biddle's copy of the computer disc had been burnt, along with the money, in the fire at the villa. The only other copy Wright knew of had been sent to Dent at his office by Biddle and would, by then, have arrived there. That was his only remaining hope: break into Dent's office and steal the disc from there. He began to ponder how he might go about doing it.

Monday morning dawned in Caracas several hours after it had in southern England. John rolled over in the double bed in the PanContinent Hotel and felt the warmth of Angela's body lying alongside him. For a brief second he, too, was content, but then his memory kick-started itself too and started reminding him of all the things he did not want to remember—the fire, the explosion, the cell in the police station and the questioning that had followed on from the night that he and Angela had spent there. He had been suffering from mild concussion when he had been woken up in that cell from the sleep of the dead to be confronted with what the warder told him was breakfast. His stomach churned at the sight of it and he did not tempt providence by trying to eat anything. On the other side of the cell Angela looked terrible. She had not slept a wink out of worry for what would happen next and she could not face the prospect of food either.

Some time later they were taken from their cell to two separate interview rooms. Angela was looking wretched and desperate as they parted, as if a death sentence had already been passed on her and was about to be carried out. John was led into a small room and told to sit down at a table with two chairs, one positioned on either side of it. He sat down as the warder who had escorted him there left, closing the door behind him as he went. The man sitting on the other chair was sharply dressed in a light grey suit and white shirt, with a neatly-knotted plain dark grey tie. He looked as cool as a cucumber—a man very much in control of himself on a day that was already beginning to heat up.

He introduced himself as Lopez; no title or rank; no "good morning"; and no handshake.

'Your name is Biddle, John, yes?' Lopez asked him, in accented English.

'Yes.'

'You are citizen of the United Kingdom?'

'Yes.'

'And you are here, in this building, because . . . ?'

'I don't know,' John told him. 'My house burnt down last night. The police came to the fire, arrested my wife and I and brought us here. Now I'm here, talking to you, and I have no idea why.'

'And why are you here, in Caracas?'

'I . . . we . . . came here to see if we liked it,' John said. 'If we did we were going to stay. If not; then we'd go back to the UK.'

'What do you do for money?'

'Ah . . . well . . . I had some cash, but it burnt in the fire; so now I suppose we'll have to go back anyway.'

'With your passports and your open return tickets you managed to save from your fire, yes?'

'Yes,' John confirmed.

'So how did your fire begin?'

'I don't know for certain, but I think someone broke in and tried to open the safe, with an oxy-acetylene torch.'

'What is this; this ocksy-settling torch?'

'What is it? How can I describe it? Ah! I know; a welding set. Gas bottles, pipes, torch, flame; for welding; for cutting metal.' And he tried to describe the shape of the bottles, the pipes, the flame, the heat, the sparks, with his hands.

'How you know this?' Lopez asked him.

'Because I saw the bottles and the torch; lying on the floor, in front of the safe in the study when I went in there.

The fire was already burning the paint off the outside of the bottles.'

'Why did you go inside there?'

'To see if I could put the fire out and save the house, of course. It wasn't ours, it was rented. I felt responsible.'

'You were responsible? For your fire?'

'No: I *felt* responsible; for the house,' emphasising "felt". 'My parents taught me to look after things that belong to others even better than I look after things that are mine. I felt responsible for the house, so I went inside to see if I could put the fire out.'

'But you could not.'

'No,' John said, 'I could not; it was too big; so I grabbed the passports and tickets and left.'

'And then the house, it blew up.'

'Yes, it blew up.'

'Why?'

'Why? Because the gas bottles got too hot and exploded; taking the house with them.'

'Was the house insure?' Lopez asked, changing the subject suddenly.

'I hope so,' John said, thinking about it for the first time. 'We didn't insure it, so I hope the owner had.'

'What was in this safe you say your "thief" tried to break into?' John did not like the way Lopez emphasised the word 'thief', as though he did not believe there was one.

'Some money; papers; the usual kind of thing. And he did get it open, but he set light to the contents; that's what must have started the fire.'

'But it did not hold your passports and tickets.'

'No; they were in the sideboard, next to the door. That's how they survived; I grabbed them on the way back out of the room.'

'Wait here please Senor Biddle. I will return shortly,' Lopez said as he stood up. Then he turned and left the room.

When he came back, ten or so long minutes later, he was looking more serious than he did when he left. He lowered himself into his chair, leant forward and stared intently at John as he spoke.

'What was the bomb for?' he asked.

'Bomb; what bomb?' John asked, incredulously.

'The bomb you have made; the bomb that blew up when you don't expect it and destroyed the house.'

'There was no bomb,' John told him. 'The explosion was caused by the gas bottles . . . '

Lopez cut him off in mid-sentence. 'So you tell me; but your lady friend, she say different. She tell us about your bomb. Now you tell me also. What was it for?'

'You're lying. There was no bomb, so she couldn't have told you about one. We came here to start a new life, away from the madness of the UK. We thought we could be happy here, but the house we rented was broken into by someone with a welding set, who tried to open the safe, but set light to the house instead, and the fire made the gas bottles blow up, destroying the place. That's what happened. That's what she's told you; it's what I'm telling you; and if you can't see that it's the truth then you're not much of a detective,' John shouted angrily, his head beginning to pound painfully from the after-effects of the concussion.

'No!' Lopez shouted back, standing up suddenly and banging his fist down hard on the tabletop. 'You are conspirators! You are terrorists! You make your bomb to make war on the innocents!'

At that point there was angry shouting in the corridor outside and the door of the room burst open. A uniformed policeman looked in round the doorpost and spoke to Lopez in Spanish. Lopez followed him out of the room and was harangued by another man in the corridor. John did not understand the words in Spanish, but the tone of what was being said was clear enough. Then his neighbour the lawyer appeared at the door, beckoning him to leave. Outside, he was reunited with Angela and the few possessions they had saved from the fire and they were taken out of the building to a long, black limousine that was waiting for them. From there they were driven back to the PanContinent Hotel, escorted by their neighbour, who was full of apologies for the way Lopez had behaved.

'I am so sorry,' he said. 'That man is not a policeman. He works for the government, in the counter-terrorist branch of the security services. Even there he is seen as something of an extremist. He is paranoid; everywhere he sees terrorists and conspiracies where there are none. I have been inside your house. I have seen what is left of the safe and the, how do you say, bottles of the gases. I know there was no bomb. So now you are free to go, and I am sorry for your pain and suffering.'

John and Angela thanked him for his kindness, for his hospitality the night before and for his help that morning, and he left them at the desk of the hotel, checking back in, just over a week and a half after they had done the same thing for the first time.

After they had all left him, Lopez went back to his office, in the basement of an annexe to the Ministry of Justice, and started trawling the internet for information on how a viable bomb could be made from oxy-acetylene bottles and a container the size of a safe. John and Angela spent the rest of the day and the evening in their room, resting, and trying to work out what to do next.

Now it was Monday morning and John got up, knowing that he had to come up with a plan: stay there or go home; those were the only two options open to them just then; stay or go. If they stayed, they could both sell their UK properties—his house and her flat—buy a place in Caracas and live off the five thousand a month that he had told Wright he wanted from Perma-way in addition to the million in cash. And it was at that point, as he thought of Wright for the first time in over a week, that the penny dropped and he realised they were in a far worse position than he had been supposing. The singed and smoking man he had passed at the foot of the drive was Wright; he was suddenly certain of it; even though the Arse man had changed his appearance. That was why he had uttered the word "Bastard" as they had passed. Wright had somehow found them, and burnt down their house in a bungled attempt to grab back the money and the computer disc.

Fighting down the feeling of panic that was beginning to well up inside him, he went into the bathroom, picked up the phone that was hanging on the wall, dialled "9" for an outside line, "44" for the UK, then the number of Everest's office in North Downham, the number he had committed to memory ready for when their routine contact was to be made—or for just this kind of emergency. After a silence of barely thirty seconds or so the phone on the other end of the line rang, and was answered promptly by the little old lady he recognised, from her voice, as Margaret; Everest's elderly secretary.

'Hello,' she said quietly. 'Everest and Goodbody.'

'Good morning,' John said. 'Can I speak to Mister Everest please.'

'No dear; I'm afraid that won't be possible,' she told him.

'Oh, isn't he in yet? What time do you think he'll be there?'

'I'm afraid he won't,' she told him. 'I'm afraid he passed away, unexpectedly, a week ago. Are you a client, or is this a personal call?'

For a moment John was completely unable to speak. 'C . . . client,' he stammered. 'How did it happen?'

'A heart attack, the doctor said. Out of the blue; just like that; there one minute and gone the next.'

'Were you there?' John asked her.

'Me? Oh no; I'd gone home by then. He was here on his own; so he died all alone. Unless the police are right,' she almost sobbed.

'The police?' he said.

'Yes. They don't seem to think it was just a straightforward heart attack. They've been asking a lot of odd questions; and then there's the tape recording.'

'The tape recording?' John prompted.

'Yes; the emergency call for the ambulance that Mister Everest is supposed to have made; only it wasn't him; it was someone else; the police had a recording of it; it was someone whose voice I've never heard before.'

I'm willing to bet I have, John thought to himself, beginning to feel slightly sick. Though how he found poor old Everest is anybody's guess.

'I'm sorry to raise this just now,' John told her, 'but do Mister Everest's clients have access to the papers and other things that he was holding for them and dealing with on their behalf?'

Now she really did sob. 'No, they don't,' she said. 'He hadn't made any arrangements about that before he died, because he didn't expect to be going so soon; and I don't have any keys or passwords or anything to the bank accounts and safe deposit boxes he used to use. Lots of people have been asking that question, and all I can say is "no". I expect I'll have to employ another solicitor to try to sort it all out; and who'll pay for that?'

'I'm sure Mister Everest's estate will pay for that; but if I were you I'd do it as soon as possible; before people start to get frustrated and angry.'

'Yes, I suppose you're right. I'll start looking this morning. If you'd like to leave your number I'll get them to phone you first.'

'That's very kind,' he said, 'but I'm abroad at the moment. I'll ring you again as soon as I get back.'

She thanked him. He thanked her and rang off, putting the phone handset back in its cradle on the bathroom wall.

When Angela got up, she found John in the bathroom, sitting on the end of the bath next to the wall-phone, his head resting in his hands. He looked up at her as she came in, his face a picture of dejection and misery.

'It's all over,' he told her. 'All gone: nothing left. It was Wright Arse who started the fire; he was the man we passed at the bottom of the drive. He found out where we were somehow, broke into the villa, tried to open the safe and managed to set fire to everything. And now Everest is dead and we've lost it all. We'll have to go home; to Asham; there's nothing else we can do.'

She sat down next to him and he told her about the phone call to Everest's secretary and finding out from her about the heart attack. 'If the police think that it was more than just a heart attack, then it seems a fair bet that Wright was involved in it somehow; otherwise it's just too much of a coincidence,' she said.

John agreed, but said 'I don't see how Wright could have found out from Everest where we were, though, because he didn't know; I never told him where I was thinking of going, only that I was going away somewhere.'

'Then he must have found out some other way,' she said. 'Either way, does it make any difference?'

'No,' he agreed. 'Not really. Wright found us; the money and my disc have gone; the disc and the documents Everest had are locked up where it doesn't sound as though it's going to be possible to get to them—not in the near future, at least. We have no money, and I don't suppose there's any chance at all of getting the extra five thousand a month I told Wright I wanted, now that he knows where we are.'

Angela agreed so, reluctantly, they decided that they would have to return home, to Asham, while they waited for Everest's affairs to be sorted out: not to John's house though; to Angela's flat. So later, after breakfast, John phoned the office of Novice Airlines and booked two seats on their Tuesday midnight flight back to the UK, in Super Class, of course, using the return portions of their open tickets.

The rest of that day and most of Tuesday they spent in subdued mood, passing the time away as best they could, wandering around the city on foot looking at all the sights that were free, as they only had enough cash to pay for the taxi back to the airport plus the minimum for food and drink over the two days they had left there. The hotel bill they would have to settle with a credit card; then worry later how they would pay it off once they arrived home. Eventually the time for leaving came, and they took a taxi back down to the airport, and this time they had no difficulty making the driver understand where they wanted to go, as the word 'airport' is almost universally understood across the globe, wherever it might be said.

The midnight flight back to Britain seemed endless to them when compared with their journey in the other direction, and the gloomy, overcast weather of a late, dull afternoon at High Weald International Airport, coupled with the slight feeling of disorientation caused by flying eastwards through a foreshortened night and day just added to the depressed mood they were both in when they arrived there. With no luggage to collect they sped through the terminal building and were soon descending the escalator towards the station platform from where they would catch a train to Asham: or rather from where they hoped to catch a train to Asham; but the railway had other ideas.

'Your attention please,' boomed the speakers of the public address system. 'Due to a security alert on the line between South Suburbia and High Weald International Airport, all trains are subject to delay, alteration and cancellation at short notice this evening. Would customers please refer to the destination boards and listen for further announcements. Thank you.'

This all seems depressingly familiar, John thought as he and Angela reached the bottom of the escalator and were spat out into the back of what appeared to be just a solid wall of bodies, and what was promising to be a long wait began.

In his office in Overway House, Stephen Dent watched the screen of his computer gradually turning red again as more and more trains were affected by his company's continuing use of The Book of Reason, and their corresponding lines of text on the South Coast Trains information screens were turned to red to show it. Fines would be levied by OFFTOSS for the delays, but money would be coming in from the Roamer-Phone deal. On balance, the phone deal brought in more than the fines that had to be paid, so it was worth putting up with the bad publicity the railways got for the money it all produced; and the same applied to his own little nest-egg too, from the part of the scam that only he knew about.

That evening, in his flat in the suburbs of South Suburbia, Adrian Wright was finalising his plans for breaking into Stephen Dent's office. His original idea had been to do it that very night, but after giving some thought to the problem of how he would get into Overway House in the first place, he had decided that it would be best to wait until morning, when there was more chance of getting in undetected, amongst the crowds of workers arriving there at the start of another long day at their desks, in front of their computer screens. In the time he had been working with Perma-way, Wright had often noticed the way that their staff gained access to Overway House, mostly arriving in groups on the trains, rushing up the ramps from the platforms, through the ticket barriers, then in through the doors of the foyer and across it to the bank of lifts behind the reception desk, with nothing more than a cursory wave of their security passes at the receptionist who, if she was busy attending to a visitor, often took no notice of any of them at all. During the time he had been working with Perma-way, the fact that this had been happening, and his client's refusal or inability to do anything about it, had been galling to him; but now his interests had changed so dramatically he saw it as a positive feature that he should take every advantage of. And when Stephen Dent had so unceremoniously evicted Wright from the back of the car after collecting him from the police station, the Perma-way director had been far too preoccupied and angry to give any thought to mundane matters such as security passes, so Wright still had his; and although the picture on it no longer matched his appearance, that would not matter because no-one was going to get a close enough look at it to notice.

Out in the street, a passing car slowed down to a crawl as the driver leant over to gain a clear sight of the front window of one of the houses on his left. Having seen what he wanted, he sat up and accelerated away, pressing the buttons on his mobile phone as he did. It was answered as he turned the corner at the end of the road and started to head for home. 'Hi Sash,' he said. 'It's me. The light's back on again; so it's definite; your man's back home again. Over to you.'

In the morning Angela got out of bed at her normal time, having conceded that she had to go back to work before her employer decided she had no job to go back to. When she had left to go to Caracas with John, she had not resigned but, being as conservative in many respects as he was, had agreed with her manager an extended leave of absence to deal with a family crisis that had suddenly and unexpectedly blown up. Now they were home, with no other means of support, she had to go back; so she did.

John stayed in the flat, Angela's flat, which was now, for the time being at least, his home as well as hers. After she had left, he had eaten breakfast, watched the news on TV, had a shower and got dressed; then settled himself down at her computer, turned it on and connected it to the internet, using the passwords she had left for him when he told her he wanted to use it. He began slowly, using a popular search engine to look for entries under the headings "Adrian Wright" and "Stephen Dent"; the internet equivalent of thinking out loud rather than doing anything he really thought would be useful. Just as he expected, nothing useful came up. So he continued to think out loud on the keyboard and found himself typing "train delay, Lord's Copse"; then hitting the return key. Nothing happened for a while, then a list of links appeared and he started to look down it.

The story had, he found, been quite widely reported, with some coverage even reaching as far as the national dailies. Longer, more detailed stories were presented by the local papers, with pictures; of the station, of stationary trains, and of Wright, the arse, being led away in handcuffs by the police. One of the locals even went as far as identifying Wright by his first name, and carried a picture of the street in Pooley where he lived. Now that is interesting, John thought to himself.

In his office at North Downham Police Station, DCI Flagg was waiting for the phone call that would tell him that Wright was back at home, having instructed motorplod, as he liked to call his colleagues in Traffic Division, to keep an eye on his suspect's flat. They, not having been told why or how they should go about it, had been driving past religiously, twice a day. The first time was just before three in the afternoon each day, when there was no need for Wright to have a light on in his sitting room. The second was just before three in the morning; well after the time that Wright turned off his lights and took himself off to bed. And their chances of seeing any other evidence of him being there ranged from slight to negligible as they simply drove past on the road at the front, not having been told about the back entrance and the alleyway at the end of the garden.

John worked entirely alone, and so had to be more resourceful than Flagg was. He also knew how to use the internet, which Flagg did not, and it took him no more than a few hours to decide that he knew almost exactly where Wright lived. He worked this out using the photograph printed in the local paper, street maps that showed him the location of all the parks in and around Pooley, and websites that held reams of photographs of the area, taken at various times through the past century or so.

On the street maps he found that there were three parks either in or close to Pooley itself, that could be described as being "in the area". From there he made a list of the names of all the streets that ran along their outsides, that might be the one he was looking for. Then he used all those street names to search for photographs he could compare with the one in the newspaper article, to tell him which of them it was.

Before starting his search he would never have guessed how well the history of the suburbs had been recorded by photographers, and how accessible most of their output would turn out to be. For each of the streets he had listed there was a multitude of images to be looked at, starting from either the earliest days of photography or the earliest days of development of the area, depending which of them had come first. There were pictures of Victorians mourning; Edwardians celebrating; soldiers marching off to wars, triumphantly expectant; and returning home afterwards, depleted in both numbers and spirit. There were pictures of children playing; builders building: tradesmen delivering; road menders working; and groups of residents posing proudly in front of the cameras, in celebration of some notable event or the other. And although John found the subjects of these pictures fascinating in their own right, they were not the focus of his interest, as it was the backgrounds against which they appeared that he really wanted to see.

One by one, street by street, he worked his way through the images he conjured up on Angela's computer screen, staring past the solemn or smiling faces, the children playing and the workmen toiling, to look at the fronts of the buildings beyond them, trying to see if they could have been the ones that appeared in the newspaper article about Wright—the arse. Some, he could see straight away, could not have been the ones he was looking for, because their shape, or style, or materials were wrong; but many appeared the same or similar enough, as the style of building used and the time that they had been built were common throughout the area.

Eventually, after working away at it solidly for several hours, he had narrowed his search down to just two streets, adjacent to two parks, one on either side of the town centre in Pooley. And with a little more searching he found the image that decided the matter, on a website carrying an article on Pooley during the Second World War, published in the early years of the conflict. The photograph, printed in black and white, had been taken from almost exactly the same spot as the one in the local newspaper, but this one, rather than intending to show the street itself, was there to document Pooley's historic sacrifice to the war effort, as workmen removed the park's ornate iron railings, to be taken away and melted down for guns, or bullets, or bombs. And because the location and angle of view of the photographer had been more or less the same as that of the person who had taken the later picture, the terrace of houses across the street from the park appeared on the left in both of them and, despite the time that had passed between the taking of the two pictures, they were clearly the same houses, facing the same park, and lining the same street; Park Terrace South, in the South Suburbia suburb of Pooley.

It was too late in the day to do anything about it right then, but the following morning, armed with this new-found knowledge, John left the flat and drove northwards to Pooley in Angela's car, the keys of which she had left for him when she had set out to walk into the centre of Asham to go to work. Following the directions he had written down for himself from the maps he had found on the internet, it took him just over an hour to complete the journey in the light post rush-hour traffic of a bright summer's day, and in what seemed to him to be almost no time at all he was turning into Park Terrace South.

The road he found himself in was a long, straight one, with the park on one side, his left, and terraces of tall, red-brick-fronted Victorian houses on his right. Those houses had once been grand; occupied by the reasonably well-off who could afford to live well and employ staff to help them do it. Now almost all of them were divided into four floors of flats; the only way they could survive without falling into terminal disrepair and decay.

At its far end, Park Terrace South gave way to Park Terrace East at a T-junction. John stopped there, then turned right, stopped again and reversed into a vacant parking space on the left-hand side of the road, almost immediately opposite the end of the terrace in which Wright's flat was located. John took stock of his situation, imagining himself to be like one of his fictional or TV detectives on a stake-out. On his immediate right-hand side he had a clear view along the pavement running in front of the terrace, so if John was vigilant he would see the arse if he chose to go out that way. Across the road, diagonally forward and right, at the end of their back gardens, John had clear sight of the mouth of the alley that served the rear entrances to the houses, just like the one he had behind his own house. He knew without having to look that this alley ran the full length of the back of the terrace and led out into the road at its far end, as well as the one he was parked in, so if Wright decided to leave his flat by the back way, there was only a fifty-fifty chance of seeing him. Still, covering two of the three possible ways out was better than not covering any of them, so he would just have to trust to his luck.

As it turned out, his luck was good, and after just over an hour of waiting, his attention was drawn to the movement of a familiar figure emerging from the end of the alley. The hairs on the back of his neck prickled and stood up as he took in the short, dark hair, the leather jacket, the polo shirt and casual trousers, all of which he had seen in Caracas the week before; but above all it was the face he remembered most; familiar, even without the moustache. With a conscious effort of will he pulled his hand away from his car's ignition key, knowing that however tempting it might be, running Wright over at that point was not going to help him get back the money or the computer disc or, preferably, both of them. So John just sat patiently and watched, as Wright paused briefly at the end of the alley and looked furtively around, then crossed the road, climbed into a small, dark, saloon car parked on the same side and a short way ahead, started up, pulled out, and drove off down Park Terrace East. John pulled out as well and followed him at a respectable distance. Wright went shopping at his local supermarket, and John went with him. Then Wright returned to his flat, and so did John.

Wright, of course, had been far from idle himself. On the morning of the day before that, at just about the

time that John had sat down at Angela's computer, he had
arrived at South Suburbia station on the bus to make his
attempt to re-enter Overway House. Dressed in his former
"uniform"—blazer, grey trousers, white shirt and regimental
tie—in an effort to blend in with the crowd of suits and
"business-casual" clothing everyone else would be wearing,
and carrying his black leather briefcase, he made his way to
the edge of the station concourse, from where he could look
into the foyer of the Perma-way office building and wait for
his moment to arrive.

It was not long in coming. Several groups of workers
had already stomped their way in through the front doors
and disappeared into the lifts when the hoped-for visitor
arrived, just ahead of the next wave of commuters rushing
towards their desks. Wright joined them as they coursed in
through the doors, and was swept across the foyer with a
cursory wave of his security pass towards the receptionist,
who was busy interrogating the would-be visitor, and into
one of the lifts. Which floor Wright got out at was not
important to his plan, so he chose the lift's second stop,
then made his way to the men's toilet and into one of the
cubicles there. It was not that he wanted to use the toilet
just then, although he would undoubtedly need to from
time to time during the course of the day to come, but that
was where he planned to spend the working day, hidden
away in various toilet cubicles up and down the building,
until the day reached its end and the offices began to empty
out again. So began his long day of waiting, made just
about tolerable by the reading of a novel he had wanted to
tackle for some time, but had never got round to opening,
punctuated every fifteen minutes or so by a move from
floor to floor, from cubicle to cubicle, so as not to attract
attention or concern by spending too long in any one of

them. Each move was carefully timed, to be made when the toilet he was leaving was empty, to reduce the chance that he would bump into anyone who knew him.

The day passed slowly, but it passed, and at about nine o'clock in the evening, when he had had more than enough of War and Peace, and thought that even the most seriously-damaged workaholics would have packed up and gone home, Wright emerged from his last lair and began to make his way to the floor where Dent had his office. Thankful that he knew the way the security staff in the building operated, and hoping that nothing had been changed in the weeks since he was last there, he walked up the stairs and emerged into the corridor leading to the offices of Perma-way's directors. Checking carefully for lights, noises or any other signs of life in each of the offices as he passed them, he walked towards Dent's office door. When he reached it he paused, hardly daring to breathe, to make sure there was no light to be seen shining under or around its edges and no sound to be heard coming from behind it. There was neither, so he reached out, pushed the handle down and opened the door a crack—just to make absolutely sure—this was no time and no place to get caught if he was to have any hope of achieving his aim of getting his hands on that disc.

Inside the office it was quiet and dark. Wright opened the door a little further, slipped inside and pushed it closed after him. Standing with his back to the door he pulled his torch from his jacket pocket, turned it on and directed its beam at the wall on his left, where he knew Dent's safe was located, behind a large print of the Flying Scotsman belching smoke and steam as it pulled out of a station somewhere back in time in the golden age of steam. Knowing the location of the safe was one of the benefits of having been nosy when he had been working there for Dent, on the grounds that you never knew when what you found out might turn out to be useful. He walked to the wall, reached out and flicked the concealed catch high up on the left-hand side of Dent's picture, out of sight behind its heavy, wooden frame. With the lightest of touches the picture swung away from the wall on its hinges, revealing the front of the safe behind it. It was not a modern or sophisticated model, and it took Wright no time at all to open it, using one of the keys on the huge bunch he had brought with him, inside the leather briefcase that also held his copy of War and Peace. He bitterly regretted not having had the foresight to take those keys with him to Caracas, although he knew that his chances of getting them through the security checks at the airport were slim, and he would be loath to lose them as it had taken him most of his working life to collect them, and was confident that he stood a good chance of opening almost any conventional lock with something, somewhere in his collection. And if he had been stopped while carrying them through the airport he might have found it difficult to explain them away to the satisfaction of the police, and the security services, had they got involved. At least he had them now though, and that gave him a fighting chance against Dent, Biddle and all the other bastards who were responsible for making him suffer so badly.

With a mixture of hope and anticipation he scrutinised the lock on the door of the safe, then holding his torch between his teeth he sorted through his collection of keys and selected one of a group he thought were most likely to be the ones he needed. Two minutes and several keys later he had the door of the safe open, had emptied it, and was sitting at Dent's desk with his back to the wall rifling through its contents. He started with the collection of papers, looking between each of the sheets in case the disc he wanted was lodged there. It was not, so he turned his attention to the box the papers had been resting on. Slowly, carefully, he lifted the lid and slid it to one side. Inside the box, wrapped in an oily cloth, was a revolver, of the kind once issued to officers in the British Army. This had once belonged to Dent's Grandfather and had been passed down through the generations of Dent menfolk as a memento of his life. Dent kept it there because his wife was firm in her belief that all such instruments of violence should be destroyed, and would not acknowledge its right to exist; let alone entertain the idea of having it in her house. Wright held it up and examined it carefully. It was not loaded and there was no ammunition in the box or the safe. That did not mean that Dent could not get some from somewhere, of course. But there was no disc.

'Bugger it!' Wright said under his breath.

He leant back in the chair, fighting back a strong urge to vent his frustration on the inside of Dent's office and trash it. That, the logical part of his mind told him, would be counter-productive if he was to have any chance left of finding the disc anywhere else, because alerting Dent to the threat of losing the disc was the last thing he needed to do right then. Where could it be? he asked himself. The obvious answer; the only possible answer, unless Dent had been stupid enough to entrust the disc to one of his fellow Perma-way Directors, was at his home, and Wright did not for one moment think that Dent was stupid. There were many things he might be, but stupid was not one of them. So where do you live, Mr Dent? Wright asked himself. And who's going to tell me? There was a large desk diary beside the computer screen in front of him, as Dent was old enough and stuck firmly enough in his ways not to have adopted computerised scheduling of his appointments completely. Wright pulled the diary towards him and flicked open its front cover, looking for the section where places were provided for the owner to insert their name, address, and a lot of other information that might be useful to a potential diary-thief. It was blank. Finding it filled-in had been too much to hope for. The same was true of the section at the back set up as an address book. Where else? he asked himself.

Wright shone the thin torch beam around the inside of the office and brought it to rest on a second door, set into the far wall; not the one he had come in through. Of course, he told himself: a secretary. He got up, walked round the desk, across the room and opened the door. Beyond it was, indeed, Dent's secretary's office, with a neatly laid-out desk making it easy to find another diary, just like Dent's; but this one, unlike his, had the back section filled in, and right there, just where it should have been, was Dent's home address, phone number, mobile phone number and wife's mobile phone number; in case of emergencies. Wright found a pen and wrote it all down on a piece of paper that he then folded and tucked away in his inside jacket pocket. Now; what are you up to Mister Dent? Wright muttered, flicking the diary's pages open at the current week. There was nothing there that looked to be of any great interest until he got to the Saturday evening, where there was an entry that read "Rail Industry Awards—London Criterion Hotel".

He turned and walked back into Dent's office and opened his diary to the same pages. This was even more forthcoming, giving not only the same brief information, but also the time of the taxi that was to pick Dent and his wife up from their house to take them to the hotel, and the taxi that would take them back home again on the Sunday morning, after a relaxing night of cosseting in a first-class London hotel. Wright smiled broadly, knowing that this was his chance to find what he was looking for, that he now knew must be somewhere in Dent's house; and he had all night to find it, provided there was no-one else living or staying with the Perma-way director and his wife. There's only one way to find that out, he told himself. Get up there and stake the place out.

Rising from Dent's luxuriously-upholstered chair, he picked up the papers and box, and returned them to the safe. Then he shut and locked the door and swung the Flying Scotsman back into place. He walked back to the office door, turned off his torch and stood, listening. There was nothing to be heard, so he opened it a crack and looked out into the corridor. There was nothing to be seen either, so he opened it further and looked round the door-jamb in the other direction. Still nothing, so he slipped out, shutting the door behind him, and made his way back to the stairwell. This was the tricky part; getting down the stairs and out of the building without being seen, as it was where he was most likely to meet one of the building's overnight security guards doing his rounds. He did, however, stand more chance of hearing them coming towards him than they did of hearing him coming towards them, as all of them were elderly and overweight and made a considerable amount of noise when climbing the stairs. And if they were coming down, they would never catch up with him because it was almost as much of an effort for them to go down as it was to go up.

He made it down to the bottom with only one minor scare, when he almost tripped over one of the guards coming out of the lobby on one of the floors on his way down to the next. Wright realised what was happening as the lobby door began to swing open—just in time for him to do a swift about-turn and skip back up the stairs to the back of the landing above, from where he could not be seen. The guard snuffled, snorted and grunted his way down the stairs to the floor below and disappeared into the lobby there to make his rounds. Wright waited until he was sure the man had gone; then carried on down the stairs to the bottom, where there was a door that opened out onto the street above the station.

The doors were solid, so when Wright began to push one open he was taking pot luck on what he would find on the other side. Just above the rail he was pushing on was a sign on the door that said

"This door is alarmed"

But he knew it was not; the sign was just a way of trying to scare people into not using it, and going out via the approved route, the front entrance, where they could be glared at by the over-officious receptionist. Wright looked at the other door, that had no sign, and wondered what it would say if it did have one. If its nerves were any better than its partner it might say

"This door is mildly concerned" or

"This door simply couldn't give a toss".

The door he was pushing on opened a fraction then stopped; bumping up against something that was both soft, but at the same time unyielding. He pushed harder, but met the same resistance. Not wanting to have to spend all night inside Overway House, or have to leave by the building's front entrance, he applied his full weight and gave a mighty heave. The tramp who had fallen asleep in the alcove the doors were set into shot across its floor and was deposited unceremoniously onto the pavement outside in a spirit-smelling, ragged heap. 'Wasssawassaaaa!' he moaned, grabbing at Wright's leg as he tried to walk past. Wright stumbled, straightened up as he regained his balance, then kicked out hard with his free foot, making a good, solid contact with a soft part of the tramp's anatomy. The moaning turned into a high-pitched wail and the bony hands released their grip on Wright's ankle. Heads turned up and down the street at the sudden sound. Wright strode briskly away and was swallowed by the darkness of the street running along the side of the station before anyone else could reach the stricken tramp to find out what had happened. Inside Overway House, all of this passed by without any of the guards hearing a thing.

The following day Wright went to the supermarket, and that was when John Biddle started to follow him. Jim, without realising he was doing it, followed both of them. Later on in the afternoon all three of them set off again from Pooley, this time to go to Dent's house, although only one of them knew it for certain, one suspected that might be where they were going, and the third had no idea at all. The route they followed took them out of Pooley, across the southern end of South Suburbia, and up into the hills to the east, where the houses grew large and stood further and further away from one another, and the area became generally more rural than urban.

Wright knew where he was going. John simply followed him at a discreet distance. Jim, who started off third in the convoy, soon became suspicious that he was not the only tail that Wright had; a suspicion that was more or less confirmed as they left the suburbs, the traffic thinned out, and the small, dark saloon in front of him continued to make all the same turns that Wright did, staying around the same, discrete distance behind him. Jim dropped back and began to follow the follower, thinking that it was most likely to be the police if it was anyone, and not wanting to get in their way if it was.

On the road that ran across the front of Dent's house, Wright slowed down. As he passed the entrance to the drive he started to signal, then turned left along the small lane that ran down the side of the property, looking for the entrance to the National Trust car park on the opposite side that he had seen on the internet maps and aerial photographs he had used to do his preliminary reconnaissance of the place. He turned right onto the gravel surface of the car park and ran on slowly, coming to a stop in a secluded spot among the bushes on its far side, where his car would not be visible from the road. John carried on past the cark park entrance for a short distance, rounded a bend to the right, then pulled off onto the verge on the side of the road, where his, or rather Angela's, car would not be seen by Wright. Jim had no choice but to carry on even further before stopping, to make sure that whoever it was in the second car would not see him. As he got out he phoned Sasha to update her on what was going on.

'I've followed Wright out into the country, to a big house.' He gave her the details of where he was. "He's picked up another tail . . . no I don't know who it is. I suppose it could be the police, but I don't think the driver's anyone I know.' He described Angela's car and gave Sasha the registration number.

'OK,' Sasha told him. 'I'll try to find out who that is and let you know. In the meantime, you stick with them and see if you can find out what they're up to. Oh, and keep your head down, just in case the tail is the police. I don't want to have to stump up the bail money to get you out for being a peeping Tom.'

Jim walked back up the road towards the house, keeping to the verge, ready to step into the bushes and trees beyond it if he saw anyone looking in his direction. Ahead of him, the second car came into sight, as did its driver, a nondescript-looking man, who seemed to be doing the same thing that he was. John walked back up the road towards the entrance to the car park, also keeping to the verge and ready to step back out of sight if Wright came into view and looked his way. Wright left his car and began the work he had gone there to do, as oblivious to the presence of John Biddle behind him as John was to the presence of Jim behind him.

Wright walked slowly along the verges of the two roads that bordered Dent's property, making an appraisal of it from the point of view of a burglar who did not want to get caught as he went about his business. The house was a large, mature, detached, mock Tudor affair standing in its own landscaped grounds. The front garden was large, with tall hedges growing on the inside of the waist-high, close-boarded, wooden boundary fence, and a number of leafy bushes in neat beds set into lush, green lawns; all of which served to mask the view of the house along the gravel drive that curved towards it from the gateway leading in off the road. The place was perfect for approaching without being seen from the inside, and breaking into without being seen from the road. Having seen all he could from the front, Wright turned and walked back in the direction he had come from, making John and then Jim step back quickly into the bushes so they did not get spotted. Wright passed within feet of where John stood without seeing him, and the temptation John felt to pick up a fallen log and beat the arse to death with it was almost more than he could resist—almost, but not quite—and Wright carried on walking; oblivious to the threat to his life, but at the same time safe from it.

Beyond the end of the back garden there was a field, and then a small wood. Wright continued walking until he was level with its edge. He paused, looked around him to make sure he was alone, then disappeared in amongst the trees. For the next hour or so Wright stood just inside the edge of the wood with a small pair of binoculars trained on the back and along the sides of the house, looking at the windows and doors, paths, fences, gates, and everything else he needed to know about to ensure that his forced entry would go as smoothly as possible when he attempted it. The house had a burglar alarm, of a type he recognised. It also had Tudor-style leaded-light windows, properly made in the traditional way, with tiny panes of glass held together with strips of lead. That, he knew, would make it easy to get into without tripping the alarm. At the end of the hour or so he moved on, finding it much more tricky to get to a suitable vantage point from which he could observe the front of the house without being seen himself. In the end he settled for a spot just inside the front garden, inside a leafy green bush, from where he could see the front door and the area that the family's cars would be parked in when they came back that evening. His observations from the back had convinced him that there was no-one home, so he reasoned that if he sat there long enough he would see the arrival of everyone who was currently living there.

By midnight, Wright was satisfied that he was right, and he had seen everyone, so he got up, stretched his cramped and aching muscles and joints, went back to his car and drove home. John and Jim both followed him, and when they were satisfied that they knew where he was heading, they peeled off in turn and went home to their beds. Wright was at home and safely tucked up in bed asleep with the lights off long before the regular motorplod patrol went past his flat, so his presence there went undetected again, and DCI Flagg was still not told that he was back.

In the time that Wright had spent sitting in his latest bush hide-out he had seen both Dent and a woman he assumed to be the Perma-way director's wife arrive home, but nobody else. Before he left the place, all the downstairs lights had been turned off, followed by the one that had come on in one of the upstairs rooms, so it seemed safe to assume that only Dent and his wife were in residence, meaning that when they both got into the taxi to go to the Rail Industry Awards the following evening, they would be leaving the house deserted, with only the burglar alarm to protect it.

The same impromptu convoy left Pooley again in the early evening of the following day and repeated, more or less exactly, its journey into the well-heeled Suburban suburbs. Wright parked his car in the same place as before, only this time he turned it round first so he could drive it straight back out again, in case he needed to make a quick getaway. His follower and his follower's follower carried on down the road a while before pulling in and stopping.

Wright made his way round to the front of the house, sauntering slowly along the footpath beside the wooden fence, looking around him as he did, adjusting his pace so he arrived at the gateway at the end of the drive during a lull in the traffic and when no-one was looking his way. With one last, quick glance behind him he slipped inside and crept through the undergrowth to the bush he had sat in the day before. He waited inside his bush until the day ended, the evening arrived and wore on and the daylight faded into darkness, leaving the house and garden bathed in the soft glow of moonlight falling from a cloudless sky. At the appointed time the taxi had arrived, turning in off the road and crunching its way along the gravel drive to the front door of the house. Dent had come out, dressed smartly in his dinner jacket and bow tie, accompanied by his elegant-looking wife. The front door was slammed, The Dents got into the back of the taxi, which turned away from the house, made its way back down the drive, pulled out onto the road and was gone, leaving Wright on his own in the garden—almost.

He waited a long time before moving, just to make sure the Dents were not coming back for anything they had forgotten and until it was dark. Then he crawled forward out of the bush, stood up, brushed himself down and walked towards the house. On reaching the front of it he turned to the right, away from the drive and made his way round to the back along the foot of the right-hand gable wall. Once there, he stopped in front of the window through which he had decided to make his entry into the place. He put his hand into his jacket pocket and pulled out a craft knife. Its new, razor-sharp blade glinted silver in the moonlight that bathed the back of the house. He lifted the knife, slid its blade into the tiny gap between one of the panes of glass in the window and the lead strip that contained it, pushed harder and began cutting.

The first cut was not too difficult, while the edge of the blade was still keen, but it got progressively more difficult as the sharpness was blunted, even by cutting into the relatively soft lead. He had to stop and change the blade for a new one several times over, but even so it was not too long before he had cut away the outer layer that was holding the glass in place over a large enough area to allow him to make a reasonably-sized hole. The next stage was to take out the glass by pushing back what was left of the lead and levering it out, pane by pane. This took him a little while to do, but time was not an issue, and if it enabled him to bypass the alarm, then it was time well spent. And at the end of that time the reasonably-sized hole was glass-free and ready to be used.

Wright turned on his tiny torch, leant in through the hole and examined the inside of the window frame, looking for the magnetic contacts that operated the alarm. As he had hoped, they were mounted on the back of the outer frame, and not on the inner frame of the secondary double glazing he had been sure he would find there. Using a long and sturdy screwdriver he had also brought with him, he levered on the frame of the double glazing until the catch snapped open. He slid the glass back out of the way, reached up, and pulled himself in through the hole. Once inside, with his back to the window, playing his torch slowly around, he could see that he was in a small sitting room or parlour: not, he thought, what he was looking for. He crossed the room and went out into the large, parquet-floored, wood-panelled hall beyond it. One by one he tried the doors leading off it, looking into each room by the light of his torch until he found the one he was looking for—was sure that he would find—Stephen Dent's study. He walked in and scanned the walls with his torch.

'Oh Stephen; you're so wonderfully predictable,' he said out loud, without fear of being overheard in the empty house. On the wall he was facing was another painting of another steam engine, this one captured travelling at speed, crossing a verdant, picturesque landscape, but obviously painted by the same artist as the one on the wall of the office in Overway House. He stepped forward, pulling a chair away from the small desk as he passed it, then climbed up to reach the top and sides of the frame of the painting. He found the concealed catch, pulled it, and the whole thing swung away from the wall on its hinges in a repeat of the events of two nights before. Wright's strong feeling of deja-vu was reinforced as his torch light showed him another safe of exactly the kind he had found in Dent's office, no doubt installed at the company's expense and to company standards.

'You deserve to be burgled Mr Dent, you really do,' Wright muttered as he pulled out his trusty bunch of keys, thinking again that if could have found a way to take them to Venezuela, none of this would have been necessary. Seconds later the safe door was open and the prize he had been seeking was his. He lifted the entire contents out, stepped down from the chair, turned, and spread it all out on the desk in front of him. There was a small pile of computer discs, a number of sheets of paper connected together with a treasury tag threaded through a hole punched through their top left-hand corner, and three large, hard-backed books that looked like desk diaries. Wright looked at the discs first, quickly finding the one he was looking for, conveniently marked on one side with the single word "Biddle" in bold letters in black felt-tipped pen. Wright gave a triumphant whoop at the sight of it and turned his attention to the rest of what he had found with it.

Even before the sound of his exultant outburst had finished echoing around the hall and stairwell of the luxurious and elegant house, unbeknown to Wright, a number of miles away from where he was standing, a red panel began to flash on a computer screen and an alarm began to sound. A pair of electrical contacts he knew nothing about had parted company when he had swung the painting out of the way, starting a thirty-second countdown within which he needed to press a concealed button he also knew nothing about, if he was to cancel the alarm that would then sound in the control room of the company Dent had hired to look after the safety and security of his house and his belongings. Thirty seconds passed, during which time the operator monitoring the computer screen reached out and pressed a button to call up on his screen the address of the property where the alarm had been triggered, lifted the receiver of the phone that stood on the desk next to the screen and made ready to call the police.

Wright turned his attention to the rest of the contents of the safe. The books were not diaries, they were ledgers, of the kind an accountant might use. He read swiftly through the first few pages of each one, then turned his attention to the other papers. They were bank statements which, together with the ledgers, told a story revealing exactly how devious this slimy character Stephen Dent really was. Having seen enough for the time being, Wright gathered together everything he had taken from the safe and slid it into a plastic carrier bag he pulled from his jacket pocket. He turned away from the safe, walked back through the dark hallway, through the small sitting room or parlour, and climbed back out through the hole he had made in the window. He paused momentarily on the window ledge, hopped down onto the grass below and straightened up; and that was when John Biddle stepped out of the undergrowth and hit him across the back of the head, with a log taken from a stack of firewood piled up not far from the back of the house.

John bent down and picked up the plastic carrier bag; obviously containing what Wright had gone into the house to collect. Standing over the sprawled-out figure of his adversary—not out cold but sufficiently senseless enough to lay groaning softly without making any effort to get up—John pulled out the contents of the bag and examined it by the light of his own small torch. He saw the computer discs; he looked at the ledgers and bank statements; he rapidly reached the same conclusion that Wright had—arse though he might be. He slid everything back into the carrier bag and turned to walk away; around the side of the house and back to his car. As he did, he realised that he could hear the wail of sirens, not far off and approaching fast, and could just make out the flashing blue lights that went with them, through the trees and bushes of the woods along the road not far away. He quickened his step, and that was when Sasha slipped out of the undergrowth and hit him across the back of the head; also with a log taken from the same stack of firewood, just as she had seen him do to Wright only moments before.

Sasha stepped forward to Wright and reached down to pull him to his feet, as he was showing signs of returning to life, if not health. 'Adrian,' she said urgently. 'Get up. The police are coming. If you don't want to be arrested again get up! We need to get out of here!' By then Wright had recovered enough to take in what was being said, and grasped the implications of the increasingly loud sirens and garish blue flashing lights, flicking off the trees along the road. Groggily, he dragged himself to his feet and staggered towards the bastard Biddle. He bent down and grabbed the plastic bag as Sasha pulled on his arm urgently, telling him that they really ought not to be there. Half walking, half running, they staggered away into the bushes along the side of the back garden, Sasha half-carrying Wright to stop him falling over again; heading towards the road and Sasha's car and as far away from the end of the drive, where the police would arrive at any moment, as they could get in as short a time as possible.

John came to his senses just in time to avoid being arrested himself. He got up and followed the path Wright and Sasha had taken, just as the first car swept through the gates and roared up the drive. All the police found was the hole in the window and the open, empty safe.

CHAPTER SEVEN

Detective Chief Inspector Flagg was standing on his own in the middle of Stephen Dent's study when the Perma-way director came in from the hall. It was Sunday morning, almost twelve hours after the burglary. Flagg had been there for some time and was looking around after the Scene of Crime Officers and the fingerprint boys had done their stuff. Dent had only just arrived. He had turned his mobile phone off the evening before and given instructions to the hotel staff that he was not to be disturbed, either during the awards ceremony or overnight in his room, so it was only in the morning, at breakfast, that he had been told about the break-in. He left the hotel immediately and took a taxi back to the house, telling his wife to follow on with their overnight bags. For a few moments after Dent entered the room, the two men just stood and stared at one another without saying anything; then Flagg broke the awkward silence.

'So; we meet again Mr Dent. How have you been since our last meeting? Lost any more sack-fulls of money?'

'I'm not sure I particularly like your tone Inspector,' Dent snapped. 'What are you doing here? I've asked the Transport Police to look into this for me, and they're on their way here now.'

'They're going to be disappointed when they arrive then, because this is outside their jurisdiction. It's on my patch; not on railway property. That makes it mine, not theirs; whether you, or they, like it or not. Now, if you wouldn't mind, could you please tell me what's been taken?'

'Nothing,' Dent snapped, far too quickly for Flagg's liking, after only the briefest of glances at the open, empty safe.

At that point they were interrupted by Brennan, who had come into the house to tell Flagg that there was something outside he needed to look at. They left Dent on his own in the study and went out into the front garden. Brennan led the way out to the road, then along the two footpaths that ran across the front of the house and down the lane at the side, to the car park opposite, where he had found Wright's car.

'Do you recognise this, Guv?' Brennan asked, tapping gently at the front number plate with his foot.

'I do indeed, Brennan. It's our friend Wright's, isn't it? Now I wonder what that's doing up here; or more to the point, I wonder why it's still here when its owner quite clearly isn't. Come to that, I wonder where he *is* right now.'

'No idea, sir,' Brennan said. 'Do you want me to find out?'

'Good idea,' Flagg said. 'Take uniform down to his flat. If he's there, take him in for questioning. This is just one coincidence too many. And while you're at it, give motorplod a bollocking for not telling us he was back.'

The two walked back to the house in silence. Brennan went off in one of the patrol cars. Flagg went back into the study, to Stephen Dent. 'Now, Mr Dent, where were we? Oh yes; you were just about to have a good look around and tell me if anything's missing.'

'I have; and there is nothing missing; just as I told you.'

'Don't you think that's just a bit odd? Because when I had a look around upstairs earlier on, just to make sure there was no-one lurking up there I should know about, I found a lot of jewellery and other valuables in drawers and cupboards, all very poorly protected, but still there. Are you really trying to tell me that whoever broke in here simply opened your safe, which you're saying was empty at the time, then left in disappointment without looking anywhere else for anything else they could have taken?'

'I can't say: I wasn't here. Perhaps the alarm disturbed them.'

'The main alarm didn't go off. They, whoever they are, bypassed it by cutting the glass out of the window in the room across the hall. And the alarm on the safe, the one that did go off, doesn't sound here, so that's not the answer.'

'I don't think I should be expected to give you the answers to these questions,' Dent said. 'You're supposed to be the detective. If you were conducting the investigation which, I repeat, you're not, I'd be looking to *you* to provide *me* with the answers, not the other way around.'

Flagg let it pass and changed tack, a thick skin being an essential in this kind of situation. 'Do you know a Mr William Everest?'

'No, I don't think so. Is there any reason why I should?'

'But you do know Adrian Wright, though,' Flagg said, ignoring Dent's question.

'Yes; you know I do.'

'When did you last see him?'

'The day I collected him from you; after the fiasco on the train.'

'When precisely did you last see him on that day, and where?' Flagg asked.

'When? About ten minutes after we left your office. Where? God knows: somewhere on the road between your police station and my office.'

'And do you know where he is now?'

'Look; I don't see what any of this could possibly have to do with the reason why you're here now, and in any case, as I've told you, this is nothing to do with you; the Transport Police are going to deal with it. So I'd like you and your men to leave, now, before you manage to trample my garden completely flat and the carpets into ruins.'

'And as I explained to you.' Flagg said, struggling to contain his irritation with this bumptious overbearing upstart of a man, 'It's not in their jurisdiction, it's in mine.'

Flagg and Dent glared at one another; then both looked round in response to a light tap on the door. As if on cue, another policeman walked into the room; this one dressed in the uniform of an inspector in the Transport Police. Behind him were the two PCs who had accompanied Dent when he had collected Wright from the police station.

'At last,' Dent snapped. 'Flagg, this is Inspector Sands. He'll be taking over now, so you're free to go.'

Flagg stepped towards Sands. 'Detective Chief Inspector Flagg,' he said, emphasising his full title; holding out his hand for the inspector to shake. 'I'm afraid Mister Dent is labouring under a misapprehension. He seems to think he can decide who has jurisdiction here, but as I've tried to explain to him, that's not the case. This isn't a railway matter, it's a straight forward break-in, so it's mine. And while we're at it, I'll be taking over the train investigation as well.'

'No you bloody well won't,' Dent erupted indignantly. 'You're exceeding your authority. That's a railway matter, so my men will deal with it!'

'I'm sorry to disappoint you Mr Dent, but I have a dead body, on terra firma, not railway property, whose demise, in my opinion, is linked together with the unsavoury incident on your train and with this burglary, and that puts it all within my jurisdiction, so I'm pulling rank and taking over the investigation of the whole lot of it. Now that may not suit you, and you may not like it, and you may well be best buddies with the Chief Constable and the Home Secretary and play golf with both of them every Sunday morning for all I know, but it doesn't change the fact that it's all mine now, until I decide, or events prove, that it isn't. Am I making myself clear?'

Dent, taken aback by being spoken to in a manner he was not used to, surrounded as he was most of the time by the yes-men who worked with and for him, stayed silent. Inspector Sands may well have been one of Dent's yes-men, but he also knew Flagg was right, so he stayed silent too.

'I'll leave you two to say your goodbyes,' Flagg said to both of them, and walked out of the room. As he crossed the hall and went out into the front garden he could hear the sound of raised voices in the study behind him, but not what they were saying. Flagg's phone rang. He pulled it out of his jacket pocket. 'Hello,' he snapped into it. 'Flagg.'

'Hello Guv; it's Brennan. I'm at Wright's flat with uniform. He's not here. His landlady let us in with a spare key, so we've been able to have a good look round. Either his bed's not been slept in or Wright made it this morning before he left. There's no way of knowing whether he's taken any clothes or anything, but his toothbrush is still in the bathroom and its not wet, so it hasn't been used this morning, and probably not last night either. My guess is that he's not away on holiday or anything, but he wasn't here last night.'

'OK,' Flagg said slowly. 'Get hold of the lovely Withers and stake the place out again. If he shows up there, pick him up and take him in. While you're doing that I'll think about what we should do about this sanctimonious prig Dent. Keep me in touch with what's happening.'

'Will do, Guv. Speak to you later.'

Flagg turned his phone off and slipped it back into his pocket. There was nothing more he could do there; Dent was adamant that nothing had been taken and the break-in appeared to be a clean one, with no obvious clues to point towards the person who had done it; except Wright's car, of course. It was time to leave, but at least he could annoy Dent just a little more before he did. He went back into the house, just in time to find Sands and his PCs leaving, and Dent stalking across the hall towards the kitchen looking thunderous. Sands gave Flagg a brief nod and a resigned smile as they passed.

'Mr Dent,' Flagg said, following him into the kitchen. 'We need to take your fingerprints, and those of anyone else who lives here, works here, or visits on a regular basis.'

'Why do you want to do that?' Dent snapped at him, clearly annoyed by his continuing presence there.

'So we can eliminate you: from our enquiries that is. Now; whose prints do we need to take?'

'Is this really necessary?' Dent asked, finding it impossible to prevent his exasperation from showing as he spoke.

'Yes, I'm afraid it is,' Flagg told him. 'We've collected a number of sets of prints from both your study and the room they got in through, so we need to eliminate those we think aren't from the burglar, leaving us free to look more closely at those that might well be.'

'So when is that going to happen?' Dent sighed.

'Oh, anytime really—as long as it's sometime today,' Flagg told him, smiling over-politely. 'So; when your wife gets home, would you both be kind enough to come down to the station please; and bring with you the names and addresses of anyone else we might need to consider not arresting on the grounds of breaking and entering or aggravated burglary?'

'I really don't see the point of this farce Flagg. As I've already told you, nothing was taken, and as for the suggestion of this being part of a . . . of a . . . conspiracy of some kind, well that's just ludicrous; a nonsensical suggestion.'

'I think I'll allow myself to be the best judge of that,' Flagg replied stiffly. 'Now if you could find time in your no-doubt busy schedule to do as I ask, sometime today, I'd be very grateful; otherwise we might have to come up and get you; and although the nearest houses are some distance away, the sound of sirens tends to carry a long way in the early hours of the morning, as does the effect of our pretty blue flashing lights.'

'Are you trying to threaten me, Flagg? because if you are, you've chosen the wrong man!'

'Oh, I don't think so, sir; I think you're entirely the right man; I just don't know what you're the right man for just yet; but I will; oh yes, I will. I'll look forward to seeing you later then.' With that Flagg walked out of the room, out of the house, got into the front passenger seat of the waiting patrol car and was swept out of the front gates with a roar of its powerful engine and the scrunch of tyres on gravel.

Inspector Richard Sands was fuming as he left Dent's house. He had disliked the man instinctively from the moment they had first met, and Dent had done nothing to help him alter his opinion since then. Sands was in complete agreement with what he could see DCI Flagg thought of him; and because Dent had been instrumental in appointing most of his fellow Perma-way Directors and had picked people who were as close as they could be to mirror images of himself, Sands felt the same way about all of them too. Unfortunately he had to take a more diplomatic line with them than Flagg did, as they, and Dent in particular, were influential characters in the railway world, particularly with the upper echelons of the Transport Police. Sands had to tread carefully when dealing with any of them, therefore, but given a chance would have liked nothing more than the opportunity to bring one of them, the whole lot of them, down a peg or two, or three, or four . . .

John arrived at London River Crossing Station on the train he had taken from Asham in the middle of that bright, sunny Sunday morning. He did not really understand why he was there, other than having the feeling that he needed to connect in some way with Stephen Dent, and with what he had found out during his swift reading of the papers and ledgers that Wright had taken from the Perma-way Director's house and then, subsequently, from him. One thing he did know was that Wright now had an accomplice, because it was not the arse himself that had hit him over the back of the head—Wright was still lying on the ground at John's feet when that surprise had been sprung.

The train slowed as it approached the platform and then stopped, as the guard completed the usual unnecessary and unwanted airline-style announcement by thanking all of those on board for choosing to travel with South Coast Regional Trains that day. It sounded formulaic; insincere; as though it was being read by someone who really did not believe in what he was saying—what he had been told to say—which it probably was. The doors slid open with a hiss of compressed air being released and John stepped out onto the platform. Above him and around him the station, rebuilt only a few years before, sparkled and shone in the dappled sunlight that glittered down through the high glass roof with its semi-transparent fabric sunshields, perforated by thousands, or tens or hundreds of thousands, of tiny holes, stretched out underneath. He walked towards the exit at the head of the platforms, all paved with the light grey granite flooring that had replaced the dour, dark asphalt that had been there before the rebuilding/refurbishment began.

John crossed the open area at the head of the platforms, on the far side of which stood the first rank of shops, or "retail outlets" as they had become known in modern phraseology. He stepped onto the first of the three gleaming, stainless steel and chrome escalators that would carry him down to the new station concourse level three floors below, past more and more shops, and moving image marketing placards (large TV screens) depicting Mediterranean holiday scenes, towards the rotating turnstiles at the bottom, through which the masses of workers the trains brought into The City every day disgorged during the course of each morning rush hour, like lambs to the slaughter; only to rush back in again at the end of each day, desperate to get back home while there was still some small part of the day left for them to enjoy. Like lambs to the slaughter, he said to himself, and shuddered. Just like I used to be; and might well have to be again. And as this depressing thought struck him, his head began to throb again from the blow it had received the night before, and the face of his oppressive boss, Roland Smythe, rose up in front of his eyes to haunt him like some kind of ghoulish spectre.

John reached the bottom of the three flights of descending escalators and then, instead of making his way out of the station as he might have been expected to, he turned round and stepped onto the bottom of the first one going back up. Rising up from the artificially-lit bowels of the station into the bright, natural sunlight above, he felt as though he might be ascending onto some higher plane. The vision of Roland Smythe faded, and John thought that this was the way Stephen Dent must feel about the place, even without the escalators and the sunshine. For here, John knew, was the source—or maybe just one of a number of sources—of the crooked Perma-way Director's private nest-egg. As he went further and further up through the station into the light, John could see names that were familiar to him—not just because the shop-fronts they adorned were the well-known high street names and speciality stores that congregated in modern shopping centres, airports and stations—but because they were also the names that were listed in the papers and ledgers that John had scanned through rapidly by torchlight in Dent's garden before Wright's accomplice had hit him and they had been snatched away from him.

John had not had much time to take in any more than the fact that the names were listed as the headings of rows in a table that connected them with dates and what appeared to be amounts of money. And it was not too difficult to see how it all worked: Dent's Book of Excuses delayed the trains; the marooned and frustrated commuters phoned home—'Hello; it's me. No I'm not on the train yet; the bloody thing's been delayed again; dead cow in the driving seat of a train at Howard's Heath or some such nonsense. No I don't know when I'll be home. Don't worry about me—you go ahead and eat—I'll grab something here.' And from there they went into the pie shops and the bars and the newsagents, to eat and drink and buy books or papers or magazines to help while away the time; and for every purchase made, Dent's under-the-counter agreement with the shops, restaurants and bars made him just a little bit richer—tax- and conscience-free, of course.

John reached the top of the escalators, walked over to a bench and sat down to think. He knew what Dent was doing; but what was Wright up to? Who was the arse's accomplice; and where would it get him if he knew the answers to those questions? Wright had gone to Caracas to find him and to get the disc and the money. At first John had thought that it was to enable him to return them to Dent, but what Wright had done after he had got back to the UK had shown that this was not his intention at all: he wanted them for himself. Why? Why would anyone want a million pounds? Stupid question. Wright had failed in Caracas but, with the help of his mysterious accomplice, he had succeeded in getting hold of the disc in Dent's back garden, despite John's gallant efforts to stop him. He had also got himself evidence of Dent's second scam, involving the shops, bars and restaurants here, and possibly in other places as well: after all, if it worked here, why would it not work in the other London terminal stations, in South Suburbia, at the airport, at Bridges Junction, and everywhere else there was a newsagent, a coffee shop, or any other place a frustrated passenger might go to relieve the boredom of a long wait for a train that might or might not turn up at some unspecified time in the future?

Wright was about to copy what John himself had already done: he was going to blackmail Dent. That was now abundantly clear: blackmail Dent for money he had no right to: money that should belong to him, John, and not to the arse Wright. John vowed there and then that he was not going to let that happen; that he would somehow stop it and take back what was rightfully his, as payment for all he had suffered over the years of torment at the hands of the railway companies and his bastard boss. Then he and Angela would be free to take off and start all over again. And this time there would be no mistakes. He stood up and began to walk across the heads of the platforms, staring up at the destination boards, looking for the train that would get him back home in the shortest time. He had to go back to Asham to prepare; then on to Pooley to stake out Wright's flat and wait for him to set out to meet Dent, to swap the papers and disc for the money.

When Wright woke up in Sasha's bed that same Sunday morning she was not in it with him, and nor had she been; she had been up all night working at her desk and on her computer. Being a reasonably good newshound, with instincts to match, she had recognised the scent of a good story in the person of Adrian Wright from the very beginning, when she had first seen him, being marched off the train at Lord's Copse. That was why she had befriended him, followed him to Dent's house, rescued him from the assault on him as he left the place and the police arrived, and why he was now snoring loudly in her bed as she worked her way through the papers and computer discs he had taken from Dent's safe.

When she and Wright had escaped from Dent's garden, through a hole she had made in the hedge between it and the lane that ran along its side, she had had to half drag, half carry him because he was still only half with-it—from the blow on the head that John Biddle had given him. Letting him attempt to drive his car was out of the question, so she took him straight to hers, pushed him into the passenger seat and was racing away down the lane at high speed before the police had even made it as far as Dent's front door. On the way back down into South Suburbia, Wright showed no great signs of life and Sasha thought that it would be unwise to leave him on his own at his flat, so she decided to take him straight to hers: protecting her investment as it were. Luckily she lived in a first floor flat, in one of the outer western suburbs of Suburbia, so when they arrived there she did not have to manoeuvre him up too many flights of stairs, and after she stopped the car in the street outside it was no more than a few minutes before he was undressed and stretched out in her bed snoring loudly, and she was able to sit down and take stock of what had happened that night. After a quick visit to the kitchen to make herself a coffee, she slid into the padded leather chair behind her desk, and in the quiet of the night, in a pool of soft yellow light thrown down by the desk lamp in the cocooning darkness of her study, she began to read the papers Wright had taken from Dent's safe, in an attempt to find out what was going on.

The papers were interesting, but not of much use on their own. The first batch seemed to be about the sales figures of various shops at various times through the previous few years. The next batch were bank statements, for an account in the name of Stephen Smith. They showed no withdrawals and a constantly increasing balance, with deposits being made regularly, always in cash, but always for different amounts. Sasha knew instinctively that there must be some connection between the two sets of figures, but no matter how hard she tried she could not find it. She spent a long time reading and re-reading the names, dates and amounts, to fix them in her mind, so that when she moved on to whatever was on the discs, she could readily make connections—if there were any connections to be made, that was. That was one of the key things she had learnt about journalism over the years—connections are everything.

When she had grown tired of reading the data on the papers, and was no longer taking anything in, she moved on to the discs, and then everything began to become clear. One, in particular was crucial, because it held the key to it all. When it was installed in the computer and its contents displayed on the screen, Sasha could see that it held just five files, labelled First, Second, Third, Fourth and Fifth. Following what she took to be instructions telling her the order in which the files should be opened, she used her mouse to point the cursor on the screen at the icon representing the first file and double-clicked the left button. The cursor was replaced by the hour-glass symbol and the little green light on the computer flashed on and off to show that something was happening inside it. After a minute or so the screen was filled by a new window, showing that the file labelled "First" was a media file; something she would have to watch and listen to. She leaned over and opened the left-hand desk drawer, pulled out a small set of headphones, plugged in and put them on. The screen was ready, so she clicked on the 'play' button.

The file that ran was sound-only and was obviously home-made. The voice was John Biddle's, but she did not know that because she did not know him—had not even heard of him at that point. What she heard was the voice of an ordinary-sounding man, one she might have called 'a punter' in the office, telling her, hesitantly at first but then with growing confidence, about what she would find on the other files on the disc; The Book of Excuses; his own train diaries; the spreadsheet that gave the profit and loss information for the Roamer-Phone deal (all profit, no loss); the Perma-way work order sheets that connected the mobile phone giant with the delays, and The Book. Finally, without giving away anything about himself, he told of his connection with it all—the project to develop a computer-based system to maximise the income and his involvement in that. All-in-all it was quite a story.

For next few hours Sasha stayed glued to her computer screen, scrolling through page after page of documentary evidence to support everything that the disembodied voice on the disc had told her. Instinct told her that it was genuine. It could have been a hoax; but if it was it was one heck of a hoax: and what would be the point? And if it was genuine it was one heck of a story. Working on the principle that her instinct did not usually let her down, and it could not do her any harm anyway, she delved through her desk drawers until she found an unused memory stick and made herself her own copy of the files on the disc. Then, in the light of her new knowledge, she turned her attention back to the papers Wright had taken from Dent's house, and quickly fitted them into the picture, deciding that "Stephen Smith" had the same deal going with the shops at the stations as he did with Roamer-Phone: delays pushed up sales figures, and some of the increases in profit found their way into Mr Smith's (until very recently) very private bank account. Lucky old Mr Smith! Now there were two more things she had to do:- (1) make copies of all of these papers to put with her copy of the files on the disc, and (2) work out a way to find out where Adrian Wright fitted into it all—and she had all the equipment she needed for both of them.

For what little was left of the night, Sasha remained at her desk, scanning the papers sheet by sheet and storing the file she put them into on the memory stick. By the time she had finished it was light outside and a new day had begun. She got up and stretched; running through in her mind what she had to do to set the scene for the next part of what was now her new plan. Very quietly she left her study, crossed the hall and went into the bedroom, where Wright was still asleep, but might begin to stir at any moment. She reached down and pulled her nightdress out from underneath her pillow, screwed it up, then draped it casually over the top, trying to make it look as though she had got up, slipped out of it and just left it there. Then she pushed down the quilt on her side of the bed for the same reason. Satisfied with her work, she crept back out into the hall, then went into the bathroom to have a shower, which she genuinely needed.

When Wright woke up in Sasha's bed that morning she was not in it with him, but she had made a decent job of convincing him that she had been. He opened his eyes and found himself in a bed that was not his, in a room he did not recognise, and spent the next few minutes wondering where he was, and why his head felt so sore on the outside and throbbed so much on the inside. One by one he ruled out the possibilities: he was not lying bleeding in a gutter somewhere, so he had not been mugged; his tongue was not glued to the roof of his mouth and he did not feel the urge to discharge the contents of his stomach into the gap between the nearest post-box and the wall behind it, so the demon drink was not to blame; he did not think he had been hit by a train because he was still in one piece rather than many; but the thought of trains brought something back to him, and then he remembered it all, right up to the moment when someone had hit him on the back of the head: beyond that it was just a thick, impenetrable fog.

He sat up and looked around him at the room he was in, lit up by the soft summer daylight that filtered in through the lightweight fabric of the curtains at the window. His head spun and he groaned quietly. The room was a woman's; that much he could see from the clothes and shoes strewn carelessly across and under the chair in the corner, the items of make-up and skincare on the dressing table against the far wall, and the crumpled nightdress lying on the pillow next to him. He reached out and touched it, and found it was cold. He heard movement outside the bedroom door and pulled his hand away quickly. Sasha came into the room, her body wrapped in a large, fluffy towel, her tousled blonde hair still damp from the shower.

'Sasha', Wright exclaimed in surprise.

'Were you expecting someone else?' she asked, a playful grin spreading across her face. She flopped down onto the bed next to him, leant over and kissed him lightly on the cheek. Having no clear memory of how he came to be there and what might have happened during the night he had no idea how he should respond to that.

'Yes . . . I mean no . . . I mean I had no idea what . . . who to expect. What happened? How did I get here?'

Sasha smiled. Her ploy was going to work: he had no memory of the key part of the night; the key part for her, at least. She looked down, and made a pretence of being embarrassed.

'I was following you,' she said. 'You went to that house, and went in through the window. I waited outside. When you came out, someone came up behind you and hit you.

I got so angry I hit him too. Then I picked you up and brought you here, to look after you.'

'You were following me?' Wright said. 'Why?'

Now for the tricky part, Sasha thought, hoping that male vanity would see her through. 'Like I said when we first met, I've been looking for Mr Right. I thought you might be him, but I wanted to find out more about you first, in case you were a pervert or cross-dresser or something: I've stumbled across some right weirdoes in my time, believe me: but it's OK; you're just a good, old-fashioned, down-to-earth burglar. That I can cope with; as long as you don't get caught and go to jail; that would make the sex a bit difficult.' And she leant over and kissed him again; this time full on the mouth. He fell for it, and for her; hook line and sinker.

'I'm not a burglar,' he said. 'Yes, I broke into that house, but not for the reason you think. I'll tell you about it later. First I need to ask you something. When I came back through the window I was carrying something. Do you know what happened to it?'

'Yes,' she said. 'It's here. I figured that's what you went in to get, and if it was important enough for you to get beaten around the head for, I thought I ought to rescue it; so I did.'

'What was it? What did you get?' he asked anxiously.

'Some papers and computer discs.'

'You darling! You angel!' he cried, and this time it was his turn to kiss her.

She pulled away before he got too carried away. Later, it might be a pleasant distraction, she thought. He wasn't bad looking, a bit old perhaps, but she hadn't had a boyfriend for a while: and if it helped to keep him where she wanted him, why not? But not right then. She needed to keep him keen to get the story out of him. And there was a story; she knew full well there was. 'I need to get dressed,' she said, sliding out of his grasp and off the bed. She walked over to the dressing table and pulled some clothes out of the drawers—underwear, a pair of jeans and a T-shirt. Keeping her back to the bed she deliberately let the towel drop and posed provocatively as she dressed, showing him what might be his later if he was a good boy. Then she skipped out of the room and into the kitchen.

Wright joined her at the dining table a few minutes later for toast, black coffee and strong painkillers. His head was spinning, and not just because Biddle had hit him; he was trying to come to terms with everything else that had happened to him since the evening before; particularly with Sasha and the promises that her body was making to him.

'So what's going on then?' she asked him, chewing on her toast. 'What's the story?'

He took a deep breath before speaking: in for a penny . . . 'The bottom line is that I'm about to blackmail someone for a considerable amount of money.'

'Tell me more,' she said, leaning forward towards him across the table. 'Who? and for how much?'

'How much is easy; a million pounds.'

'Hmmm,' she said dreamily. 'Maybe you *are* my Mr Right.'

'"Who" is a bit of a longer story.'

'I'm in no hurry,' she said.

'The trains always seem to run late,' he said, after a pause to think about where to start.

'Tell me about it. They're awful. Someone deserves to be shot for it.'

'You're right,' he said. 'But not for the reason you think. They run late, yes; but not because they have to. They run late because they're made to.' Then he told her the whole story, about Dent and his fellow Perma-way Directors, The Book of Excuses, the deal with Roamer-Phone, about the bastard Biddle, the blackmail plot, the ransom, the episode on the train at Lord's Copse—although he glossed over the worst part, the bit about the leather bondage gear—and about their first meeting. He paused. Sasha stayed quiet, knowing that there was more to come.

'I traced the bastard Biddle to Caracas, where the idiot got married. That's how I found him; through the marriage licence application. He and his squeeze were living in a villa in the suburbs. I waited until they went out and broke into the house and the safe, but he had it booby-trapped, and when I opened the safe door a fire bomb set light to the contents and destroyed it. Then I knew that the only remaining disc was here, with Dent. I couldn't find it in his office, so I broke into his house to steal it.' He left out the part about the unfortunate man-mountain Everest and his own part in the solicitor's premature demise.

'So who was it that hit you outside this Dent's house then?' Sasha asked him.

'I suppose it must have been Biddle,' he said. 'He must have come back from Caracas to get the last disc back from Dent so he could run the blackmail scam again, to replace the money that got burnt. Only, thanks to you, he hasn't got it—we have—so it's us who can blackmail Dent and run off with the money this time.' In his mind he and Sasha were already together; a team; an item.

'Do you think Dent will pay up a second time?' Sasha asked.

'I think he will,' Wright told her. 'Because this time there's more to it than there was last time; Dent's got more than just the mobile phone deal going on; and this time he's ripping off his partners in crime as well; not just the mugs on the trains.'

Sasha tipped her head to one side in a questioning pose, waiting for him to carry on, even though she already knew what he was about to say.

'There were two sets of papers in Dent's safe with the discs: bank account records and balance sheets from shops. I only had time for a brief flick through them, but I'm pretty sure that Dent has his own personal scam going with the shops at the big stations—mainly the ones in London. When the trains are delayed, and trade goes up as a result, he skims off some of the profit into his own personal bank account, and not even his fellow crooked Directors know about it. So if, when, I tell him to pay up, I can tell him he'll have the other Directors to worry about, as well as the police, if he doesn't.'

Sasha's mind was racing. This was what she had been waiting for—a chance to get to the National Dailies with a blockbusting story—the exclusive that would put her name right up there in lights; would bring her the fame and fortune she craved so badly. All she had to do was work out how to make the most of it all; to make sure that what she had was the biggest blockbusting story she could possibly make it.

'So what happens now?' she asked, taking another sip from her coffee.

'I need to come up with a plan for making the exchange and then getting away with the money. It can't be too difficult; after all, Biddle's already done it once, and he's as thick as they come.'

He can't have been all that thick, my love, Sasha thought, or we wouldn't be sitting here now, having this conversation.

But she refrained from saying anything because to do so might have been damaging to her cause.

'I need to get my car first,' he said.

'Do you think that would be wise?' she asked. 'This Biddle character, if it was him that hit you last night—and I think we have to assume that it was—must have known it was you, and must have been watching you to know that you'd gone to Dent's house. Who's to say he won't have found your car and be watching that?'

'That's true; I hadn't thought of that. And I suppose the same goes for my flat too. That's a bit awkward isn't it?'

'Well you could always stay here; with me; that might be . . . nice,' she said, feigning coyness. 'Then perhaps I could help you.'

He thought for a moment, weighing up the advantages of being with Sasha with the disadvantages of not being able to work on his own, which was always his preference, but he could see that the two went together, and if his flat was being watched he could not go back there; not to live, anyway.

'That would be great,' he said. 'As long as you wouldn't mind.'

'Of course not,' she told him, continuing with her reluctant virgin act to make it look as though it was something she would only do if it was really, really necessary.

'I will need to go back there though,' he said. 'I've got nothing to wear, and there are a few other things there I need besides clothes.'

'But that could be dangerous if the flat really is being watched; and it might not just be John Biddle that could be watching; it could be the police as well. They could have found the car and traced your address through the DVLA.'

'You're right,' he said. 'This just gets worse and worse. I need the things I've got in the flat if I'm going to do this properly, and I don't really have any alternatives,' and he lapsed into silence.

'Let me think about it for a while,' she said, getting up to fill the kettle and make more coffee. They sat in silence on either side of the table, drinking the coffee and thinking. Wright frowned as he concentrated, his mind running round and round in circles, unable the find a way through that he could convince himself would work. Sasha sat opposite, looking as though she was having a happy daydream as she tackled the same problem, but with a different set of resources to call on. After a while she reached out and put her hand over his on the table. She squeezed it reassuringly. 'I've got an idea,' she said. 'You get yourself a pen and a sheet of paper from the writing pad in that drawer there,' pointing towards one of the kitchen units. 'Start writing a list of all the things you think you're going to need, and exactly where they are in the flat. I'm going to make a phone call.'

Wright did as she said, thinking carefully through the plan that was beginning to shape itself in his head; writing down the things he thought he might need at each step; not realising how closely what he was doing mirrored the way John Biddle had done the same thing while he was deciding how to rob the Perma-way directors of some of their ill-gotten gains the first time round.

Sasha went into the bedroom, pushed the door closed, pulled her mobile phone out of her handbag and phoned Jim. 'Hi,' she said when he answered. 'Do you still have your shady contacts . . . ? Good, there's something I want you to do . . . No, I'm not sure it's legal, but after I've told you why I want you to do it, you won't be worrying about a trivial little thing like that. Now listen . . . '

Sasha strolled back into the kitchen with a wide grin on her face. Everything was beginning to take shape and come together. Wright looked up and asked her what she was smiling at. 'Good news,' she told him. 'I've found a way to get what you need from your flat.'

'How . . . . ?'

'I don't think I'll tell you yet,' she said. 'You're not the only clever one in this partnership; and I'm a woman of many mysteries and surprises. Now put that pen down and come with me: I've got a job for you.' It was, she had decided, time for her to take the final step: to bind him to her, in ties of trust and lust. She stood up, reached out and took his hand, pulled him up out of the chair, then set off towards the bedroom.

CHAPTER EIGHT

When darkness fell across the outer southern suburbs of London that Sunday evening, the principal players in this sordid little story of greed and lust had divided themselves neatly into two groups; the watchers and the watched.

Flagg was watching Dent: or to be more precise he was watching the end of Dent's drive, from an unmarked police car parked in a lay-by on the opposite side of the road a short distance from the Perma-way Director's house. Dent's reluctant visit to the police station with his wife, on Flagg's orders, to have their fingerprints taken, had done nothing to improve his mood, particularly as Flagg had given instructions that the two of them were to be delayed and inconvenienced as much as, and in whatever way possible, while they were there.

In the meantime, Flagg had taken himself back to Dent's house to make use of the time that the fingerprinting process would give him. Walking round to the back of the place he climbed in through the hole in the window that Wright had made, that Dent had not had time to do anything about filling properly. Once inside, Flagg set about carrying on with his search of the house; a search he had been in the middle of, but had had to abort when he heard the scrunch of gravel on the drive and looked out of the front window to see Dent's taxi arriving, bringing him back from London. Flagg was absolutely convinced that Wright, Dent and the late Mr Everest, and maybe Dent's wife and possibly as-yet un-named others too, were involved in some perverted kind of sexual activity. Now that was not illegal in itself, as long as the participants were consenting adults, but unlawful killing, manslaughter or murder, and causing mayhem on the rail network; all that most definitely was. Flagg had no idea what it could be that they were all up to, but he was determined to find out, and the next step in doing that involved resuming his search for the damning evidence he was sure he was going to find inside Dent's house.

Having had a good look around upstairs before Dent had arrived at the house the first time, he started again where he had left off; in the downstairs sitting room at the front. He looked in magazine racks, in sideboard drawers and cupboards, at DVD and CD cases. He looked for secret hiding places under chairs and inside the tops of occasional tables. Even Dent's wife's embroidery bag did not escape his attention. He found nothing, so he moved on into the study. This was a modestly sized room, not lavishly furnished, so the search was not overly time consuming. Again it revealed nothing of the kind that Flagg was hoping to find and he had to pin all of his dwindling hopes on the dining room and kitchen. The dining room dresser cupboards and drawers contained nothing more exciting than cutlery, crockery, tablecloths and placemats. He had just begun in the kitchen when his phone rang.

'Flagg,' he snapped into it.

'It's Bob,' said the voice on the other end of the line—the desk sergeant back at the station. 'Mr and Mrs Dent have just left and are on their way back up to you. And he's not a happy man, I can tell you.'

Flagg looked at his watch. 'Thanks Bob,' he said. 'You've done a good job. I owe you one.'

'You owe me *yet another one* you mean,' he replied and rang off.

Flagg looked cursorily in another few potential hiding places, knowing that he was wasting his time, then made his exit from the house and the garden and walked back along the road to his car. He settled into the driving seat to await the arrival of the Dents, and the start of what could be a long vigil. Looking down the road he could also see the head of the lane that led to the car park where, until the middle of that afternoon, Wright's car had been standing. It had been taken away on his orders, and now sat in one corner of the back yard at the police station, waiting to see if Wright would be bold enough to try to claim it or report it stolen.

'Let him come to us if he wants it,' Flagg had told Brennan when the subject had come up during the course of a phone update at the end of the morning. 'That way we get two chances to nab him: one if he shows up here to collect it and a second if he comes down to the station when we tell him we've got it.'

Brennan had agreed, and Flagg sat in his car, staring alternately at Dent's gateposts and at the end of the lane alongside the house; knowing that when the day ended and it got dark, everything would become so much more difficult.

Brennan and Withers sat side by side in silence in the front seats of Brennan's car in the street outside Wright's flat. Brennan was happy to be there, and was wondering if the girl beside him could possibly feel the same way. When they had been together before, he had been pretty sure that she had come to like him. But in the days that Wright had been away, when they had not been working together and their different shift patterns had not allowed them to see very much of one another, his confidence had waned, and he was beginning to think that he might have imagined it all.

For her part, WPC Withers would have been regarded by many people as a bit of a strange girl. Pretty from a young age, she had grown up to be what most men would call "a right stunner", but without being aware of it. The attention her looks had drawn, particularly from those of the male persuasion, had just served to make her self-conscious and awkward, rather than the opposite, because she could not understand why they were looking at her, and was easily embarrassed by it. And because of all that, she had never had a proper boyfriend. Neither was she "one of the lads" where her workmates were concerned—she did not have the outgoing personality for it—so she was seen as being slightly aloof. And because she was so good looking and no-one could believe that a girl that was so good looking would not have an equally good looking man in tow, it was assumed that she kept her work life and private life separate, and was spending her off-duty hours with some Ferrari- or Porsche-owning merchant banker or stockbroker whom she would leave the force to marry and breed with at some point in the not-too-distant future. So as far as her colleagues were concerned, she was "off the market" and none of them even bothered to try to compete with the non-existent merchant banker. For this reason Brennan was far closer to achieving what his fevered imagination was making him dream about than he could possibly have realised. And all he had to do was ask, and the delectable Withers would become his steady date, and he would know what it felt like to be that merchant banker—without the money and with only an old Mondeo to his name, of course.

Outside the car the sky had grown dark and the streetlights had come on. Everything was quiet and peaceful. Suddenly, Withers leaned across, reached out and grabbed the front of Brennan's jacket, pulled him towards her and started to kiss him. He responded, and all of his ambitions to found a new dynasty with this stunning-looking woman were fully restored. On the pavement next to the car, an old man walked by with his small dog sauntering along beside him, pulling gently on the end of its lead.

'Sorry,' she said breathlessly when their lips finally parted company. 'I saw movement in the mirror and thought it might be him.'

'Quite right,' he said. 'Better safe than sorry.'

'And good to get the practice.'

'Yes.' And then they were practicing again; for quite a long time; and after a while they began to get quite good at it.

'When this is over, and we get the time, would you like to go out with me; to the pictures or something?' he asked when they came up for air again.

'Love to,' she said, and moved her hand, to rest it on his, on the top of his gear stick.

Further along the road, John Biddle was sitting quietly in Angela's car, also waiting for Adrian Wright arse to show his ugly face. When John had got back from London, he and Angela had sat down and discussed what they should do next. The options seemed to be quite straightforward—return to their former lives, or go on with the hunt for the last disc and try to repeat the blackmail plot. Angela would have settled for the former if she thought John would have been happy, but it was clear to her that her new husband was not going to accept that path as his future, and wanted to continue with what had now become the quest to find Wright, because he had the disc. They knew where he lived, and that it had two entrances, one at the front and one at the back. There were two of them, so the division of labour was obvious. Angela had insisted on taking the first shift at the back, walking slowly along the alley until she came to a collection of dustbins that she thought would provide her with a good hiding place. She stopped, looked around to make sure there was no-one nearby to see her, and ducked down behind them.

Nothing happened until well after midnight, when the hustle and bustle that normally breaks out when the pubs turn out had all died down. Angela was the first to be alerted as someone turned the corner at the bottom of the alley and began to walk towards her in the darkness. She could clearly hear the scrunching of feet on the loose stones of the unmade surface as he or she walked towards her, in spite of their efforts to tread softly and silently. As the bins that formed Angela's hiding place were positioned between the bottom of the alley and the gate at the end of the garden of the house that Wright's flat was a part of, whoever was coming up the alley was going to have to walk straight past her to get there, if, indeed, that was where they were going. She almost did not dare to breathe as the footsteps approached, then passed, then stopped, at roughly the place where she thought Wright's gate must be. The latch clicked. The hinges squeaked. There was a short period of silence, long enough for someone to walk the length of the garden, Angela thought; then the sound of glass—cracking, rather than breaking. Angela pulled out her mobile phone and dialled the short code she had programmed into it for John's. 'John. It's me,' she whispered into it when he answered; as softly as she could but as loudly as she dared to. 'Someone's here; at the back of the house; I think they've just broken into the flat.'

'OK,' he said. 'You stay there, out of sight. I'll cover the front. If he comes out your way, follow him and send me a text as we agreed. I'll come and find you. If he comes out the front I'll do the same. And Angela; be careful; he can be a bastard when he wants to.'

'I will, but what if it's not him?'

'Of course it's him. Who else would it be?' They lapsed into silence and she put her phone away. Her heart was pounding hard inside her chest. Was it with fear or excitement? She had never been involved in anything like this before, and thought that it must be a bit of both. She settled down to wait, to see if the intruder would come back her way.

Outside in the street, John was ready, but Brennan and Withers were relaxed. Brennan was firmly of the view that if nothing had happened by midnight then it was not going to, so they might as well call it a night and go home. She kept saying that they should give it a bit longer, just in case, and as he did not want to catch the sharp edge of Flagg's sarcastic tongue if they missed something important by not being there, he had reluctantly agreed with her.

John was watching when the front door of the house opened—just a little at first, then a little more and a little more, until it was wide enough to let a shadowy but cagey figure slip out onto the landing at the head of the steps. The figure looked around, making sure that he—John was sure it was a 'he' from the profile he could see—was not in imminent danger of being grabbed by anyone lurking nearby. Guilty behaviour if I ever saw it, John thought. Then the figure ran; down the steps; turned sharp right, then along the pavement on the opposite side to John, Brennan and Withers. John let him go by. He was past the other two before they realised he was there. All three of them jumped out of their cars and gave chase: John to follow; the other two to apprehend.

The decoy that Jim had selected after the phone call from Sasha was someone he had met one dark night while the little scrote was trying to break into his car. Basically a sly coward who slunk around in dark corners committing his nefarious deeds, this lad was fleet of foot (his main attribute) but not quite quick enough for Jim's athletic turn of speed. When Jim had finished shaking him warmly by the throat and promised to rip his head off completely if he ever tried anything like it again, Jim offered the scrote a chance to redeem himself and earn some pocket money by keeping him up to speed on the misdeeds of the local small-time criminal fraternity. When Jim had tracked him down in his local earlier that evening and told him what was needed and how much it was worth, the scrote said he was up for it. Jim filled him in fully on the details, then arranged to pick him up later to give him a lift. That way, Jim would know that he had got there and had not just ducked out with the fifty percent advance Jim had given him; the rest to be delivered once the job was done.

His brief from Jim was to draw anyone who followed him away from the flat without getting caught; running just fast enough to stay ahead to make them think they were in with a chance, to lure them as far away from the flat as he could. He ran down the street to the T-junction at the end and turned right, ran past the end of the alley, crossed the road and took the next on the left. His aim was not too difficult to achieve. Brennan was no Olympian and Withers, who had subconsciously dressed to impress her new partner, was wearing unsuitable shoes. John was even less fit than Brennan, and the four of them, the decoy scrote in the lead, then Brennan, then John, then Withers, were soon strung out along the road, heading directly away from the flat and the alley behind it. When the heel of one of WPC Withers' shoes gave way, she left the swiftly disappearing Brennan to it and, wondering who the other man in the chase could have been, turned round and limped back towards the car.

Back behind her bins, looking out, Angela had seen four people, one of whom she recognised as her husband, run across the end of the alley, as clear as day in the stark orange light spilling down from the streetlights. About ten minutes later the figure of the one girl amongst them returned, hobbling badly on what appeared to be a broken shoe. She passed out of sight, and Angela settled back into her hide, wondering where John was, and when she should venture out to start looking for him. It was then that she realised that she could hear another set of feet approaching, scrunching softly on the stony surface of the alley, coming from the opposite direction to the first one—from the top coming down. The footsteps carried on coming towards where Angela was sitting; then stopped. The latch clicked and the hinges squeaked again, then there was silence. Angela, acting on a hunch, stood up, slipped out from behind the bins, walked up the alley and across to its far side, and felt her way along the fences there until she found the gate that was partly open. She walked forward through the gateway into the garden, straining her eyes to see where she was going.

At the top end of the garden, where the back wall of the house loomed up and cast an impenetrably black shadow over everything, the path led to a small flight of steps that rose upwards to the back door. Angela stumbled, banged her shin badly on the step and had to bite down hard on her lip to stop herself from swearing out loud. Slowly, carefully, she groped her way up the steps to the top, where she found that the door was also open. Inside the house it was equally dark, but looking down the corridor that the back door opened into, Angela could see a sliver of light, moving gently from side to side underneath one of the doors that opened off it in the depths of the ground floor—the door to one of the flats. It was the light cast by a torch, in the hand of someone who had obviously just gone into the house from the alley, and who was apparently looking for something. Angela had no idea at all what she should do next, so she did nothing, and just waited. Rapidly, she ran through all the alternative variations of what she was watching, making subconscious decisions about what she should do, depending on which of them turned out to be true. If it was Wright and he was staying, he would have put a light on in the flat. If it was Wright and he was using a torch so as not to be seen, he would soon be leaving again; which meant he was staying somewhere else and she should follow him to find out where. If it was a burglar, then she was wasting her time and would probably be about to follow someone she had no interest in at all. But how could she find out which it was, a burglar, or Wright?

Indecision kept her where she was, standing in the dark shadows at the end of the corridor, which was just as well because, after about ten minutes or so, the door of the flat opened and a shadowy figure emerged. The torch snapped off, but not quickly enough to prevent Angela from seeing the profile of the man she had seen just once before, in Caracas on the night of the fire. It was Adrian Wright. Angela was rigid with fear in case he turned towards her, because he was certain to walk straight into her in the darkness of the narrow corridor: and then what would happen? She did not like to think about it. Wright pulled the door of the flat shut and, without even so much as a glance in Angela's direction, walked away from her, towards the front door of the house. He opened the door a little and looked out. Then, obviously happy with what he saw, or did not see, he opened it further and slipped outside. In the light that spilled in from the street, Angela could see that he was carrying a bag, a large holdall of some kind, presumably full of the things he had come to the flat to collect. He pulled the door closed behind him. With her heart in her mouth, Angela crept forward along the corridor towards the front door. When she got there she peered through the peep-hole, and looked out at the distorted image of the man John despised so much. What was he doing?

Wright was looking up the road, raising his torch to waist height and pointing it in the same direction. It flashed twice; then dropped. For half a minute or so nothing more happened, then Wright moved off down the steps, just as a car came down the road and stopped sharply, in line with the bottom of them. He walked swiftly round the back and got in on the passenger side after throwing the bag he was carrying over the seat into the back. Angela flung the front door open and ran down the steps towards her car, fumbling in her pocket for her set of keys, as Wright and his driver roared away down the road in a cloud of exhaust fumes. Jim, standing in the shadows of the trees in the park opposite the house, saw and photographed Wright's exit and the pick-up in Sasha's car; saw and photographed

Angela frantically running after them; then saw two more cars, one carrying Angela and the other carrying a mystery woman, pull out from parking spaces and speed off down the road without lights in pursuit of Sasha and Wright.

Sasha had no idea that she and Wright were being followed; she was too intent on driving, and the two cars behind her kept their lights off, to begin with at least. And Jim could not phone and tell her, at least not just then, as he and Sasha had agreed, when she had phoned him to set up the stunt with the decoy, that Wright had to believe that she was helping him on her own. Shortly before the appointed time, she had driven herself and Wright to his flat, parking a little way up the road, from where he had easy access to the top end of the alley running behind the house, and they had a good view down the road to the front of it. They settled down to watch for the watchers, that they knew must be there somewhere, even if they were tucked away out of sight in their cars just then. Sasha had not told Wright exactly what was going to happen, just that she was taking him to his flat to collect the things he needed, and she had arranged for whoever might be watching to be distracted while he did.

They sat and watched until the decoy emerged from the front door and ran, followed by two men and a girl, who jumped out of two cars further down the road. Then Sasha told Wright to go to his flat, using the alley at the back, collect his things, then come out through the front. At the signal with the torch she would drive down and pick him up and away they would go. She stayed in the car and waited, but she was so wrapped up in her own success and how well everything had gone, so intent on watching for Wright to emerge from the front door of the house onto the top of the steps, that she failed to see Withers hobble back across the end of the road and slide into the driving seat of Brennan's Mondeo. Wright came out the house and flashed the torch. Sasha started the car, pulled out and drove down to meet him. He came down the steps as she pulled up, walked round the back of the car and got in. She accelerated away, turned left at the first junction and right at the second, then picked up speed on the main drag through Pooley.

'Did you get what you wanted,' she asked.

'Yep,' he said. 'Everything I need to set it all up and collect from Dent. That worked well. How did you do it? Who was the decoy?'

'It was my cousin,' she lied. 'He's a light-fingered tea-leaf. I owed him a favour. I gave him your address and told him to break in—in through the back and out through the front. Oh, I hope he didn't take anything valuable or do too much damage,' she said, as if she had just realised that might be possible.

'He wouldn't have been able to find anything important, and nothing else matters any more. You did well; very well,' he told her, full of love-struck admiration. She smiled, but not for any reason he might have imagined.

Behind them, Angela paused at the second junction and put her lights on. Traffic was light and she would not have too much of a problem following the car in front of her, so she waited a second or two before pulling out, keeping a reasonable distance between herself and it: less chance of being spotted, she thought. Behind Angela, Withers did the same thing, thankful for once that Brennan had been consistent in his otherwise silly habit of leaving his keys in the ignition of his car. As soon as she had pulled away from the kerb and found herself behind another unlit car turning the same way that the car Wright was travelling in had gone, she realised that her target had another tail.

Like Angela, she also paused at the second junction to put her lights on—no point getting stopped if she could avoid it—then pulled out to follow the tail, hoping that they, whoever they were, would not lose Wright and whoever was driving him.

A short while later, the three cars arrived in the western suburb of South Suburbia where Sasha lived. Sahsa parked. She and Wright got out and went into her flat. Angela saw them stopping and slotted into a space some way short of where they had parked. Withers drove past and turned left at the next junction. She turned round at the first chance she got and crept back along the road, taking station on the corner, from where she could just see the front of the group of buildings she thought the occupants of the first car had gone into. Withers turned off her engine and lights, pulled out her mobile phone and called Brennan. He was walking back from his failed pursuit of the decoy; out of breath and not in a particularly good mood.

'Where are you?' he asked Withers when she had said who was calling.

'In your car, in a road in South Suburbia,' and she named it.

'What are you doing there?' he asked her. She told him.

'OK; you hang on there. I'll call Flagg and see what he wants to do. If Wright's got an accomplice and we still want to pick him up we'll need back-up. I'll be in touch again later. If anything happens and you can't raise me, call for help.' He called Flagg on his mobile.

'Any luck?' the DCI asked him when he answered.

'Yes and no,' Brennan told him. 'Wright showed up all right,' but he's got an accomplice, and now they're holed up in another flat; this one in South Suburbia. Withers is down there now, keeping watch on the place. Oh; and they've got another tail; not just us.'

'What?' Flagg exclaimed. Who the hell is that, then? It can't be Dent; he's safely tucked up in bed with his wife: has been for several hours.'

'What do you want me to do?' Brennan asked.

The silence at the other end showed that Flagg was thinking. Brennan knew better than to interrupt when he was.

'Where are you right now?' Flagg asked eventually.

'Outside Wright's flat.'

'And he's definitely not there?'

'No; he's definitely in the flat in South Suburbia with his accomplice.'

"Right: get yourself into his flat and give it a good going over on the pretext of there having been a burglary.'

'What am I looking for?'

'Anything that might give us a clue as what the bloody hell is going on; anything that might tie Wright into the death of Everest; and anything that might tell us who this accomplice is. Now: did the delectable Withers use her brains instead of her tits and get the registration number of the other tail?'

'No: not possible. When she was close enough to see it, neither of them had their lights on; then when the lights did go on it was too far away. She didn't want to be spotted.'

Flagg swore: paused. 'OK.' he said. 'Give Wright's flat a going-over then get down to join Withers. And stay awake. I want to know who the accomplice is, who the other tail is and what this is all about; and I want to know quickly; got that?'

'Yes, Guv,' Brennan told him, then rang off and walked towards the front door of the house that housed Wright's flat.

When Angela had parked up and watched Wright and a woman she did not recognise go into one of the blocks of flats, she had phoned John. Like Brennan, he was breathless and unhappy. She told him what had happened and where she was.

'OK,' he said. 'Stay where you are; I'll get a cab down there to join you.'

Brennan walked up the steps to the front door and pushed on it. It swung back easily on its hinges, left open by Angela when she shot through in pursuit of Wright and Sahsa. In the hallway it was dark and still. He walked in, leaving the front door open to let as much light in as possible. Stepping forward slowly and carefully, he made his way towards Wright's front door. Suddenly the light came on, bathing the hallway in a stark yellow light from the single bare bulb hanging from the light rose in the ceiling. He swung round.

'Stay where you are you hoodlum; or I'll let you have it,' said the little old lady who had been standing behind the front door brandishing a short metal fire poker, before promptly fainting. Brennan recognised her as Wright's landlady. When she recovered, luckily quite quickly, she recognised him as "that nice policeman" who had been there earlier in the day. He helped her back into her flat and made her a cup of tea.

'What were you doing behind the door, luv?' he asked her.

'I heard noises in the hall, looked out and saw the doors were open. I thought we'd been burgled, so I came out and hid behind the front door with the poker, in case whoever it was came back.'

'Why didn't you just shut the doors and lock up?'

'The glass in the back door was broken; they could easily have got back in again; and you hear such terrible stories on the news and Crimewatch; that's such a wonderful programme, don't you think?'

Not if it just scares the pants off old dears like you, Brennan thought. 'Why not call the police then? he asked her.

'I don't have a telephone, she said, looking sheepish, as though she had been caught out, doing something she should not have been doing. 'I can't afford it. I'm seventy-seven you know, and I only get the pension.'

Brennan reached into his pocket and pulled out a twenty pound note. He put it under a vase on the dresser. 'Get yourself a pay-as-you-go mobile phone with some credit on it. Once you've bought it, if you don't use it, it won't cost you anything, and as long as you keep it charged up it'll always be there ready in case you need to make a 999 call. Now, I need to borrow the key to your friend Mr Wright's flat again if that's OK.'

'Of course dear,' she said. 'It's in the pot on the mantelpiece.'

He took it and went out into the hallway. Before going into the flat opposite he went to the front door, and then down the corridor to the one at the back, to make sure they were properly closed and locked. The bolts at the top and bottom of the back door were stiff from lack of use, but he worked them loose enough to slide them across to lock it.

On the way back he called out: 'I've shot the bolts on the back door.'

'Oh don't do that dear; I'll never get them open again; they're very stiff,' she said, coming to the door.

'In the morning I'll get someone to come over to sort out the window and those bolts,' he told her. "Now lock your flat door and try to get some sleep.'

He turned away, opened Wright's front door, went in and turned on the lights. Inside it was in disarray, but it had not been burgled. Brennan had seen a lot of burglaries in his time, and this was not one of them. Wright had been back to collect things—clothes, and what else? He began his search; slow and systematic; looking for . . . what exactly?

Inside her flat, Sasha was watching Wright unpack. Most of what he had collected from his place was clothing, but there were also toiletries and a couple of other essentials. The first was a tattered address book, containing details of his friends and acquaintances—and the contacts he had made over the years in the various jobs he had worked in. This was what he thought of as his 'resource list', one he was planning on using later that day. The second essential item was a gun, a second world war Mauser pistol, found while he was serving in Germany and brought home as a souvenir. When he had found it, left to rot with a pile of other rubbish in a damp and deserted hut once used by the German Army, it had been in poor condition and looked unlikely to be of any use for anything other than as an ornament; just an interesting discussion-piece. When he set about cleaning it up, though, he found that the deterioration was all on the outside; its workings had been well-oiled when it had been dropped or discarded, and that had helped to keep its most important parts in good condition, even under the layers of filth and corrosion on the outside. As a hobby, he set about cleaning it up and restoring it, and he still remembered, with a feeling of pleasure and pride, the first time he had taken it to the firing range and found not only that it worked almost perfectly, but also that it was more accurate than anything he had ever shot with before.

Sasha looked down at the pistol as it lay on the bed, resting on the piece of cloth he always kept it wrapped in. 'Do you think that'll be necessary?' she asked, for the first time feeling that she might be getting in over her head.

'Not really,' he said. 'It's just my insurance policy; just in case things don't go the way I want them to.'

In her pocket Sasha felt her mobile phone vibrate as its silent alarm was activated. She discreetly looked at the screen; incoming call from Jim. She left Wright to unpack and locked herself in the bathroom.

'Hi Jim,' she whispered. 'What's up?'

'I take it you can't easily talk,' he said. 'So you listen and I'll talk. I did as you said and stood in the park. I've got some good photos of what went on down here tonight, including the two tails you picked up as you left. Any idea who they might be? They both followed you in cars, but they had their lights off and it was too dark to see the number plates. I didn't get a clear sight of what kind of cars they were either, it all went off so quickly. That's about it for now. I'll ring again if anything else happens. If there's anything you want you can always text,' and he rang off.

Sasha stayed in the bathroom for a while, thinking, before she flushed the toilet and went back to the bedroom. Two tails? One she could understand; that would be this John Biddle character, or someone working with him. The second, though, was a bit of a mystery. Could it be Dent?

She supposed it could be; he would know the disc and papers had been taken from his safe. He would have two likely candidates for the theft in mind. One was Biddle, the other Wright. He would know where Wright lived, or be able to find out easily enough, because Perma-way had used his services for a while, so they would almost certainly have a record of his home address. Yes, she told herself, it's probably someone working for Dent. And now they know where we are; so perhaps having the pistol isn't such a bad thing. She made a note to herself that she should get her copy of the contents of the disc and Dent's papers out of the flat to a place of safety first thing in the morning. It was too late to do anything about it right then. She went back to Wright, who had stowed everything away and was getting ready for bed.

Outside in the street, John had arrived and found the car with Angela sitting in it. 'Well; what are we doing here then?' he asked rhetorically as he slid into the passenger seat.

'Trying to work out what to do next, I suppose,' Angela said. 'Look; are you sure this is such a great idea? Couldn't we just forget all this—tell ourselves Caracas was a holiday and go back to life the way it was before this all started?'

John laughed; not at her, but at the idea of going back. 'That's just not possible for me,' he said. 'I think it would drive me completely off the rails; and frankly, I think I'm over halfway there already.' They lapsed into silence, looking out through the windows of the car at the silent, deserted street. In the block of flats that Wright and his accomplice had disappeared into, the last light went out. Nothing else was going to happen that night. After a while John broke the silence.

'Wright's going to try to use the disc and those papers of Dent's to blackmail him; just like I did. As I see it we've got two choices: we could try to get the disc and papers back from Wright and use them on Dent, in the same way that he plans to; or we could wait, and try to steal the money from both of them when they meet to make the exchange. Whatever happens, it's going to be over in a few days. Give it that long. If we end up with the money, then we don't need to go back to our old lives. And if we don't get it . . . ' He tailed off into silence. Angela sighed; then agreed. It was just a couple of days, and then things would be settled. They began to work out how they could maintain a round-the-clock watch on Wright and his accomplice.

Back in Wright's flat, Brennan was coming to the end of his search, which had turned out to be fruitless. Nothing of any significance had turned up; certainly nothing to connect Wright with any of Flagg's sexual depravity theories. The only thing Brennan had found was the letter Wright had received from his employer telling him he had been fired. He phoned Flagg. 'Hi Guv; still awake?' he asked.

'Evidently so,' Flagg told him.

'Anything happening?'

'Not a sausage,' Flagg said. 'How did the search go?'

'Nothing. He's about as clean as it's possible to be.'

'What; nothing? Are you sure?'

'Absolutely, Guv. I did it twice; just to be sure. The only thing I found out is that he's been fired from his job with "Amalgamated Risk Services Europe", which abbreviates to the word Arse.'

'That's appropriate,' Flagg said, laughing, his skill at solving cryptic crossword clues enabling him to make the connection between the words somewhat more quickly than

Brennan had managed to. 'That makes him Wright Arse!' Having been cheered up by this small piece of silliness, Flagg seemed to forget to be grumpy about Brennan's lack of success in the search.

'His toothbrush is missing now,' Brennan said. 'So it looks as though he's planning not to be here for a while.'

'Right,' the DCI said. 'Get yourself down to join the delectable WPC Withers; and make sure you can keep your hands off her long enough to do some work while you're down there,' and he laughed as he rang off, as if he thought he had cracked a good joke.

CHAPTER NINE

Dawn broke over South Suburbia on another bright Monday morning. John yawned and stretched, having been awake all night watching the front of the block of flats that Wright and his accomplice were holed up in. Beside him, Angela was asleep: how he envied her the ability and peace of mind to be able to do that in the cramped conditions of the front seats of her car. He looked out at the street in front of him, or rather the part of it he could see past the car that was parked ahead of them. When he had first arrived there the night before, he had thought that their task was going to be impossible; two of them watching twenty-four hours a day over a building that probably had two entrances at least. How would they sleep? Where would they sleep? Where and how would they eat and carry out all those other necessary human functions? But now he could see that that was not going to be such a problem after all, as the blocks of flats had only one entrance each, so they were going to be far easier to watch than he had feared.

The building Sasha lived in was quite new; one of a group of four identical blocks that had been built on a narrow strip of land that had been left when the old terraced houses that used to stand there were demolished.

Each block housed four flats on each of its four floors, all opening onto a single staircase that in turn led down to a single entrance front door, in the centre at ground level. The only way in or out was through that door; unless you lived on the ground floor, of course, where the windows were also an option. Having seen the lights on in the early hours of the morning, John knew that Wright's accomplice lived on the first floor of the second block along from where he was sitting. At ground level, each block sat in its own car park, which only opened out onto the road where Angela's car was parked. At the back was a high and solid brick wall that separated the plot the flats had been built on from the yards of the industrial estate beyond. Anyone entering or leaving any of the blocks would be clearly visible to anyone watching from the road outside.

John waited and watched, but nothing stirred. When Angela woke up a while later, he left her to watch while he went off in search of facilities in the local area. In the street one turning back behind the car he found a small park with a coin-operated public toilet that, miraculously, had not been vandalised and was still in working order, which came as a great relief to him. On his way back to the car to tell Angela, he noticed a small hotel, operating in one of the terraced houses that lined the street, with a 'Vacancies' sign hanging in its front window. It was too early to knock on the door and ask about a room, but he doubted that he would be beaten to it by delaying for an hour or so, not first thing on a Monday morning, so he went straight on back to the car.

Angela, when she went to use the facilities in the park, was away for quite a while. When she came back she looked quite fresh, having washed her face and brushed her hair as well as tending to the immediate essentials, and she brought with her some croissants and coffee she had bought from a baker's shop further along the road from the park. She and John sat in her car and had breakfast.

At the end of the next side turning in front of Angela's car, in his unmarked Mondeo, Brennan sat on his own, also watching Sasha's flat. After searching Wright's place and speaking to Flagg he had called the police station and asked for a car to pick him up and take him to where Withers was parked. He took over from her for the rest of the night and told her to go home and get some sleep; an order she obeyed willingly.

Flagg was in a bad mood; something Brennan was quite familiar with having to deal with on a regular basis. The DCI was bored, stiff and uncomfortable and no further forward with his investigation, which annoyed him because he was very much the type of person who needs to be making progress, even if only a small piece each day, in order to stay happy. At least he was not facing the whole of the new day sitting there in his car, though, because Dent would, at some point during the course of the morning, be going to work, at which time Flagg would ring his secretary and invent some pretext for finding out where he would be going and what he would be doing all day.

Inside her flat, Sasha woke early; then lay still in the bed alongside the still-sleeping Wright, wondering what this new day had in store for her. Any brief doubts she might have had about what she was doing she pushed quickly to one side, telling herself that she was doing a service to the public, as well as securing her own future. If someone was ripping people off, then everyone had a right to know about it, and it was her job to make sure that they did; at a reasonable price, of course. When Wright awoke he found her already up and dressed, sitting at the computer in her study, drinking coffee and flicking through news websites, just as she did at the start of every morning. She looked up and smiled as he appeared at the study door. 'So what happens next?' she asked him.

'I have some thinking and planning to do,' he told her. 'Will it be OK if I use your computer for a while; when you've finished, of course.'

'No problem,' she told him. 'I'm only surfing the news channels; just to keep up-to-date with what's going on in the world.' She nearly slipped up and told him that by the same time the next day he could be making the news himself, but stopped herself just in time. That was her plan, not his. If his plan worked, no-one would ever know about it, apart from him, her and Dent. 'I've got to go out in a while to do some shopping, so I'll leave you to it when we've had breakfast.'

Dent drove away from his house at about seven-thirty, followed at a distance by Flagg, who was heartily glad to be on the move again. Flagg followed Dent's car down into South Suburbia and left him when the Perma-way director turned into the entrance to the Overway House car park. Flagg carried on for a few hundred yards more, took the next side-turning, and parked. At eight-thirty he phoned Overway House, asked for Dent, and was put through to his secretary, just as he had hoped he would be. 'Good morning,' he said when she answered. 'This is Detective Chief Inspector Flagg from North Downham Police Station. I need to see Mr Dent today. Can you give me an appointment please?'

'I'm sorry Inspector, but I think that might be a little difficult; Mr Dent has a full day of meetings scheduled, with only a few minutes between them, here and there.'

'Are they all in Overway House?' Flagg asked.

'Yes; they're all in this building,' she confirmed.

'Oh good,' he said. 'I only need a few minutes of his time. If you could tell me when those few minutes' gaps are supposed to be, perhaps I could drop in and see him during one of them?'

'Yes, well I suppose that will be alright,' she said, and read out a full list of Dent's appointments. 'Shall I tell him you're coming?' she asked.

'No, I don't think that'll be necessary,' Flagg told her. 'Then he won't be disappointed if I don't make it. Police business can be a little . . . flexible at times. There is one thing you could do for me though,' making it sound like an afterthought, whereas it was really no afterthought at all. 'If Mr Dent's plans change, could you let me know; so I don't come all the way down there and find he's decided to go out.'

'Yes, of course. How can I contact you?'

He read out his mobile phone number. 'Thank you very much for your time and your help,' he said, and rang off. He could afford to be generous; now he would know exactly where Dent was all day without having to sit and watch him: virtually an impossibility in a place like Overway House anyway.

Angela and John sat and watched the inhabitants of the street leaving their houses and flats to go about their daily business—to work, to school, to go shopping, wherever it was they might be going that day, but they did not see Wright. At just about the same time that Dent was arriving at work, they saw a blonde-haired woman leave the block they were watching and cross the road to the line of cars parked ahead of them. Angela stiffened. John looked at her enquiringly. 'What's the matter?' he asked her.

'That's the car I followed last night. The one that woman has just got into. She must be Wright's accomplice.' Sasha started her car, pulled away from the kerb and drove off down the road. 'What do we do?' Angela asked.

'Stay here,' John told her. 'It's not her we're interested in; it's him.'

At just after nine o'clock, when he was pretty sure they were not going to see Wright emerge from the front of the building, John went back round the corner and booked himself and Angela into a vacant room in the hotel he had spotted earlier. That gave them a base; a place where calls of nature could be answered and one of them could get some sleep while the other one stayed on watch in the car.

On the next corner, Brennan was relieved by the return of WPC Withers so he could go home to eat, sleep and shower. He promised to be back in a few hours.

Inside the flat, Wright was struggling to come up with a plan for confronting Dent and escaping with the money. However hard he tried not to, he kept coming back to the bastard Biddle's plan and the way it had all worked so smoothly. Eventually he grudgingly conceded defeat and decided to try to produce something similar. Why re-invent the wheel? he asked himself, when the wheel's already been shown to work so well. Having decided that, he began to find the planning process a whole lot easier. He trawled websites, looking at maps and satellite photographs, and studied timetables. He found what he thought was a good place, and the rest of it just slotted together like a jigsaw; in theory at least.

Sasha stopped her car just inside the entrance to the hypermarket car park. Jim pulled the door open and got in. She drove to a parking space, stopped and turned the engine off. 'Morning gorgeous,' he said, handing her one of the take-away coffees from the cardboard tray he was carrying; just bought from the shop's cafe. 'Now; tell me what this is all about.'

She reached down into her handbag, squeezed down in the gap between the seat and the door, and groped around for the memory stick she had copied Dent's secrets onto. She pulled it out and held it up in front of him. Then she told him what was on it, what they were going to do with it, and what it was going to do for them. She also told him that when they had finished there she wanted him to take it to the office and put it somewhere safe; somewhere really, really safe.

'That's quite a story,' he said. 'What chance do you think this Wright character's got of pulling it off; of actually getting away with the money?'

'I don't know,' she said. 'And don't go getting the idea that sharing it with him or ripping him off for it after he's got it is as good a deal as selling the whole story to the dailies and then staying on to play in the top league with the big boys. That's where the real money is.'

'So what's the plan then?' he asked her.

'Wright's going to set up a meeting with Dent somewhere, sometime, to exchange the money for the disc and the papers. We need to gatecrash that party and catch them in the act; get photos, the lot.' She paused and thought for a moment. 'Or what if we could do better than that?'

she said, as an idea began to form itself in her head. 'Look,' she said," I need you to do me a favour. Go into the shop and get me some shopping; a couple of days' worth—fruit, veg., meat, bread, milk—you know, the essentials. I'll give you the money later.'

Jim looked at her in an amused, questioning way, waiting for an explanation.

'When I left Wright I told him I was going shopping. How would it look if I went back without any?'

'And while I'm looking after your domestic arrangements, you'll be doing what, exactly?'

'I've got some phone calls to make: now move it.'

'Yes madam,' he said, tugging his forelock in a parody of domestic servitude. He got out and walked away across the car park. Sasha got out her mobile phone and the thick notebook she kept her extensive lists of contact numbers in and dialled the number of Overway House. It rang for a moment or two before being answered by an operator on the switchboard. She asked to be put through to David Law, the Communications Director. There was a click and more ringing, then a sing-song voice said:

'Good morning. Office of the Communications Director. Debbie speaking. How may I help you?'

'David Law please,' Sasha said, imparting her voice with as much gravity and authority as she could muster.

'May I ask who's calling?' Debbie asked.

'The Press Complaints Commission,' Sasha snapped back. 'I have a serious matter I'd like to discuss with Mr Law.'

'Hold the line please.' There was silence for a short while; then a man's voice answered.

'David Law. Who am I speaking to?' he asked abruptly.

'Not important,' Sahsa told him. 'Now listen carefully; I have a serious accusation to make.' The words she used and the way she spoke were both designed to engage Law's attention and stop him from ringing off before she had delivered her message. It worked.

'An accusation . . . about what?' he asked.

'About money; and about your Financial Director, Stephen Dent.'

'What about him?' Law asked, cagily.

'I have it on very good authority that he is about to abscond with some of your money.'

'He's about to abscond with some of Perma-way's money,' he repeated slowly.

'That's not what I said,' Sasha told him. 'I said some of *your* money,' emphasising the word 'your'. 'And by that I mean money that you think belongs to you, and him, and seven other Perma-way directors; whose names I could give you if you insisted; but I don't need to because you already know who they are.'

'Who are you? How do you come to know what it is you think you know?' Law gabbled, lurching towards incoherence.

'Not important and not important,' Sasha told him. 'My advice to you would be keep an eye on Dent, and keep an eye on your money.' Then she rang off; satisfied with the way it had gone. Over the next half an hour or so she made contact with as many of the other crooked Perma-way Directors as she could, posing as a string of high officials to get their attention, then telling them exactly what she had told David Law. That, she thought, should set the cat amongst the pigeons. And she was right; even as she was speaking to the last of them, frantic whispered conversations were already taking place in dark corners and empty corridors throughout Overway House, and urgent phone messages were being left for the Directors who were elsewhere that day. The only one not included was Dent, for obvious reasons.

While all of that was going on, David Law was in contact with the bank: not the bank that Perma-way used for its legitimate business; this was the London branch of the Swiss bank that the crooked Directors were using to deposit their ill-gotten gains. When he had identified himself, given the account number and the correct passwords, he asked if it would be possible to stop anyone from making withdrawals from the account for the time being.

'Oui, Monsieur,' the bank official said. 'If you can provide this instruction in writing, signed by all the account holders, we can apply it within three working days of receipt of your instruction.' Two problems:- too slow; and Dent was one of the account holders, so it would require his signature.

Next question:- 'Who is authorised to make withdrawals?'

'Any of the account holders, provided the request is counter-signed by the key account holder,' the official told him.

'And the key account holder is . . . ? Law asked, fearing that he already knew the answer.

There was a rustle of paper at the other end of the line. 'Monsieur Stephen Dent. He named himself as the key account holder when he first opened this account.'

'And does the key account holder need anyone else's signature when he wants to make a withdrawal?'

'Non Monsieur; just his own.'

So Dent could make withdrawals just on the strength of his own signature, without reference to any of the others, and it would not be possible to stop him for at least three days, even if he was willing to sign the instruction to stop himself. There was only one thing they could do, if the bank would agree.

'Would it be possible for you to notify me if you receive any requests to withdraw money from this account?'

'Oui, Monsieur; that is part of the service we provide for all our joint account holders. We find it helps them all to . . . understand each other's financial transactions.' Meaning that the bank must deal with a lot of crooked or half-crooked operators working together on scams like theirs, who could not bring themselves to trust each other. 'Which telephone number would you like us to use?'

Law gave the man the number of his personal mobile phone, then thanked him for his time and rang off.

Law dialled Dent's secretary's number next, and asked her to let him know if Dent's plans for the day changed. That way he would know where Dent was all day. She confirmed that she would, and told him that he was the second person to make that request that day.

'Really?' Law said. 'And who was the first?'

'Well it's a bit odd really: it was the police.' Law breathed in sharply. 'I wonder what they could want with him.' She did not know about the break-in at his house: no-one in Overway House did, and Dent was not about to tell any of them. Law was confused and disturbed by the news, immediately jumping to almost the right conclusion, although he did not know it.

Meanwhile, back in the hypermarket car park in South Suburbia, Sasha was ringing the Transport Police. 'I have some information about an incident that occurred on a train at Lord's Copse Station a couple of weeks ago,' she told the operator she was put through to.

'Hold the line please caller, I'll transfer you to the officer who deals with that area.' There were sounds of a computer keyboard being used in the background, followed by a series of clicks, then a male voice asking how he could help.

'It's about the incident on the train at Lord's Copse.'

'Yes, madam; what about it?'

'It was part of a scam, to steal a substantial amount of money from Perma-way. That scam will be reaching its conclusion very soon and the money is about to be moved. The Perma-way Directors are involved. If you watch them, you'll find the money. The evidence you need will show up later.'

'Do you have any names you can give me, or anything that might show us that what you say is true?'

'The names are the evidence. The Perma-way Directors are Stephen Dent, Bill Taylor, Colin McFee, David Law, Irwin Lee, Peter Davis, Alan Perkes, Gordon Harper and Richard Keane. The other name is Adrian Wright, of a company called Amalgamated Risk Services Europe—abbreviated to Arse.'

'Are you sure you aren't trying to pull my leg?' the policeman asked. 'Wright; Arse?'

'No, it's genuine. Check it out and you'll see.'

'OK. Now can I have your name please?'

'No,' and she hung up. They could do what they liked with it; she still had the story and the evidence. If the arrests were to be made at the same time that her story broke, so much the better, it added to the sensation value—pictures of Perma-way Directors being dragged from their homes in the small hours of the morning by the police—but if arrests came later the story lasted longer; either way worked just as well for her.

After his mystery caller had rung off, the policeman she had been talking to followed his instructions. He was not there to decide what was and was not genuine and relevant; he was there simply to take information, extracting as much of it as he could from the people who called in, then pass it on to the right person to be evaluated. He typed up what Sasha had told him and sent it by e-mail to the collator for the division in whose area Lord's Copse Station fell.

Inspector Sands' sergeant walked into his office an hour or so after that e-mail had been sent, carrying a copy that he had printed off and marked up, with a large, bold red ring around the name of Adrian Wright. He put it on the desk in front of Sands, who leaned forward and read it. 'Why the red ring around Wright's name?' he asked.

'It was never released to the press,' the sergeant said. 'We know it because we've got the transcripts of his interview at North Downham, but no-one else has got it.'

'So you think this call is genuine?'

'Could be. Someone with inside knowledge and a grudge against one or more of the Perma-way Directors phones in to tell us something we usually wouldn't take any notice of; only they also show us that they know something they shouldn't know, unless they're on the inside themselves. It's tempting to believe it could all be true, don't you think?'

'OK. Find out where all these Directors are today. Most of them should be in Overway House. If they are, take a couple of the lads down to the station in plain clothes and stake the place out. If any of them leaves, let me know and we'll decide what we do from there. Oh, and see if you can nab a pickpocket or two; it'll justify your being there, in case anyone asks.'

Wright flicked through the pages of his address book, looking for a particular name and phone number; someone he had dealt with on and off for a number of years. The man in question was known to his friends and associates as Klepto because he was able, given time, to get his hands on almost anything anyone wanted him to find for them. Wright dialled and waited for an answer.

'Hello Klepto,' he said. 'Adrian Wright here.'

'Adrian; how are you? I haven't heard from you for a while.'

'No; and in case anyone asks, you haven't heard from me now, either.'

'Like that is it? OK, what can I do for you?'

'I need some . . . items; and I need to have them today.'

'Right: tell me what they are and I'll see what I can do.'

'Two smoke canisters; big ones, for outdoor use. A decent pair of handcuffs; standard Military Police issue should do. A length of chain; light but strong; say two metres long; with links big enough to slip onto the 'cuffs before they're done up. Ammunition; for a World War Two German Mauser pistol; one clip.'

'No problem. I'll get back to you in a couple of hours.'

Then Wright phoned Dent, catching him in his office, before the start of his first meeting. 'I've got some things that belong to you,' Wright told him.

Dent swore, using a string of profanities so foul that as an author I'd be embarrassed to write them down, even in a book like this where there's been so much bad language used already.

'Yes,' Wright said. 'I'd probably say something similar if I was in your position, but it won't help you at all.'

'What do you want?'

'I think you probably already know the answer to that,' Wright said, and laughed. 'I want the same deal Biddle got, for the same reason. You give me a million in used notes today and I give you the disc Biddle made about your mobile phone scam. As an added incentive, I'll also forget about some papers that belong to you; that I took out of your safe on Saturday night. They're very interesting, and I think your fellow bent Directors would be interested in them too. I hope none of them are violent by the way; I hear that some criminal types take very badly to being duped or double-crossed.'

'I can't do it,' Dent told him. 'Too much money has gone already.'

'Bullshit,' Wright snapped. 'I know that's not true, and you know I know it; so stop trying to bullshit me. Just get the money and wait for instructions.'

'I can't,' Dent spluttered. 'There isn't time.'

'More crap and you know it. Get yourself up to London to the bank; get the money and wait up there for my instructions.'

Dent conceded defeat and sighed deeply into a disconnected line—Wright had rung off. Dent bitterly regretted having let him find out too much about the workings of the scam while they were dealing so unsuccessfully with the bastard Biddle.

Wright put the phone down, leant back in the chair and reflected on his progress. He had done everything he could for the time being. Dent would be going to London to get the money; Klepto was dealing with the hardware; Wright had his plan pretty well sorted out and the place identified. There was nothing left to do. He turned to wondering when Sasha would be back.

Dent had to work hard to suppress a momentary panic, and try to think about what he should do. He only had a short time to work something out, because his first meeting was about to start. He quickly decided that he had to make arrangements to get the money from the bank, then he would have longer to work out how not to have to give it to Wright; but at least he would have it with him if the worst came to the worst and it turned out that he did have to give it away. He phoned the bank and gave them his instructions. They said it would take time to organise, but could be done, and would he like to contact them again later in the day? Then he phoned his secretary, during the first break in the first meeting, and told her to cancel all of his afternoon appointments, as he would be going out after lunch and would not be back. No, he would not be contactable—if anybody wanted him they would have to wait until the next day. Oh, and could she tell security that his car would be in the car park all night and they were to keep an eye on it. Last time he left it there it was damaged and he did *not* expect the same thing to happen again. End of conversation. The secretary phoned David Law, as she had promised, and then Flagg.

'Did he say where he was going?' the DCI asked casually.

'No, but I think it's probably into London. He said he'd be leaving his car in the office car park. He always does that when he goes into London. He hates the traffic there, so he goes in by train.'

Flagg thanked her and rang off.

While Dent's secretary was talking to Flagg, David Law took the call from the bank that confirmed his worst suspicions: it told him that Dent was making arrangements to withdraw a substantial amount of money from the account in cash—they would not be specific about the amount—and that he was expected in London to collect it sometime later that afternoon or evening. Law was not exactly shocked, more numbed, because he had been told that this was going to happen by his mystery caller, but until the call came from the bank there had been no proof, and he could fool himself into not believing it if he chose to. Now he had spoken to the bank, disbelief was no longer an option; he knew what the woman had said must be true. And with an outsider knowing what they had done, and with the police showing an interest in Dent as well, Law was feeling the beginnings of an icy fear that the whole thing was starting to unravel itself.

When Flagg had spoken to Dent's secretary about her boss's impending trip into London, he was already inside South Suburbia Station, sitting at the coffee bar on the upper concourse, so all he now had to do was keep his eyes open to spot Dent leaving through the main entrance of Overway House, and make sure that he was not spotted himself.

David Law and his colleagues posted "sentries" from amongst their number around the inside of Overway House so that, whichever way Dent decided to go when he left, one or more of them would be in position to follow him, reporting back on his movements to the others by mobile phone so they could tag along and catch up. They had decided not to confront him until they were sure he had been to the bank and collected the money, because without it as evidence he was sure to find a way to argue his way out of his guilt. Everyone waited for Dent to leave the building.

Sasha returned to the flat, with the shopping Jim had bought for her, later in the morning. Wright was waiting for her. When she had packed everything away and made coffee for them both, they sat down at the kitchen table and Wright outlined his plan to her, describing the phone calls he had made while she had been out, and what he had planned for Dent and the money. They went over it several times to make sure it made sense and would work properly. When they had finished, Sasha excused herself and went into the bathroom. She sat down and started to compose a long text message to send to Jim.

Everyone waited for Dent to leave the building, which he did at about half past two in the afternoon, walking out through the front doors, across the station concourse, through the ticket barriers and down the ramp onto platform two, where the next train to London River Crossing was expected to arrive within the next few minutes. Flagg followed him down the ramp, always keeping a number of people between the two of them; always trying to stay behind the Perma-way man. Several of the other Perma-way directors did the same thing, while phoning the others to report the fact that Dent was on the move and they had him in their sights. Two PCs from the Transport Police also did the same thing, one of them phoning their superior officer and being told to tag along and see what was going on. The train arrived and they all got on it.

The journey into London was uneventful. At the end of the line they all got off; Dent first, then Flagg, followed by the Perma-way Directors and the Transport Police. Dent led them along the platform and down one flight of the escalator, where he got off and went into a shop selling luggage—suitcases, flight bags and the like. Five minutes later he re-emerged pulling a brand new, small, wheeled suitcase, and resumed his passage down through the station towards the exit. Flagg and the others tore themselves away from window displays, which up to that point had all seemed to be thoroughly engrossing, and followed Dent at a distance, still oblivious to one another's presence.

Dent left the station and walked across the bridge spanning the river. On the north side he took a flight of steps leading down onto The Embankment, then turned east and headed towards The Tower. Part of the way along he stopped and sat down on one of the wooden benches provided for tourists to sit on to stare at the back of the river wall. He took out his mobile phone and rang the bank. 'My name is Stephen Dent,' he announced. 'You're expecting my call.' Then he gave them the account number and passwords.

'Monsieur Dent,' the Deputy Under-Manager said when the connection was made. 'We have executed your instructions. The money we expect to be here at nine o'clock this evening. If you wish we can send a car for you?'

'That would be helpful,' Dent said, then gave the name of a budget hotel not far away from The Tower, which he had booked himself into by phone not long before leaving his office. He had stayed there before; it was no-frills cheap, clean, reasonably comfortable and, most importantly, anonymous; no-one was interested in who you were or why you were there; it was just a place to sleep in. Having finished his call to the bank, Dent went straight to the hotel and checked-in.

Nothing more happened until nine o'clock in the evening, when Dent was picked up by the car that took him to the bank. Flagg was not there: he had been clever and called in a favour from a mate who was quite high up in the City police force and, as a result, Dent's car was followed by an unmarked patrol car manned by two young officers who fancied themselves to be the next Starsky and Hutch, or Bodie and Doyle, or a pair of budding Bonds. The Perma-way directors had no such outside resources to call on. They were all now present in London, and had split themselves into groups of two, taking it in turns to watch the entrances to the hotel while the others ate, drank and waited in a bar nearby. When Dent appeared at the front door at nine, the two on duty there simply hailed a cab and made the driver's day by using that hoary old cliché "Driver; follow that car". Behind that cab was another cab, whose driver's day had also been made in exactly the same way.

Outside Sasha's flat it had been a long and boring day for the two groups of watchers on stake-out duty. The people who lived in the street had gone out, gone about their daily business and come back home again. The day had run its course and darkness had fallen. At half past ten the front door of the block of flats opened and Wright came out. Withers poked Brennan hard to wake him up. John picked up his phone and was about to dial Angela to call her back from the hotel, but he stopped, because Wright had stopped too, and was standing still on the edge of the kerb, looking up and down the road as though waiting for something. In the distance a pair of headlights appeared and approached the point where Wright was standing. The car slowed down and drew to a halt. The engine stopped. The lights went off. Wright got in. All anyone watching could see inside was the two dark heads of two people talking. This lasted for just a few minutes, then the engine restarted, Wright got out, the lights came back on and the car accelerated away. Wright walked back to the block of flats and went inside, carrying the bag he had collected from the driver.

Dent was away from his hotel for almost two hours, during which time his bankers filled up his suitcase with the used banknotes he had asked them for, to the sum of one million pounds. The City police and four men in two cabs kept watch while he was inside the bank, and as he returned to his hotel in the bank's car afterwards. Shortly after his return, Flagg appeared in the hotel lobby flashing his warrant card at the night porter and demanding (1) a chair in some quiet corner of this establishment that was comfortable enough to sleep in, and (2) to be woken and told immediately if 'the man in this picture and your room number forty-two so much as farts in his sleep'. A little later one of the Perma-way directors came in and made a similar request, with cash on offer instead of a warrant card, and contact to be made by mobile phone, as a back-up to the two sentries still posted out of sight outside.

As it turned out, the porter's services were not required, because Dent did not move again until well after dawn's early light, when both Flagg and Dent's colleagues were all up and about, waiting patiently for his next appearance. By that time, Dent had been awake for a number of hours, having been woken by the shrill tone of his mobile phone ringing. Straight away he was wide awake. He sat up stiffly, still fully dressed from the night before so he was ready for this call when it came. He looked at the illuminated clock built into the base of the television set; it was three o'clock in the morning, an hour he did not see on a regular basis. Outside it was still dark. He reached out, picked up his phone and answered it. It was Wright. 'Where are you?' he asked.

'I'm in a fleapit hotel just off the north end of Tower Bridge,' Dent told him resentfully; the place was clearly not up to his usual standards.

'Wait there until I call you; and be ready,' Wright snapped, and rang off.

Wright studied the map of London he had lying open on the desk in front of him. He measured the distance from the end of Tower Bridge and estimated how long it would take Dent to walk, then added a few minutes to allow for delays and made a note on his timetable.

Dent sank back onto the bed, his mind in turmoil, desperately trying to find a different way out of the mess he found himself in, but coming back every time to the only one he could think of; the service revolver he had in his jacket pocket.

Wright slouched back in the desk chair, also wide awake, thinking through the details of his plan, again and again, envisaging himself doing this and doing that, but always ending up with the money. He set the alarm on his watch to wake him when it was time to begin, just in case he nodded off. There was no point in taking chances.

CHAPTER TEN

The leafy green outer London suburb of Woodhill is, and always has been, a quiet place. Originally a wooded hill, as its name suggests, over time it first gained a house or two, then grew to become a village, then a small town. In the early years of the twentieth century it was swallowed up by the rapid expansion of the London suburbs as the city overflowed its boundaries and flooded out into the countryside that surrounded it. Its story is by no means unique, as the same thing has happened on all sides of the capital, not just in the south, where Woodhill is to be found, about halfway between the City of London and the pale imitation of it that is South Suburbia. And as is the case with many places like it, the act of being swallowed whole by the greatness of the metropolis to the north and the commercial draw of Suburbia to the south served to rob it of its centre, as its inhabitants were enticed to desert it each working day by the lure of the bright lights and fatter pay-packets of the firms that had set up their head offices in the one and regional centres in the other. And in this they were ably abetted by the railways, as Woodhill is crossed by not just one line, but two, and blessed with a fine Victorian station that serves them both.

The first line to be built was on the surface, crossing the hill from east to west, following the crest of a ridge of high ground, running for many miles in both directions into the counties on either side; a ridge of which the hill is a part. This line is now the slow way into London—a single track in each direction winding its way across the bottom edge of the city before turning inwards to make its way into Queen Elizabeth, the terminal station in its south-west quadrant. The second line to be built offers a more direct route in and out, taking a more or less straight line between Suburbia and the City, charging straight through the green hill in a deep cutting and passing underneath the first line, which now runs over it on a high, elegant, brick-built viaduct.

Woodhill station sits at the intersection of these two railway lines and is really two stations, linked together by many stairs and a long footbridge that runs across the cutting from one side to the other. Woodhill High Level has two platforms, one on each side of an island built between the tracks and running the full length of the viaduct, serving the up line on the one side and the down line on the other. Woodhill Low Level has four platforms on two islands, serving slow up, fast up, fast down and slow down lines respectively, although only the slow trains stop there now, the fast trains just streaming through on the two centre tracks without so much as a pause. The viaduct stands high above the southern end of the low level platforms. The footbridge crosses the cutting in front of it at an intermediate level, above the lower station but below the higher, and is connected to both by flights of iron-framed stairs with heavy wooden treads—still just the way the Victorian railway engineers had built it. This arrangement offers passengers alighting there the opportunity of leaving the station on either side of the cutting, to west or to east, or, if they prefer, taking a second flight of stairs to transfer from one set of platforms to the other.

The station manager was proud of his establishment. He ran a tight and disciplined ship, keeping his staff, his station and his passengers—he was one of the old school of railwaymen who still had passengers rather than their more modern manifestation as "customers" or, even worse, "clients"—in good order at all times. His platforms were always clean and well swept; his stairways and passageways were clear of obstruction and sound underfoot; his wood- and metal-work was always well cared for with no signs of rot or rust appearing through their paintwork. The trains were received and despatched with brisk efficiency, so if they left Woodhill Station late it was only ever because they had arrived there late in the first place, and not because they were delayed by anything he or his staff might or might not have done while they were there. His flower arrangements had been known to win awards. Everything in the small piece of the world over which he had control was just that; controlled, and just so.

That morning he was doing what he usually did at that time of the day; surveying his domain; watching the trains arriving and departing and his passengers coming and going in their turn. He stood on the footbridge, staring down at the platforms of the low level station, which was looking as clean and tidy as it usually did in the bright summer sunshine, despite the depth of the cutting and the deep shadow that spread across its eastern slope. Leaning forward, with his outstretched arms resting on the high handrail in front of him, he had the calm and placid look of a man at peace with the world; a man without a care in it. In reality he was not like that at all, he was very much on duty and working, mentally at least, observing the trains and passengers coming and going, closely watching the actions of his staff, and using his high-tech wristwatch, just poking out from under the cuff of his left jacket sleeve, to time the arrivals and departures, making sure that nothing that arrived on time departed late, and that nothing that arrived late lost any more time while it was there. Order and efficiency was the key to the success he had achieved in his career; what he strived to achieve; what he always managed to achieve; until that morning, that is. At that time of the day he had no idea what was about to happen. How could he? None of it had started to happen then, and had he known what he was in for, he might well have decided that it would have been better if he had taken the day off and let it all happen to someone else. For even as the station manager, satisfied with the way everything was running that morning, was turning away and heading up the stairs towards the high level station where his office was located, events far beyond his control were beginning to conspire to converge upon him.

Sasha and Wright got up, got dressed and had breakfast early, so they had more than enough time to allow for delays as they travelled to the places where they needed to be to set Wright's plan into motion. Wright had his pistol in one jacket pocket, the chain and handcuffs in the other and the two smoke canisters in the plastic carrier bag that Sasha's shopping had come back to the flat in the day before. Sasha had the disc and Dent's papers. Her role was to come to Wright and give them to him when (if) the exchange was to be made; but Wright, with his gun, secretly had no intention of making an exchange, just taking the money and running. Sasha drove them to South Suburbia station in her car, slowly enough to make sure that anyone who was tailing them could easily keep up, under the pretence of making sure she did not run the risk of being stopped for speeding.

John drove Angela's car, and Brennan fell in at the back as the other two passed the end of the side-road where he and Withers were parked. One after the other they made their way through the early morning traffic to the station. Sasha stopped. Wright got out. Sasha sped off, going quickly now in an effort to make sure she was not followed. She need not have worried; John, Angela, Brennan and Withers were all intent on following Wright, not her. They all stopped outside the station. John got out and Angela took the wheel and drove off. Withers got out and Brennan did likewise. Neither one of them went very far, parking and leaving their cars at the first available opportunity, both on yellow lines in side streets; leaving them to the mercy of the traffic wardens—a small matter in the face of the game they were playing and the stakes they were playing it for.

Inside the station, Wright had bought a ticket and sat down with a drink at the coffee bar on the upper concourse, outside the automatic ticket barriers, and was reading a morning paper in an unconcerned-looking way. John, Angela, Brennan and Withers stayed out of sight of him (and each other) and made preparations for what might follow. At different times, first Angela, then Withers, neither of whom was known to Wright, went to the ticket machines on the concourse to buy pairs of tickets to enable them to get through the barriers when (if) the need arose. Withers gave Brennan his ticket and then went to take up station on the far side of the barriers, standing not far away from Jim, who was already there to keep an eye on Wright for Sasha.

Sasha drove north from South Suburbia for around ten miles, following a route that took her straight to Woodhill Station. She had to park some distance away and walk the rest of the way there, but that did not matter because she still had plenty of time in hand. She bought a ticket, passed through the barriers, walked down onto the lower level up platform and sat down on a bench to wait.

Wright sat at the coffee bar on the upper concourse of South Suburbia Station, drinking, pretending to read and glancing repeatedly at his watch. The minutes ticked away, until the appointed time approached and finally arrived. Wright punched the number of Dent's mobile phone into his own and waited. Like Wright, Dent had not gone back to sleep after the Arse's first call, so the second one was answered before the end of the first ring.

'Dent.'

'Walk to London River Crossing Station. Do it now.' Click. The rabbit was running, and the sly dog would soon be catching up with him.

Flagg had not been disturbed during the night, so he had managed to get a few hours' sleep and was back on station outside the hotel before dawn to wait for his man to emerge. The same applied to the Perma-way Directors, who had taken it in turns to stand guard over the hotel's front and rear entrances so that they, too, would not miss Dent's exit. The two Transport Policemen had been relieved by others just like them, until dawn, when their numbers were swollen by others of their number, including Inspector Sands, who was convinced that the bizarre behaviour of the Perma-way Directors signalled the start of something important and decidedly dodgy.

Dent left his hotel with the money in the small suitcase Wright had told him to put it in, and set out to walk to London River Crossing Station across its namesake, London River Crossing. The day was bright and sunny with a light, refreshing breeze blowing along the river; but Dent's mood was certainly no match for it. Before Wright's phone call, he had still been searching desperately for a way out of the mess he now found himself in; without allies to help, even amongst his former partners in crime. But the short period of time Wright had given him since the theft of the computer disc and the papers that could damn him had not given him the chance to come up with anything, other than to take his Grandfather's old service revolver with him in the hope of waving it around and scaring Wright into giving him the disc and his papers without his having to hand over the money. Then he could put it all back in the bank and no-one would be any the wiser.

Behind Dent, some distance back, walked Flagg, trying to stay out of sight of his target—not too difficult with Dent in the heavily preoccupied mood he was in that morning.

Close behind Flagg were the assembled masses of the crooked Directors of Perma-way, doing the same thing. They could come as close as they liked to Flagg though, because they did not know him, and he did not know them.

Behind them were the ever-growing ranks of the Transport Police, dressed in plain clothes for the operation and trying to look inconspicuous; their identity only given away to those who knew the signs by their purposeful walks and identical, heavy police-issue footwear.

Dent was approaching the station when his phone rang again. He kept moving as he answered it. Wright told him what his next move was to be. Dent rang off, passed through the ticket barrier with his travel warrant, went up the escalators and boarded the train Wright had told him to get on, with thirty seconds or so to spare before it left.

Flagg saw what was going to happen and accelerated towards the manned gate alongside the ticket-operated turnstiles, waving his warrant card at the bemused railway official who was tending it, then ran up the escalator and jumped into the last carriage just as the doors slid shut.

Behind him, the Perma-way Directors, well and truly caught napping, did not make it to the train before the doors were closed and locked, and were left on the platform as it pulled away. They milled around in confusion, looking for the destination boards at the head of the platforms that would tell them where they needed to go to catch the next train heading in the same direction. They found it and all trooped round to get on, angry that they had ten minutes or so to wait before it was due to leave.

Back at the end of the platforms, Inspector Sands and his men all stood and watched in amusement as the farce developed in front of them. Then they calmly walked forward and got on the same train as the Perma-way Directors, splitting into groups of twos and threes to intermingle with and surround their quarry.

At South Suburbia Station, Wright was still sitting at the coffee bar drinking; apparently unconcerned, apparently unhurried, now the game was underway and his target was on the move; but inside he was like a coiled spring, just waiting to leap into action. In reality he was just waiting for the right time to make his move. He did not know for certain that he was being followed, but he had an uncomfortable feeling that he was—or was that just his paranoia getting the better of him? Whatever it was, he had decided not to ignore it, and was taking precautions.

He looked round slowly for what he knew must be the last time before he had to go, scanning the faces of the crowd, not seeing anyone he recognised.

Round the corner, out of sight, Angela and John huddled together, also waiting. Every once in a while Angela, the least likely of the two to be spotted, peered round the end of the wall they were hiding behind to make sure he was still there.

Round the other corner, on the opposite side of the upper station concourse where this game of hide-and-seek was being played out, Brennan was doing the same thing.

Wright looked down through the glass wall of the concourse, at the platform and tracks below, and stiffened. His time had come; his train was arriving; its coaches streaming one after another into the station, slowing, slowing, slowing; stopping. The doors opened. Its passengers began to disgorge onto the platform. He got up and ran. Angela saw him go and pulled John out of hiding as she set out after him. Brennan saw him go and ran out after him too.

Wright had been clever in the way he had done his planning. He got most of the way down the ramp to the platform before the wall of commuters coming up it hit him, and he only had to swim against the tide for a short way before he broke free and could jump through the still-open doors of the last carriage.

Angela, John and Brennan, who all started a long way back, were not so lucky, and had to struggle against the upward flow literally from the moment they got to the head of the ramp. None of them made it down to the train before the doors closed and it started off again, heading north, towards London River Crossing.

Jim and Withers, neither of whom were known to Wright or to each other, did make it though, because they were both standing at the top of the ramp when Wright had got up, and both managed to get onto the same train that he did.

John swore, loudly and long, but his offensive outburst was drowned out by the arrival of an old, slam-door train on the other side of the island platform. The squealing of its brakes was followed by the crash of the doors opening and closing as people got off and others crammed themselves on. Brennan got straight on without bothering to find out where it was going. Angela and John were left standing almost alone on the platform. The hubbub died down. Whistles blew and the train made ready to leave.

Suddenly there was a shout along the platform, from somewhere near the front of the train 'Biddle: you sodding workshy shirker! Where the hell have you been?' John looked up in shock and saw the ugly face of his boss Roland Smythe, his features distorted with rage, as he made his way along the platform. John panicked. He looked around desperately for somewhere to escape to, preferring to be anywhere other than embroiled in a confrontation with the odious Smythe. The train in front of him shuddered and then jerked forward and started to move. John shot his hand out, grabbed the nearest door handle and pulled the door open. He pushed Angela forward and shouted 'Get in!'

'Biddle. Where do you think you're going? I want a word with you, you tosser!' Roland shouted at him from much closer.

John ran forward and leapt onto the train behind Angela, slamming the door behind him, expecting to see Roland sail past on the platform at any second, but he did not, because the foul-mouthed bully had done exactly the same thing himself and was even then beginning his attempt to make his way down the packed train in an effort to find his missing employee.

'This is the South Coast Regional Train Service to London River Crossing, calling at London River Crossing only. Thank you.'

John's mood plummeted to the depths of despair. Any hopes he had harboured of catching up with Wright and taking back the disc or snatching the money had gone. They had lost him. He had got on a slow train heading north towards London River Crossing. They, as a result of his sheer panic to get away from the one man who most clearly represented the past he was so desperately trying to escape from, had got on a fast one which, although heading in the same direction, would catch up with and pass the one Wright was on within just a few minutes. Wright could get off anywhere between South Suburbia and London, and they would never know where he had gone. And where was the dreaded Roland Smythe?

After leaving the station and travelling no more than half a mile, their train slowed down and came shuddering to a halt, just short of Windward Junction, where a branch line joined the main tracks heading towards London. After the groans of frustration died down there was silence, except for the rhythmic beating of a compressor underneath one of the carriages further up the train.

'This is a customer announcement,' said the disembodied voice on the public address system. 'We're currently being held here on a red signal, waiting for a late-running service to clear the junction ahead of us. Hopefully that won't take more than a few minutes and we'll have you on your way again just as soon as we can. I apologise for the delay to your journey and any inconvenience this may have caused. Thank you.' Click. Over and out. Nothing changed for five minutes, six minutes, seven minutes; then, as suddenly as it had stopped, the train started again and picked up speed as it passed through the junction and continued its journey northwards.

At that point, Roland Smythe was just over two carriage-lengths away from Angela and John, slowly making his way through the crush in the aisles and corridors to find Biddle; to find out where he had been, and what the hell he thought he was playing at. When he reached the front end of the carriage before the one John and Angela were squashed into, the crush got thicker and his progress slowed considerably. Needless to say, the people suffering being wedged together like cattle were resentful of this shaven-headed nuisance who insisted on moving them out of the way so he could get through. To where? There was nowhere to go.

Roland passed the toilet cubicle at the end of one carriage and squeezed through the connection between carriages into the next. He pushed through the throng past the first lines of seats then came up against a man who had wedged himself into the gap between the next set of seat-ends and showed no desire to move to let Roland through. Polite requests to move (unusual for Roland, but polite he was) fell on deaf ears, so Roland tried to push past with a muttered apology. He met with stiff resistance and an aggressive glare. He glared back. To an outside observer it must have looked remarkable, because Roland and this man could have been twins. Both were stocky, shaven headed, ugly and wore pin-striped suits. Both suffered from the same handicap, of having been elevated beyond their competence into the lower levels of middle management, where they were encouraged by their bosses (when it suited them) in their belief that they were always right. This was about to become a classic example of the unstoppable force meeting the immovable object.

'Would you move out of the way please, I want to get through,' Roland said.

'No chance, pal,' Middle Manager told him. 'There's nowhere to go.'

'Cut the crap and move your fat arse out of the way,' Roland growled.

'Go fuck yourself,' Middle Manager told him.

Roland pushed.

Middle Manager pushed back.

Roland lashed out and missed.

Middle Manager lashed out and made contact with the side of Roland's head.

Roland staggered backwards, knocking people out of the way behind him as he went.

Middle Manager went after him and continued trying to hit him.

Women screamed.

Men tried not to notice and carried on reading their papers.

'It's a fight! A fight! A real fight!' squealed an over-excited out-of-work actor on his way from Bigton to London for an audition.

The guard was called, and battled his way through the crowd to see what the trouble was.

The fight continued, with both men locked together and struggling for supremacy: to get an arm free with which to land a punch on the other.

Several people dialled 999 on their mobile phones and called the police.

Another reached up and pulled the emergency chain.

The driver, hearing the alarm go off in his cab, complied with his company's emergency procedure, carrying on to the next station, applying the brakes and bringing the train sharply to a halt alongside the fast up-line platform at Woodhill Low Level.

The guard, not a small man himself, wrapped his arms around Middle Manager and tried to pull him away from Roland. He met with no success, but did manage to pin the man's arms to his sides temporarily.

Roland, now wedged with his back up against one of the doors, wriggled one of his arms round behind him, curled his fingers around the handle that worked the door lock, and pulled on it, just as Middle Manager lunged forward in an attempt to land a head-butt on him. Roland fell back; the door burst open and deposited him, Middle Manager and the train guard unceremoniously in an untidy heap on the platform. Along the length of the train, heads popped out of windows and doors swung open as passengers, alerted by the noises and shouting, tried to catch sight of what was going on. They included Brennan who, like Angela and John, had now accidentally ended up in exactly the right place at the right time, thanks to the insufferable Roland and his look-alike protagonist.

John looked out of the window dejectedly, across the platform to the other side, where a slow train was just pulling out, with lines of open-mouthed commuters staring out of its windows disbelievingly at what they were watching. The few passengers who had got off were either staring at the fight as well, or were making their way towards the stairs that led up onto the footbridge. One of them looked familiar. John could not believe his luck: it was Wright.

'Quick!' he hissed at Angela. 'Get off. It's Wright. We've caught up with him. Look!' and he pointed out of the window at the sight of the arse ascending the stairs. Angela pulled on the door handle and they both burst out onto the platform.

Wright walked up onto the footbridge, oblivious to what was going on behind him, on the platform below. He was completely focussed on the task in hand; making sure that he got his hands on the money. He did not see the tall, ginger haired man that was Jim, or the slim, attractive brunette that was Withers, both of whom had stood close to him on the train, getting off and delaying on the platform until they could see where he was going. Nor did he see Angela and John trying to stay out of sight behind the bulk of the train they had just alighted from as they, too, tried to see where he would go next.

Up on the bridge Wright pulled out his mobile phone and dialled Dent's number. 'Where are you?' he asked. Dent told him.

'Good,' Wright said. 'Listen to me; and do as you're told.'

A few moments later, later Dent's train pulled into Woodhill Low Level Station, on the slow down line platform.

'Get off.' Wright snapped into the microphone of his mobile.

The train doors opened and Dent stepped out.

'The footbridge.' Wright told him. 'Now: and no tricks.'

Flagg stood inside the open doors of the stationary train and watched Dent walk down the platform towards the footbridge. He heard another train approaching on the fast line but paid it no attention, as he had just spotted a figure he thought might be Wright, in the middle of the bridge.

In the leading carriage of the approaching train, another of the old slam-door type, the Directors of Perma-way were keeping a wary eye out for their Financial Director, watched closely but in secret by the members of the Transport Police. As they approached each station the directors stuck their heads out of the windows, thereby risking either decapitation on a signal post, or at best a hefty fine, in an effort to see if they could spot him. On the approach to Woodhill one of them did see him, walking along the platform, just about to start climbing the stairs onto the footbridge. The man reached up and pulled the communication cord as the front end of the train reached the near end of the platform. The driver immediately slammed on the brakes and the train slithered, slid, shuddered and jerked to a stop, mostly out of the other end of the station, with just the back half of its last carriage still inside it. The Perma-way Directors all began to run, back along the length of the train, followed by the Transport Police, who had no idea what on earth was going on.

Dent walked up the steps onto the bridge, one hand holding the handle of the suitcase, the other on the butt and trigger of his father's service revolver, nestling in his jacket pocket. Wright stood waiting for him, one of his hands holding the loaded Mauser in his pocket. In the background they could both hear shouting coming from the platforms on either side; from the fight that was still in progress on the up platform, and from the Perma-way Directors who were beginning to spill out of the train on the down platform; and from the far distance came the sound of sirens approaching.

Dent reached the top of the stairs and turned to face Wright. Wright pulled the Mauser out of his pocket and pointed it at Dent. Dent tried to respond but fumbled it and the revolver slipped and spun out of his hand. At the sight of Dent's gun, Wright panicked, dropped the bag with the smoke canisters inside and shot Dent in the foot.

'You BASTARD!' Dent howled as the pain shot up his leg.

The top spun off one of the smoke bombs and the plunger depressed as it spilled out of the bag and bounced across the bridge deck. Thick clouds of odious orange smoke billowed out of it and Wright's view of the world began to disappear. The shouts and the sirens got louder, and footsteps rang out on the stairs leading up to the bridge.

Then pandemonium broke out. Everyone on the station seemed to be trying to get onto the footbridge at the same time, in spite of the fact that Wright was standing up there with a gun.

Flagg, Brennan and Withers wanted to get up there because there was a gun, and dealing with it was their duty.

Sasha and Jim wanted to get up there because that was where the story was.

The Perma-way Directors wanted to get their money back and get their hands on Dent.

The Transport Police followed the Perma-way Directors up there to find out what they were up to.

John and Angela wanted to get up there because that was where the money was.

Roland Smythe had broken free from Middle Manager and the train guard and was trying to get to Biddle, pursued by his opponent, who wanted to carry the fight on to its bitter end.

The station manager and his staff poured down from the high level station, where their offices were, to find out what it was that had shattered the peace and order of their normal morning routine.

And while all this was going on, motorplod arrived, sirens shrieking, in two patrol cars, one at either end of the footbridge; eight burly uniformed officers leaping out as soon as they had screeched to a halt, and sprinting onto the bridge to join the fray.

Not far off was the sound of more sirens approaching as the fire brigade and the ambulance service rushed to the scene in force in response to a report of a major incident occurring, triggered by the sight of the smoke wafting upwards from the low level station.

Up on the bridge, Wright had lost the plot. Dent was down and incapacitated: the money in the suitcase was there for the taking; but instead of taking it, Wright threw his gun down, pulled the chains and the handcuffs out of his pocket, manically intent on making Dent suffer in the same way that he had suffered at the hands of the bastard Biddle. He grabbed Dent's wrists and pulled him across the bridge to the balustrade. He threw the chains over the metal handrail and caught the bottom ends as they dropped down behind it. Pulling Dent up into a kneeling position, he slipped the last links of the chains over the open ends of the handcuffs and snapped them in place on the Perma-way man's wrists.

Flagg was the first one to arrive on the bridge from the down platform side. As he leapt the last two steps and turned right onto the deck the smoke cleared momentarily, giving him clear sight of Dent, chained by his wrists to the handrail, kneeling in front of Wright who was frantically trying to tear the clothes off him. Flagg had been right all the time; it was about some perverted, unnatural sexual ritual, that Wright and Dent were about to try to engage in!

The smoke closed back over the scene and Flagg was bumped and jostled from behind as the Perma-way Directors, the Transport Police and motorplod all rushed past him towards the place where Dent and Wright had been. Flagg launched himself forward to attempt to impose some kind of order.

On the up platform John grabbed Angela's wrist and pulled her towards the stairs leading up to the bridge.

'Stay focussed on where that suitcase is!' he shouted to her above the noise of panic, confusion and sirens. 'That's the only thing that matters now.'

They ran up the stairs to the top and swung left onto the bridge. Behind them, Roland was gaining ground, but as he reached the top of the stairs his ankles were pulled out from underneath him by Middle Manager who had thrown himself up the last few steps in a perfectly executed copy of a flying rugby tackle. Roland went down, four motorplod officers fell straight over him, then Middle Manager fell on top of them all and started hitting out in the hope that some of his punches at least would land on the right target.

Just ahead of the fight, John pushed his way past a tall man with a beard and a camera, who seemed intent on taking photographs of everything, in spite of the smoke and confusion. John, not wanting his face or Angela's to appear in any pictures of the event, snatched the camera away and sent it hurtling over the edge of the bridge, to smash into pieces on the platform or tracks below. Jim turned to John and started to protest but stopped short as Angela, seeing that this could spell trouble, stamped her short, blunt heel down hard on his foot, right on his in-growing toenail, which he had meant to do something about but had never got round to. Jim went down shrieking, just as Dent had done moments before.

The smoke thinned again as the first canister began to expire, only to be replaced by another thick cloud bursting out of the second, that had just been accidentally crushed by a heavy police boot. That brief thinning had given John a half-clear view of what was ahead of him:- Wright still frantically trying to pull Dent's clothes off and half strangling him in the process; another man trying to pull Wright away, while fighting off the members of a crowd that John recognised as the Directors of Perma-way he had met at the meetings in Overway House. They, in turn, were brawling with another group, this one of young, burly men in civilian clothes, but wearing policemen's boots. Finally, trying to pull the whole lot apart were four uniformed police officers, who were failing miserably because there were too few of them, and who were being drawn irrevocably into the overall melee.

John ran forward, pulling Angela behind him, reaching out towards where he knew the handle of the suitcase must be. His hand groped the air, then the balustrade of the bridge, and finally came to rest on the suitcase, that no-one else seemed interested in any longer. He grabbed its handle and picked it up, wondering what he should do next. Angela solved his problem for him: while he had been concentrating on finding the suitcase, she had heard the sound of a train approaching the high level station where, in spite of the smoke, noise and confusion on the bridge below it, services continued to run. She began to pull John towards the stairs snaking up to the viaduct and the platforms above them.

Suddenly, out of the gloom of the smoke, a uniformed figure stood resolutely in front of them, blocking their way. It was the station manager, who had completely lost control of himself in the face of his complete loss of control over his station.

'Tickets please!' he screeched. 'You must show me your valid tickets or I'll have to levy a penalty fare!' He reached out to grab Angela as she approached, but she stopped dead in front of him. John cannoned into the back of her and stopped too, but the momentum of the suitcase kept it going, swinging forwards on the end of his outstretched arm, describing a perfect arc upwards until one of its corners came firmly into contact with the soft and sensitive part of the Station Manager's anatomy, between his legs.

'Nnnnnnggggg!' was all he could say as he collapsed, in such a spectacular way that in future all sacks of spuds will be described as "going down like a station manager".

Angela strode on, stepping over the sack of spuds, tugging John along after her, finding and running up the steps, out of the cloying, clinging smoke on the footbridge, arriving on the down platform of the high level station just in time to hop onto the train that was waiting there, before its doors started to slide shut.

The two of them stared down breathlessly from the windows of the carriage at the scene on the footbridge below, as the train moved off and accelerated away from the station towards the countryside beyond the outer edge of the suburbs. The smoke was beginning to clear. The fire brigade and paramedics had arrived and were helping the uniformed police to restore order. Anyone in a uniform was automatically on the side of the right and the good. Anyone not in uniform was a villain until proved otherwise, and was being lined up and handcuffed pending further enquiries. That included Wright, Flagg, Brennan, Withers, Sasha, Jim, the Perma-way Directors, Inspector Sands and his men, Roland and Middle Manager. Dent was, of course, already handcuffed and could stay that way for the time being. Sorting out that little lot was going to take somebody quite a while; by which time Angela and John would be a long, long way away.

EPILOGUE

The story broke in the national newspapers the following day. After her arrest, Sasha forwent her right to summon legal representation to contact Cliff Maxford, to file her copy with him and tell him where he could find the corroborating evidence for her story. He used his considerable skills and numerous contacts to negotiate deals with all of the major papers, enabling all of them to run exclusive stories on the subject the following morning.

As a result of their actions on that day, the evidence made available to them on John Biddle's disc, documents seized and statements taken during raids on various railway premises and the headquarters of several mobile phone companies and some well-known retail outlets, the police secured convictions against the persons of a number of those companies' executives and chief operating officers. Two middle managers from companies not related to the scandal were bound over to keep the peace for a year, and banned from using the railways for the same period. Two police officers, one a sergeant in the CID, the other a uniformed WPC, got engaged and subsequently wed. Perma-way's spreadsheet was destroyed and the pilot copy of the computerised replacement for The Great Book of Excuses was wiped from all the hard-drives, memory sticks and floppy discs it had found its way onto. The Book itself was donated to the Railway Museum in York where it remains under lock and key. No-one ever heard of or from Mr and Mrs John Biddle again.

The railways were returned to the care and management of people who really loved them, and thought they should be run for the benefit of the people who used them and not just for profit; people who from that day forward were referred to once again as passengers. Once that had all happened, the railways were fully restored to the models of order and efficiency they always should have been, and no train ever ran late again.

Well, what did you expect? This is a work of fiction, after all.